I0534646

ISBN: 978-0-9766231-5-1

Published by Red Raptor Productions, Inc.

BLOOD LEGACY: ORIGIN OF SPECIES Vol 1, 2011. FIRST PRINTING.

Office of Publication: Long Beach, California

BLOOD LEGACY it's logo, all related characters and their likenesses are ™ and © 2011 Kerri Hawkins and Red Raptor Productions, Inc.

What did you think of this book? We love to hear from our readers.

Please email us at: **khawkins@bloodlegacy.com.**

# BLOOD LEGACY: ORIGIN OF SPECIES

RED RAPTOR PRODUCTIONS, INC.

## _Also available from Kerri Hawkins_

THE STORY OF RYAN
BLOOD LEGACY I
(ISBN: 978-0-9766231-7-5)

THE HOUSE OF ALEXANDER
BLOOD LEGACY II
(ISBN: 978-0-9766231-0-6)

HEIR TO THE THRONE
BLOOD LEGACY III
(ISBN: 978-0-9766231-1-3)

ZEN 12
(ISBN: 978-0-9766231-8-2)

THE DARKNESS: VOLUME I
(ISBN: 978-1-58240-797-5)

*visit us on the web at*
**www.bloodlegacy.com**

# BLOOD

# LEGACY

## ORIGIN OF SPECIES

*by* **KERRI HAWKINS**

# CHAPTER 1

THE AIR WAS VERY STILL AND THICK. The sky in the distance was dark with amorphous, swirling clouds. A strange tension squeezed the woman's stomach, compressed her lungs and clutched her heart. She smiled nervously at a passing neighbor but the other woman would not meet her gaze and hurried past.

The woman continued on, glancing about the street. It was oddly empty and silent for this time of the morning. Merchants should be out hawking their wares in the center square. Children should be running about chasing stray dogs or the occasional pig. The clink of the blacksmith should be a welcome background to the musical hum of the crowd.

Perhaps it was the approaching storm, the woman thought to herself. Bad weather made people act queerly. It was evident she would not be able to buy the bread she had hoped to find in the square; the baker was nowhere to be seen. She turned on her heel and hurried back to her hut.

She paused in the doorway of the simple dwelling. It was a poor home, but at least it had a wooden door instead of a flap at the entrance. She pushed through the door to check her children. Two girls and a boy sat at the table finishing the meager breakfast she had provided. Her husband had left early to hunt in the forest so, god willing, they would have meat for dinner.

The woman brushed the hair from her eyes. She was pretty in a plain sort of way, wavy brown hair, full lips, fair skin that she tried to keep soft with tallow. Her figure would have been curvaceous were times not so lean. She was remarkably ordinary with one exception: the startling green eyes that peered from that unremarkable face.

Those green eyes surveyed her children who glanced up curiously. They did not seem to feel the tension of the coming storm and for that she was grateful. She stepped back out of the house and into the street, assessing the approaching weather. She bit her lip at the sky in the distance. Her husband was beneath that blackening sky and the storm appeared to be worsening.

The woman could not take her eyes from the clouds. They seemed to be growing in strength and number, and the storm front now took up the entire western sky. The shape of the clouds was unusual, less like water vapor and more like a churning, twisting mass of fury. As the front moved closer the clouds grew stranger, less like clouds and more like some great swarm of insects.

The wind shifted and with it came an eerie, leathery flapping and high pitched shrieking. The woman looked back to the storm front, a chill rising in bumps on her skin. Her eyes were good and she could just begin to make out the black shapes within the cloud, at the same time realizing the black shapes were the cloud.

"What is that, mama?"

Her son had followed her out and now clutched the hem of her worn skirt. For a moment she stood wordless, unable to respond. And in that moment of silence the ground began to vibrate, then began to rumble, then began to violently shake.

"Get back in the house," she said urgently, and the boy responded to her tone of voice with a quick glance of fear behind him.

She knew that she herself should get in the house, yet she could not take her eyes from the churning mass of birds that was now taking up half the sky. There were hawks, falcons, eagles, ravens, and vultures.

10

They were birds of prey and scavengers, but more than anything, they were an omen of massive death.

The rumbling increased and was now a steady roar accompanied by a rapidly approaching cloud of dust. The roar divided, the divisions became distinct, the distinctions resolved themselves into a thousand hoof beats just as the cloud of dust resolved itself into a stampede of terrified animals fleeing from some unknown horror. Wolves, foxes, cows, pigs, deer, rabbits, and squirrels scrambled for their lives. Even a bear ignored the abundant prey about him and instead fled in terror.

The woman was frozen in place. She had seen such a stampede before when the animals fled from a wildfire after the drought. But she did not smell any smoke right now.

The grasp of her oldest daughter's hand snapped her from her paralysis and she stepped into her house just before the tidal wave of animals crashed past her door. She clutched her daughter gratefully, then pushed the children back as the thin walls of their shelter trembled and shook and the dust rose from the cracks in the floor. She pulled them beneath the heavy table, the sturdiest object in the dwelling, and held them close as the roar became louder and louder. The din peaked, then began subsiding.

Her son was crying and she tried to comfort him while hiding her own terror. Although a fire would have been devastating, she wished for the smell of smoke that would tell her the threat was something understandable. As they huddled beneath the table, the rumble faded away and the flapping wings and shrieking of the raptors grew louder.

"Stay here," she said, addressing all three children.

"Mama, take this," the boy said, proffering his most prized possession, the small bone knife his father had made for him. The woman took the knife, clutched her son to her breast and kissed his tear-streaked cheek. She kissed each daughter, then pulled herself from beneath the table. She made her way quietly back to the door, opening the flimsy wooden barrier a crack.

She could see her neighbor across the street doing the same, then saw the crack disappear as the door slammed shut. She knew she should follow suit, but her desire to know what was happening was at war with her common sense. She pushed the door open a little wider.

The enormous flock of birds was blotting out the sun. The flock seemed to stop at the far edge of town, wheeling and turning about in a frenzied mass. The woman realized they were hovering over the livestock pens, and within seconds, the frantic squeals and screams of the penned animals could be heard. The woman imagined she could hear the tearing of flesh, so vicious and agitated was the attack.

Although she was trembling, she could not help but crack the door a little wider. Something was walking up the far end of the street. The gait was odd and shuffling but the outline indicated it was a man. Several other figures appeared alongside him, also staggering along. She could not make out any of their features because they were still too far away, but one figure paused in front of a hut, and then pushed to enter. Within seconds, screams were heard that just as quickly went silent.

The figures continued to limp toward her and the woman closed the door, peering only through the tiny crack that remained. One of the children made a noise and she turned to them, violently waving for them to be quiet. They shrank back under the table.

She looked back through the narrow opening, the limitation to her vision adding to her tension. Several of the figures went shuffling by her. They did not turn their heads but seemed dazed, almost as if they were sick. She pressed her eye closer to the crack. They wore gear that indicated they were soldiers and they were most definitely sick. All had a deathly pallor, lesions on their skin and festering wounds that appeared to rupture from the inside out. She choked back a scream as one man's arm fell off, detaching itself from the rotting flesh of the shoulder then falling to the ground. The man continued on, oblivious to the loss, and a giant vulture landed to claim its feast.

The woman stared at the vulture. Such creatures were hideous even in their normal form, but this one appeared to have flown from the depths of hell. It had two beaks and four eyes, three which focused on the rotting flesh it was consuming, and one that seemed to be looking right at her. She swallowed the vomit that rose in her throat, terrified to make any sound.

The parade of death continued on, the men, if they could be called that, marching onward in an endless display of deformity and mutilation. Screams and the crashing sounds of a struggle would rise above the cacophony of feasting birds, then go abruptly silent.

The woman watched in horror as her neighbor went senseless from fright and bolted into the street. She was quickly set upon by three men who tore her limb from limb in a barbarous fury, blood and flesh flying everywhere. The woman went still and the men returned to their stupor, staggering away from the pile of remains.

"Mama," her oldest daughter said, her voice trembling.

"Shhh!" the woman said, still peering through the crack.

"Mama!" the girl said, her voice terrified and insistent.

The woman whirled at the tone of voice to see a man standing behind her, facing her children under the table. With extraordinary relief, she recognized her husband.

"Simon," she exclaimed, rushing to embrace him. She wrapped her arms about his sturdy form, desperate to feel his strength.

"Mama," the girl said again, as if nothing else would come from her mouth.

Simon turned around and the woman took a step back in revulsion, the knife dropping from her nerveless fingers. He was sick as well, his skin gray and his eyes dull with fever. He did not appear as bad as the men outside, though, and the woman was momentarily hopeful. Perhaps a poultice, some herbs…

"Lia," the man said, and the woman's hope grew with the articulation of the name. Those hopes were cruelly dashed with his next words.

"Kill me," he said, pleading, clinging to the last of his reason. "Please kill me."

Lia shook her head, taking a step back. "I cannot, Simon. I cannot. Please don't ask this of me."

The man closed his eyes in resignation, and when he re-opened them, all of his reason was gone. He sprang at her like an animal, taking her to the ground with incredible strength. In an instant, he fastened upon her neck, tearing out her throat with razor sharp teeth.

Her son sprang from beneath the table and the man turned, dropping Lia like a bag of stones. Her head struck the ground hard, dazing her but unmercifully not knocking her unconscious. She lay there helpless as her husband picked up their child and swung him by the heels, shattering his skull on the hard wooden table and dashing his brains out. The eldest daughter tried to flee but he caught her by the shoulder and tore her arm from its socket. The youngest daughter crouched terrified beneath the table, but he dragged her out by her skirt and snapped her neck.

Lia lay against the door, wishing for death. But it would not come and she was forced to watch from her immobilized position as her husband killed and then began eating their children. She watched as the mindless beast chewed on his progeny, hating him and fearing him and mourning him all at the same time. And when at last he began vomiting a green milky substance and appeared to be dying himself, she cursed god for keeping her alive to see the sight.

The beautiful dark-haired man watched his fair-haired child twist in the bed, imprisoned in some sort of nightmare world. He could not imagine what she was dreaming, but whatever it was, it was causing her great suffering.

# CHAPTER 2

THE STRANGER WATCHED THE THREE from the shadows. He had initially been drawn to the trio by the red-haired one, the woman who was one of his Kind. He could feel her even from a distance, so vulnerable, so young, yet surrounded by a strange exotic power that was enticing and assailable, asking for violation. She was beautiful and luminous, and upon first sight he wanted to destroy that beauty by drinking the life from her. When he stumbled upon them, he took quick note of the older boy, also auburn-haired with a pronounced resemblance to his mother. Sturdy and handsome, the human boy was ignored by the stranger entirely.

No, his attention was now fully on the toddler with the two. The boy, or perhaps girl, it was difficult to tell, was simply stunning. Dark hair, gorgeous blue eyes, a perfect rosebud mouth, a light blush on his cheeks, the stranger could not take his eyes from him. It was not normally his nature to desire children, let alone one that appeared to be human, but at that moment he wanted the boy more than he could remember wanting anything in centuries. He fantasized about snatching the child, racing away, then bleeding and killing him at his leisure. The thought gave him such pleasure he unconsciously stepped toward them, nearly giving away his position by moving into the light. He hurriedly stepped back into the lengthening shadows.

Susan Ryerson felt a finger of unease trace its way down her spine. She looked over at her son Jason, then at Drake, who continued to play although he did glance up at her. Susan looked over at the long, black limousine parked some distance away. She had not realized how far into the playground they had moved, and how far that put her from Edward. As if he, too sensed something, the door of the vehicle opened and Edward appeared, his patrician features exhibiting a look of concern as he stared out over the top of the car at them. He glanced around, not entirely disturbed, but clearly intent on joining them.

The stranger felt the other one's presence immediately. The man approaching appeared physically older although the stranger knew him to be far older than his appearance. This one was closer to his own age and perhaps a match for him, unlike the red-haired one whom he could have easily subdued. The power of this one caused him indecision, and it was perhaps this indecision that saved his life as he was lifted bodily from his hiding place and thrown thirty feet across the playground into the merry-go-round.

Susan smothered a cry and gathered the boys to her. Edward seemed to disappear and reappear at her side. Jason looked on with wide eyes, both fearful and excited while Drake peered at the scene with interest.

The stranger caromed off the merry-go-round and landed face down in the dirt, but he had no chance to even roll over before he was snatched by the scruff of his neck like a dog and dangled several inches off the ground. He stared in terror into a pair of ice blue eyes that held absolutely no mercy. The power of the one holding him was tremendous, beyond anything he had felt before. And like the indecision that had previously delayed his movement and saved his life, the huge differential in ability between the two had the same redemptive effect. The creature holding him was so powerful, the stranger realized he was not worthy of the minor effort it would take to kill him.

Aeron saw that he had made his point and in a parental act of restraint that was completely out of character for him, decided he would not kill the cretin in front of his son. He glanced over at the toddler who was watching the exchange with mild interest and no fear, the look on his face so evocative of his other parent it was startling.

That thought brought a grim smile to Aeron's features as he turned back to the would-be attacker he now held by the throat. He tightened his grip until a crunching noise was clearly audible, then leaned forward and whispered in his ear.

"You should be thankful his mother isn't here."

With that phrase, he tossed the man aside. The stranger bounced twice, landed in an awkward and embarrassing position, then wasted no time scrambling clumsily into the underbrush, disappearing with remarkable haste. Aeron wiped his hands on his pants, then turned to approach the trio that was now a foursome with the protective presence of Edward.

Edward nodded to Aeron. He was not particularly fond of the arrogant English aristocrat, but Aeron was unrelenting when it came to his son, and they had that in common. Aeron lifted the boy into his arms, staring into eyes that were a warmer, deeper blue than his own, eyes that peered out of features that were nearly identical to his mother's. Aeron turned to Susan.

"If you don't mind, I would like to accompany you home."

Susan nodded, blushing slightly. It was difficult being around any of her Kind, but Aeron was one of the Old Ones, possessing a combination of virility and power that was overwhelming. And although she was one of the few Young Ones who would ever be around such power on a continual basis, that continuity did nothing to desensitize her to its presence.

Edward nodded his acquiescence to the accompaniment, and the five took their leave of the playground.

17

# CHAPTER 3

VICTOR SAT WATCHING HIS SLEEPING CHILD in the bed. It reminded him of a much earlier time in her life, when he had first Changed her, causing her to transition from her semi-human form into the immortal creature she was now. She did not look a day older than she did nearly seven hundred years ago, and she had looked barely nineteen then. He wondered if this sleep would be as long as that one and he sincerely hoped not. Ryan had slept almost fourteen years while adapting to her Change.

Victor leaned back. Ryan had slept so long because her Change had been particularly traumatic. Their Kind inhabited a unique, hierarchical society in which power was acquired in three ways. Strength was inherited from the one initiating the transformation; the stronger the mentor, the more powerful the offspring. Sharing blood also transmitted power. And finally power was acquired through simple age; the longer they lived, the more powerful they became.

None of those methods were truly simple, however. The very oldest of their Kind could not initiate Change because their blood was too powerful and the youngest could not because their blood was too weak. Only those occupying the middle ground were capable of "reproduction." The pleasure of Sharing intensified with power, therefore logically it would seem that the most powerful would desire to share only with others of equal power. This, too, was upended by the fact that killing another in the act of Sharing was the ultimate pleasure, and it was, at least in theory, impossible for the Old Ones to kill one another. Many Young Ones were sacrificed in the name of desire and went to their fate willingly because the pleasure was irresistible, which considerably limited the number who would actually live beyond even a normal human lifespan.

Which was why, Victor mused to himself, his child was so extraordinary. He had Changed her when he should have been far too old to initiate Change; his blood should have destroyed her. If it had not destroyed her during her transition, it should have killed her when they Shared while she was still so young, but instead it just made her more powerful. And although her seven hundred years would have put her high in their hierarchy, instead, she sat atop it because Ryan had surpassed those twice her age. She was arguably the most powerful of their Kind, indeed, even more powerful than him.

This thought gave Victor nothing but pleasure. It was partially explained by the fact that Ryan was also his biological child, something that had been considered impossible because none of their Kind were capable of reproducing outside of the Change. He had hidden the fact that he was Ryan's father from both Ryan and the Others for most of Ryan's life, and none, not even he, had an explanation for such an anomaly.

Until quite recently, Victor thought, his expression darkening. Ryan had also given birth to a child, his beautiful grandson, but it was not this thought that darkened his countenance or explained the anomaly. Rather it was the series of events that had left his child in this deep but fitful sleep. He himself had been in a similar sleep, his brought about by Aeron, the father of his grandson. But Ryan had easily dealt with Aeron in Victor's absence, then assumed the leadership of the hierarchy as had been his wish. At the very height of her achievement, however, she was taken from them by a mysterious and terrifying creature named Madelyn.

Victor's expression went from dark to black. The more powerful of their Kind could see the Memories of those with whom they Shared, and when Victor awoke from his illness, he immediately availed himself of the gift to quickly catch up with events. He had seen Ryan's sacrifice, saw her led away as a sheep to slaughter, her acquiescence an attempt to distract Madelyn from destroying them all.

And the plan had worked for awhile. Ryan's dalliance with the creature bought them time, although Ryan paid a terrible price. It was in fact her pain that brought Victor from his unconscious state, his bond with his child so great he could feel it over a vast distance. And he in turn had rallied all their Kind to battle Madelyn and her forces in an attempt to free Ryan.

Victor's expression changed, his anger transitioning to puzzlement. And this is where it had all gotten very strange. At the end of their battle, it was clear they were gaining the upper hand against Madelyn's forces, but that Madelyn herself could not be defeated. Ryan had again determined to sacrifice herself in an attempt to defeat Madelyn, an attempt that appeared doomed to failure as Madelyn overpowered her and Ryan hovered on the edge of death.

But then something had happened. Someone, or perhaps something, had intervened. No one was privy to what had actually transpired other than Ryan. All had felt Ryan's imminent death, then felt something so enormous, so powerful it was impossible to grasp. Ryan then simply disappeared, her presence just absent as if she had vaporized.

Victor stared at his child, examining the hair that was now almost white. Ryan had reappeared a short time later and it was clear something monumental had occurred. But she had merely made a cryptic comment about his mother, told Aeron it was good they had not had a girl, gathered her son to her breast, then went to sleep.

And had remained asleep for three solid weeks now. It seemed that for years now either he or Ryan had been in this position, one incapacitated, the other holding a constant vigil.

Victor was normally incredibly patient. Having lived for well over a millennium, time meant little to him. But the comment about his mother had filled him with a strange sense of dread. Victor had no memory of the woman, nor any knowledge of her existence. Earlier in his life he had assumed she had been human, a noble woman perhaps,

20

but someone whom he had never met. He thought it possible he had been abandoned at birth and simply had no memories of his childhood. As the years went by, these ruminations diminished in importance and frequency until they no longer occupied his thoughts at all.

That is until he conceived Ryan. The improbability of her birth caused him to again ponder his own origins, although the birth brought more questions than answers. Ryan's unique abilities and ascendance amongst their Kind, as well as her ability to reproduce outside the Change had caused a subtle disquiet in Victor, one he had hidden well over the years.

But now it seemed Ryan might have discovered clues to his origins, in fact, to all of their origins. He had sensed both her epiphany and the shock it had caused her system when she returned.

Victor sighed deeply. And now she slept blithely on, for perhaps weeks, or months, or even years.

The girl was drowning in an ocean of blood. It flowed into her mouth, down her throat, into her lungs and stomach. It flowed into her eyes, her ears, into her nose where the stream joined with the one flowing down her esophagus and windpipe. Strangely, although the sensation was claustrophobic, it was not unpleasant.

There were creatures here, depraved, deformed, mutilated and mutated. They somehow knew her, and with the comfortable discontinuity of the dream world, she accepted their knowledge of her as a given. It was that same illogic that made her accept without question that she knew them as well, and always had, even though she had never seen them or known of them before this moment.

The landscape shifted violently, but with the insouciance of the dreamer, the girl accepted the shift again without question or even surprise. The world was now a mass of writhing tentacles, a snarled collection of limbs lashing about with sensual and maleficent energy. She began to walk across the teeming, shifting mass, but only managed a few steps before the appendages snaked up her legs, around her torso, about her arms, lifting her from her feet gently but firmly. She was pulled down into the squirming mass, and the sensation was exactly as before: smothering but somehow not unpleasant.

As she disappeared beneath the surface, she could hear the gentle malevolent laughter of an ancient and arachnid creature. All previous contact with this creature had filled her with dread and terror, but now she was filled with an odd mixture of melancholy, longing, and resignation.

She had sensed the creature before, but it was only now she understood that it was her grandmother, knowing that the matriarch would only wait so long before she forced the girl's return.

The visions slipped away, becoming more and more ephemeral as the light beneath her eyelids became more pronounced. The final wisps drifted away as the girl opened her eyes. Although the room was dim, the minimal light seemed very bright and required a slow adjustment, causing the girl to blink, which caused her the same dream-like incongruity of a thought that blinking was not something she did very often.

She looked around the room and recognized nothing. Although she somehow knew of the subtle amnesia that accompanied the transition from dream world to real world, this seemed oddly persistent. There didn't seem to be anything in the room to anchor her and although she was waiting for a sense of "self" to materialize, nothing was forming. There were books to her right on a bookshelf, and although she knew they were "books" in a generic sense, that understanding had no more foundation than the understanding of the mutilated creatures in her dreams. It just seemed right and natural without any underlying basis that she could grasp. And although she knew they were books, she recognized none of them.

It was the same for the bed in which she was laying. She knew intuitively it was a bed but she had no memory of how or why she knew this, nor any history of knowledge of any bed but this one. And there was nothing in her mind that made this bed familiar or recognizable in any way. She turned to the bedside table, the lamp, the candles, and had the same sensation. She knew them by name, knew their purpose, but they might as well have been the very first item of their kind to ever exist.

She continued her slow perusal of the room, the paintings, the furniture, the chair at the foot of the bed—and she froze. There was a man sitting in the chair with his eyes closed. She knew he was a man as she knew of the books and the bed, but beyond that could establish no connection with him. She examined him curiously, and again words came to mind that had meaning yet no history. He was incredibly handsome, dark-haired with high cheek bones, a strong jaw and a sensual mouth. Even seated, she could see his elegant athleticism, the broad chest tapering to a narrow waist, one long leg crossed over the other. Although she lacked mooring, she understood these were desirable qualities. She was not surprised that when he opened his eyes, they were dark and beautiful.

Victor felt surprise and joy to see Ryan gazing at him: surprise that he had not sensed her awakening, and joy for the obvious reason that she had awakened. He started to get up, then stopped. She was looking at him with a very strange expression on her face, a look of confusion and slight consternation.

"Ryan?" he asked hesitantly.

The name rippled through her like a small wave, but its force was not enough to move her. It seemed familiar in the same sense as the furniture, but similarly lacked connection or context. The man stood, his concern evident. At that moment, a red-haired woman entered the room, and the girl examined her with the same curiosity and lack of recognition. She, like the man, possessed exceptional physical beauty. Her auburn hair complimented amazing blue-green eyes and fine, delicate features. The girl examined her as openly as she had examined the man, noting the lines and curves of her body.

Susan Ryerson stopped short. "Okay," she said slowly, "I've not

23

seen that look before."

Victor's eyes had not left his child. "I think there is something wrong with your patient, Dr. Ryerson," he said, his uncertainty apparent. There might have been a degree of humor in the situation were the ramifications not so serious.

Susan moved to Ryan's side. While human, Susan had been a preeminent genetic research doctor specializing in longevity and life-extension. Her life had dramatically changed when she came into contact with Ryan and her Kind, but she had continued her research out of her great love of science. That and the fact that she now had access to the holy grail of her research, Ryan herself. Although Victor initially had misgivings about Susan continuing her research, it ended up a boon as both Victor and Ryan benefited from Susan's accumulation of knowledge about their unique physiology.

Susan sat down on the edge of the bed. "Are you feeling alright?"

The girl stared at the woman. She understood the question but was not certain how to reply. Not because she did not know how she was feeling, but because it did not seem her mouth could shape the proper words. The language seemed foreign, something the girl could somehow understand but not something she could speak. The sensation was more than frustrating.

There was a commotion at the door, causing the man, the woman, and the girl to look toward the doorway. A very determined boy, perhaps all of three years old, was moving toward the bed with authority and purpose. He pulled himself up onto the mattress with far more grace and strength than he should have possessed and crawled immediately onto the girl. He gazed intently into her eyes.

The girl stared back into the deep blue depths and felt a shock of connection. For the first time since exiting the dream world she had a feeling of solidity. This boy was her son, nearly her identical twin, separated only in appearance by the differences in their ages.

The world came slamming downward upon Ryan. She instantly knew and remembered everything. It rushed back into her consciousness like a tsunami, crushing everything in its path. The knowledge was so

24

complete and sudden it caused her intense physical and mental anguish.

"Ryan!" Victor exclaimed, taking a step toward her as she winced in pain.

This time the name had meaning, context, as did his tone and his expression.

"Father," Ryan said, almost with relief. She knew exactly who he was, the only question being how she could not have. She turned to the red-haired woman.

"Susan," she said, "I—" She stopped.

Susan examined her with some concern. "Are you feeling okay, Ryan?"

The question before had seemed foreign, now it seemed incongruous. Of course she was okay. She was immortal, invulnerable, perhaps the most powerful of her Kind.

And right now, a little uncertain.

"I think I'm fine now," Ryan said. "I just had the strangest sensation on awakening."

Victor was not willing to let the odd incident pass. "You didn't seem to recognize me when you first awoke."

"I didn't," Ryan admitted, "nor did I recognize you," she said to Susan. "In fact, I couldn't remember anything at all."

Victor considered this admission with great gravity. Perhaps it was just a temporary by-product of the severe mental and physical demands that had been placed upon her. Susan echoed this line of thought.

"Between the tortures you suffered in captivity and then the aftermath," Susan said, "I'm not surprised if you have some lingering ill effects. Still," Susan said, suddenly business-like, "I'm going to have to insist on a full physical exam as soon as you're up and around."

Ryan turned to Drake, the usual twinkle in her eye appearing. "She'll come up with any excuse to use me in her research."

Victor was relieved to see the child he knew returning, her irrepressible humor and charm manifesting in full force. And although Susan did her best to frown at the gibe, she could barely hide her smile.

Ryan sat up gingerly, testing her limbs, and was relieved to see everything in working order.

"I would like to clean up a bit," she said to Victor, "then I will join you in the study. After that," she said, turning to Susan, "I will happily be your lab rat."

Victor turned as Ryan entered, pleased to see she carried herself with her usual lithe grace. The disquiet he felt upon her initial awakening had dissipated. She carried Drake upon her back and he clung to her neck, holding himself without requiring her support. She slung him around, then set him down. No sooner did his feet touch the ground then he raced to a pile of children's books, returning with one of his favorites. Ryan examined the book with mock seriousness.

"You're going to read to me about this cat and its hat?"

"Yes!" Drake exclaimed happily. Ryan was pleased to hear him speak aloud. Her mental bond with her son was so great that most times they did not need speech to communicate. He was actually quite articulate for his age and engaged in animated conversation with others, especially Jason. Ryan had to remind herself not to neglect that part of his development.

He handed her the book, then quickly returned with another one. "This one has a bear," he said with some authority, "who likes honey."

"Ah," Ryan said, "I see." He passed this book to her as well, then procured another one. This tome was quite different, however. It was thick and appeared very, very old. It was also very heavy although Drake had no difficulty carrying it.

"This one is too hard," Drake said, "even for Jason."

A shadow flitted across Ryan's face as she looked at the book. It was the story of King Arthur, one of the very first books ever printed, and it was most likely priceless. Victor had given it to her as a gift centuries before. She took the ancient text from the small boy's hands.

"Then I will read this one to you," Ryan said, "after you read to me about the bear."

26

Drake seemed pleased with this arrangement, but the books would have to wait. Edward entered, reminding Ryan that her son required food even though she did not.

"Master Jason awaits your presence at the kitchen table, Master Drake."

Food pleased Drake as much as the promise of reading, although it was clear he wanted to stay with his mother. Ryan picked him up, tossed him into the air, then handed him off to her manservant. "You go eat," Ryan said, "we'll read after Dr. Ryerson is done with me."

The two disappeared and Ryan turned back to her father. The book had stirred up a vortex of memories, some recent, some ancient, most not even hers.

"What's wrong?" Victor asked, assessing her shift in mood.

Ryan stared down at the book in her hands. There was so much to tell her father, so much information that had flooded into her consciousness. But much of it would be difficult to explain because what she had learned she had also actually experienced, making it even more challenging to sort out. One of Ryan's greatest gifts was to see through the eyes of others, experiencing their thoughts and memories as if they were her own. It was an extremely disorienting ability, though, as she constantly had the sensation of remembering things that had never happened to her and recalling events she had never been a part of. When she was inundated with information, as had so recently occurred, she had difficulty separating what was her reality and what belonged to someone else.

"It was my intent," Ryan said slowly, "to give you my blood. It would be the simplest way to show you what I've seen."

"But you're having second thoughts after your temporary memory loss," Victor deduced.

Ryan bit her lip, careful not to draw blood because its presence would most likely eliminate any restraint either of them possessed. "I took Madelyn's blood, and—," Ryan hesitated, at a loss for words. "and someone else's," she finished lamely. "I can't know what effect this has had on me."

27

Victor was silent. He wanted more than anything to lift her up and fasten himself on her neck. Not only would it give him knowledge, it would give her strength, not to mention incomparable pleasure to both of them. But he knew she was right.

"The other one you Shared with," he stopped, the words and their meaning too monumental for him to formulate. He braced himself, then continued. "That was that my mother?"

"Yes," Ryan said simply. "I believe it was."

Victor stared at his child. There was a horrible breadth of knowledge in her eyes, an understanding so deep and painful he knew that words would be inadequate to communicate it.

"She wasn't human," he said quietly, "was she?"

"No," Ryan said, "she was not even of this world." Ryan glanced down at the tome she still held in her hands and a slight smile drifted across her features. "Your father, on the other hand, was quite human, and quite extraordinary."

This startled Victor. For whatever reason, it had not even occurred to him to ask about his father. He was about to ask for more detail when he noticed that Ryan had become very pale. The book slipped from her hands and her knees buckled. A look of pain flashed in her eyes and she would have collapsed had not Victor sprang to her side.

"Ryan," he said urgently, but her eyes were unfocused and she did not respond. He did not hesitate, but gathered her into his arms to take her to the best doctor he knew.

# CHAPTER 4

LIA WISHED FOR DEATH, but death would not come. Cruelly, she lay there for days while the stink of her husband and children grew noxious, then unbearable. It was not hunger or pain that finally drove her from her shelter, but rather the putrid smell of death.

She crawled from her hut, pushing open the door she had been so proud of, the door that had offered her no protection from the parade of horror that had passed by her home. She crawled out into the smoldering ruins of her village to find herself the only survivor of the once thriving town.

She staggered to her feet. The scavengers, both human and avian, had moved on. All that was left were thick swarms of flies that hovered about the dead, feeding from them then leaving their eggs in the rotting carcasses. She stumbled toward the well, briefly wondering if it was contaminated, a thought which caused her to collapse at its edge in bitter laughter. It took a moment for her to regain control, and then she pulled herself weakly up onto the brick retaining wall.

The water level was high and she was able to lean and scoop from its surface. She drank greedily, the stagnant water the most refreshing thing she had ever tasted. She splashed water over her face, then down her throat, washing the blood from the wound that should have killed her.

The water in the well stilled, its surface becoming smooth and placid once more. The sun was at an angle that created a mirror-like reflection of the surface. Lia became very still as she caught sight of her image in the water. She leaned down in disbelief.

Her skin had taken on a leathery appearance. She leaned closer, touching her hand to her cheek. It was smooth and supple, more so than it had been before. There were tiny, repetitive patterns that looked much like scales. Lia looked down at her body. Her upper arms had taken on the same pattern, stopping about halfway above her elbows. She ripped open her shirt, exposing her cleavage. The scaliness had spread down her breasts to just above the nipple, about the same distance it had traveled down her arm.

Lia again gazed at her reflection. She realized the rash had originated from the wound in her neck and was spreading in both directions. It covered her face and head first because of their proximity to the wound, but now it was spreading down her body. She stared at her arms in horror, imagining she could see the rash spreading before her eyes.

A harsh, guttural comment behind her caused her to leap to her feet and clutch her shirt to her breasts. She did not understand the language but the disdain in the voice was clearly communicated.

Two men and a woman were standing before her, impossibly tall and dressed in the strangest clothing. One man had a deep scar across his face and the other appeared older, more refined. Both wore expressions of cruelty on their faces, expressions so habitual they had worn grooves deep into the skin. And yet somehow neither was as frightening as the woman whose striking features were untouched by time or expression, whose gaze was completely dispassionate. All three examined Lia closely, talking amongst themselves in the harsh language Lia did not understand. They seemed surprised to see her in the ruins of the town, but less surprised at the bizarre changes in her skin-tone. One of the males grasped her brutally by the arm and yanked her shirt open, causing her breasts to spill out. Lia blushed crimson with shame, but the attention the three gave her was less lascivious than clinical. There seemed to be some disagreement, with the female dismissing Lia, but one of the males maintaining interest. Finally there seemed to be some sort of compromise as the female shrugged and walked off. The male turned back to Lia and with one motion stripped the dress from her. He examined her fully and this time Lia sensed more ill intent in his perusal, now that he was no longer within the view of the female.

Lia did not have time to assess the danger of this attention because the man pierced her skin with a sharp object, and blessedly, everything went black.

Susan leaped up when Victor came into the lab carrying Ryan. She knew immediately that something was wrong, both by Victor's expression and by the limp form he carried in his arms. She swept the paperwork from the examination table to make room for the motionless figure that Victor gently set down. Edward came in the door behind them, having instantly sensed his master's distress.

Ryan was not unconscious. Her eyes were open, but she did not appear to be aware of any of them. She was very pale and her skin was abnormally cool to the touch. Susan placed her hand upon Ryan's forehead. Although Ryan's body temperature could vary wildly, this was extreme even for her. Her eyes were dark with exhaustion.

"What happened?" Susan asked.

"I'm not certain," Victor said. "She was standing there talking, then just collapsed."

Susan shined a light in Ryan's eyes, noting the near-instantaneous pupil reactivity normal to Ryan. "I've seen her like this before," Susan said. "When we were imprisoned, Madelyn would bleed Ryan almost completely. It would take days for her to recover. But this," she said, waving her hand in front of Ryan in an attempt to get her attention, "this is new."

The motion finally appeared to have the desired effect and Ryan slowly focused on Susan. Susan was relieved to see recognition in her eyes.

"How did I get here?"

"We were in the study, talking," Victor said, "then it seemed like you just faded away. It was almost as if you fainted, but without losing consciousness."

Ryan shifted on the table, then pushed to an upright position. The maneuver seemed to require a great deal of effort on her part. "I feel," she stopped, unsure exactly what she was feeling. "I feel weak right now."

Susan eyed her uncertainly. When she had been human she would have taken this statement at face value, but now that she possessed preternatural senses, the statement seemed quite impossible. She could feel the power emanating outward from Ryan and it had not diminished in any way, regardless of what Ryan was feeling. Susan turned to Victor.

"Do you feel anything different about her?"

Victor shook his head. "No, she feels exactly like an Old One, powerful beyond her years."

Edward eyed his master with apprehension. Although Ryan often seemed oblivious to her abilities, she had never expressed a feeling so at odds with the reality. The creature sitting before him possessed unbelievable power, yet seemed to have difficulty sitting upright.

"I'm going to run some tests on you," Susan said. "Fortunately I have a lot of baseline information on your anatomy, so I can do some comparisons."

Ryan sighed and reclined once more. All she wanted to do right now was sleep.

"And so this bear and this little pig, they are friends?"

Susan watched Ryan from the doorway. Drake was curled up in her arm and was reading to her slowly and methodically, his diction quite advanced for one so young. Ryan was in her bed once more, propped up on a mountain of pillows, her fatigue obvious. Susan quietly shut the door, certain that Ryan would be asleep long before the animals finished

32

their quest. She turned and stifled a cry as she nearly ran into Edward. He motioned for her to follow him, and they joined Victor in the study.

Victor sat staring into the fire, a glass of red wine untouched at his elbow. This changed when the two entered. He lifted the glass to his lips and drained it in a single drink, setting it back down on the side table. Edward grasped the decanter on the table and refilled the glass. He filled a second glass and offered it to Susan, who thought about refusing, then accepted, taking a long drink herself. Then Edward, who although always allowed, never presumed, did exactly that and poured himself a glass, also downing it in a single drink.

Victor turned from the fire to Susan. "Well, Dr. Ryerson?"

"Ryan's resting and is probably already asleep again. I'm not surprised it's taking some time for her to recover. Even as strong as she is, she's been through some pretty horrifying things. So her weakness isn't that unexpected. But the memory loss?" Susan paused, also considering Ryan's brief period of unresponsiveness. "I don't really know what to think about that." Susan took another long drink of her wine. "Now that Ryan is settled I'm going back to my lab and start analyzing the blood work."

Susan thought back to the earlier examination. Simply obtaining the sample had been an adventure since Ryan's skin was almost impenetrable and the sight of blood excited a predatory response in all of them, including Susan. It was at times like that she had to muster all of her professionalism to complete even the most mundane act.

"But you must have a theory," Victor said, pressing her, "you always have a theory."

Susan started to deny this possibility, then relented. Edward topped off her glass as she settled into the chair opposite Victor.

"I don't know how much Ryan has told you about our captivity."

"Not a great deal," Victor said. "I've had little opportunity to speak with her since she was returned to us."

"But you know of Madelyn."

Victor's expression grew black. "Yes," he said coldly, "I know a little of her. I had the pleasure of meeting her when she briefly returned to parade Ryan before us, and I know her from Abigail's memories, as well as those of my grandson."

Susan unconsciously shivered. "Madelyn bled Ryan regularly, injecting her with some type of neurotoxin to do so. Ryan swore she would not take Madelyn's blood, but I think that's exactly what she did at the end in an attempt to defeat her. Such a union would put unimaginable stress on Ryan's system."

"So you think that Madelyn has infected Ryan with some sort of disease?"

Susan was uncertain. "It's possible. It's too early for me to tell. She may just have weakened her. But I think Ryan is probably wise in her restraint on Sharing blood right now. If anyone can adapt to the attack on her system, it will be her."

# CHAPTER 5

LIA SAT IN HER CAGE. She was naked, but she had grown used to being naked. The shame had finally collapsed into numbness that was probably the only thing keeping her alive. Besides, the scales on her body now covered her entire torso and extremities. The supple, leathery surface felt almost like clothing if for no other reason it felt nothing like her skin. The skin condition would not have been that bad were it not accompanied by pain, pain that grew intense and became continual.

Like most born of her time and station, Lia was not educated. But she was cursed with a keen intelligence. Were she slow and stupid, she probably could have lost herself in the grief of the horrible deaths of her husband and children, in the madness of all that she had seen. But instead she spent day and night wondering what she had done to deserve the hell to which she had been sent. She also wondered endlessly about the demons who were her captors.

The male had come to her almost immediately and although he had done unspeakable things to her, none were recognizable as sexual. Lia was left with a feeling of violation, as if she had been raped repeatedly, yet no sex, at least in her understanding, had occurred. These visits became infrequent, then ceased entirely. Now when someone came, it was merely for observation.

Lia wished she could see herself. She could feel the growths on the side of her head, like the knotty protrusions on the head of a young goat. They were painful as well, fibrous little bumps that jutted from her skull and began to curl like the horns of a ram as they grew longer. The female looked at these with particular contempt, as if their manifestation was some sort of failure on Lia's part. Lia often wondered if it was this growth that would result in a fate like all the others.

Like all the others.

Lia had lost all track of time, yet she seemed to remember each person who came and went in the cell next to hers. All were horribly deformed, suffering. Most went mad and after a short period of observation, were disposed of with cruel efficiency. Lia could not count, so poor was her education, but at first the number seemed the size of an extended family, then that of a small town, then that of a city.

Now they seemed to her as numerous as the stars in the sky. She brushed her fingers along the bony protrusions on her head, unconsciously tracing the circular path. It was probably only a matter of time before they disposed of her as well. She hoped her death would be quick and painless, but from what she had seen of the cruelty of the executioners, efficient as they were, her death most likely would be neither.

Victor went to check on his sleeping child. He pushed quietly into her room only to find an empty bed. He passed into the adjoining room, certain he would find her curled up with Drake, but the boy was sprawled face down in the blankets alone. Victor extended his senses throughout the mansion but could not sense Ryan anywhere. He felt the stirrings of unease. He sat down on the edge of the bed and placed his hand gently on Drake. The small boy opened his eyes sleepily.

"Where's your mother?" Victor asked softly.

Drake rolled over so he could look up at his grandfather. He yawned and brushed his dark hair from his eyes. "She went for a walk." It seemed he sensed Victor's concern and sat upright, his eyes darkening.

"Is Ryan okay?"

Victor smiled. It was one of Drake's peculiarities that he referred to Ryan by her name, not "mom" or "mama" or "mother." He did the same with Victor. Ryan speculated it was because Drake had acquired language in a very unique way, not simply by repetition, trial-and-error and mimicry as did most children, but through direct mental contact with Ryan. He had absorbed her language schema before he had ever spoken a word. And although Ryan now referred to Victor as "father," she also still called him "Victor" out of habit, as she had done for centuries prior to learning that he was in reality her parent.

It did not bother Ryan in the least, and in fact, she thought it probably brought Drake a measure of protection. Although many knew that she had a son, there was no sense in inviting trouble.

"I'm sure she's fine," Victor said. He lifted the covers and motioned for the boy to lay back down, which Drake did. "You go back to sleep."

Victor left the room, but Drake did not go back to sleep. He stared into the darkness, occasionally chewing his lower lip. He more than anyone knew that Ryan was not fine.

Victor caught Edward in the hallway. "Have you seen Ryan?"

Edward identified and shared Victor's concern. "I thought she was sleeping in her room."

Victor shook his head. "Drake said she went for a walk."

Edward's response was brisk. "I will check the gardens. Dr. Ryerson is still in her lab, perhaps you should check there."

Victor nodded in agreement, but he was not optimistic. He did not sense Ryan anywhere, but that was not as meaningful as it would have been under normal circumstances. Prior to these recent events he could sense his child hundreds of miles away, but right now he was not certain he could sense her in the next room.

Moments later, Edward returned to the hallway as did Victor with

Susan in tow. Edward shook his head in response to the unasked question.

"I will access the security cameras."

Victor nodded grimly. Initially, he had thought the idea of security cameras ludicrous. No technological gadget had even close to the sensory abilities of their Kind. But Edward had been disturbed by the ease with which Madelyn and her men had infiltrated their compound when Susan and Drake had been kidnapped. And although security cameras would not have prevented the abduction, they would have at least recorded it.

Edward entered the control room and skillfully manipulated the system. The only one who was perhaps more skilled with the technology was Jason, but he was asleep right now. Victor stood back from the screens. Although he was anxious to see what, if anything, was recorded, the video playback at thirty frames per second was too slow for his preternatural eyes. Additionally, although the resolution was relatively high definition, the picture would appear to him as little more than dots, like an impressionist painting up close. Edward seemed to have found some visual work-around and quickly found what he was looking for.

"It looks like Ryan left about an hour ago," he said examining the footage. He switched camera views. "She was on foot and nothing appears out of the ordinary."

"Which direction did she go?" Victor demanded.

"She left by the east gate, a little over fifty minutes ago."

Susan was hopeful. "Perhaps she just wanted some fresh—,"

But she was speaking only to an empty corner, because Victor had disappeared.

"—air."

Susan turned to Edward. "I am constantly reminded of how much those two are alike."

The young woman was sitting beneath a tree. The sun was just beginning to peek over the horizon and light filtered through the leaves, casting shadowed patterns on the ground. The girl gathered a handful of the rich, composted soil, marveling at the coolness of the dark earth in her hand.

She glanced around. She had no idea where she was, or in the oddest sense, even who she was. It was mildly disturbing, but she was distracted by the golden dust motes floating in the sunbeams that pierced the canopy. The intricate pattern of the bark of the tree in front of her also mesmerized her, the design endlessly repeating on a smaller and smaller scale until it seemed she could see the molecular structure of the organism itself.

She glanced around. She knew all of these things, tree, sunlight, soil, but with no particular memory of how she knew them, nor any memory of knowing them before this moment. She grasped another handful of damp earth. The feel of the soil was luxurious, soft and silken in the palm of her hand. It was deathly silent in the small clearing, and although the girl sensed insects, birds, and small mammals nearby, they made no sound at all, as if something dangerous had entered their realm and all were instinctively silenced.

The girl felt something and took a moment to analyze the sensation. She thought for a moment that she was hungry, but that seemed an inadequate representation of the feeling. She considered thirst as a possibility, and that seemed closer to the mark but again somehow inadequate. It was some type of craving coupled with a desire that was sensual but not sexual in nature. This thought gave her pause because at the moment she could not quite remember what sex was.

She let the thought drift away. The heat in her body seemed to be rising, as evidenced by the steam rising from the damp earth surrounding her. The water vapor fascinated her and would have held her attention for quite some time were it not for the fact that something was approaching.

Victor entered the clearing. He was following both the physical and sensory trail that Ryan left in her wake, although the sensory signs were confusing. It felt like Ryan, yet not quite right. He was relieved to see her seated so casually, apparently unharmed; but again, something was not quite right.

The girl stared at the dark-haired man, examining him intently. She did not know him, but he seemed familiar in some vague sense, as if he reminded her of someone she could not remember. More than anything, he stimulated some devilishly predatory response in her. She analyzed the feeling with the same dispassionate interest she had held for the water vapor. He was incredibly handsome, but the feeling was distinctly non-sexual in nature. It felt more like…

It felt like she wanted to kill him. And then maybe eat him.

Victor knew something was terribly wrong, even more wrong than the earlier amnesia and subsequent weakness. Ryan did not appear at all weak at the moment. Her skin had transitioned from the previous deathly pallor to a deep flush, giving her an almost feverish appearance. Her gaze, however, was not dull with fever but penetratingly clear. Her eyes appeared almost brown, but when she shifted and the light struck her iris, Victor could see that they were actually a deep maroon.

"Ryan?" Victor said carefully, slowly moving into the clearing.

The name was like a drop of water, and had it landed in a still pool it would have rippled outward and touched shores that would have grounded her. But instead, it dripped into a maelstrom in which it had no effect at all. She simply looked at him.

Victor stepped closer, still moving slowly. Ryan stared at him, no recognition in her eyes whatsoever. A slight smile played about her lips and there was a wicked glint in her eye. It was difficult for Victor to suppress his own predatory response because he knew exactly what she was doing, even if she did not. He braced himself.

She sprang at him and even though he anticipated the move and knew how preternaturally fast she was, he was still knocked from his feet. He rolled as she dove at him, coming to his feet as she recklessly went head-first into a tree. The tree split upon impact, cracking loudly, half crashing to the ground and half remaining upright at an uncertain angle. Victor took that opportunity to tackle her, pinning her to another tree, but his grip was awkward and she flung him to the side, laughing.

He came after her again and she launched a flurry of strikes at him, ending with a kick to his midsection that sent him flying across the clearing. As she stalked toward him, he let loose his own kick which sent her staggering in the opposite direction, causing her to laugh some more. It seemed her mirth was having a more debilitating effect than his blows, but Victor did not care. He would press any advantage he had. He again tackled her around the shoulders, shoving her backward into a tree. This time his grip was sure and he pinned her with his enormous strength.

She struggled for a moment, face-to-face with him, then relaxed. She appeared more entertained by her predicament than concerned. Victor stared at his dangerously rambunctious child, torn. It had been his intent simply to bring her home safely, but her violent antics had so incited his blood lust it was all he could do not to tear into her neck and drink her dry. Any warnings Dr. Ryerson had passed on were ephemeral memories.

The girl examined the man's handsome features, the sharp cheekbones, the sensual mouth, the brooding dark eyes that were filled with a myriad of emotions. Her eyes drifted downward to the vein throbbing in his neck, but her gaze jerked further downward to a spot of red on his collarbone. It was a small cut, just a nick really, seeping just a tiny amount of blood.

The girl raised her eyes to his once more and Victor felt a sense of deep foreboding. Impossibly, he felt himself slowly and inexorably lifted off his feet. And Ryan was doing so effortlessly with a strength he had never felt in anyone. Rather than bend down to adjust her position, she was casually moving him into the position she wanted. She raised him just enough so that the wound was on level with her mouth, then pulled him forward with the same slow inevitability. Victor watched with a mixture of fascination and despair, impotence and desire.

Her lips burned on the wound, but if the effect on Victor was profound it was more so on Ryan. The second the blood touched her lips, her head shot backward, striking the tree behind her with great force. Her eyes rolled upward, then returned, unfocused. She released him and he landed on his feet, grasping her as she collapsed. He lifted her into his arms as she went limp and unconscious.

Victor stared down at his daughter, the heat from her body emanating off in infrared waves that he could see. In seconds, she had gone from that monstrously powerful creature to this feverish child lost in a delirious sleep. It was almost as if she were two different people.

He sighed, starting for home. He had the feeling this was going to get much, much worse.

Lia was awakened by someone shaking her shoulder. She recognized the man, the one with the scar that had leered at her and committed the unspeakable acts.

"Get up," he said roughly.

Lia was stunned. During her entire captivity, not one of the demons had ever spoken a word that she understood. And now this one was speaking to her clearly in her own language.

"Get up!" he repeated angrily, dragging her upright.

Lia stood, barely keeping her feet as the man hurried her through the cage door. He thrust her before him and she struggled to maintain balance, using legs that had seen little motion in the last few years. She was rushed through a hallway with solid rock walls adorned with geometric patterns, allowed no time to examine their strangeness.

The man pushed her into a room and closed the door behind them.

Lia stopped. On a slab before her was a man. He was dark-haired and beautiful, and appeared to be sleeping peacefully. His physical form was perfect, a stark contrast to her mutilation. She was very aware of her leathery skin and the horns on the sides of her head.

"Do you see this one?" the man said in his harsh, rasping tongue.

Lia nodded fearfully. She thought the demon might kill the beautiful man right in front of her, but instead he leaned close, forcing her to take a good look at the sleeping face. The demon whispered in her ear, telling a hideous story, his words brutal and impossible to believe. But as he spoke and the words tumbled out in bitter stream, Lia's posture stiffened. Her striking green eyes began to glitter, taking on the sheen and hardness of emeralds. She gazed at the dark-haired man and felt a hatred so intense it seemed it would burn her from the inside out.

The demon pulled her away, practically dragging her down the corridor. He led her through the shadows to a small side gate, then shoved her through the opening. She sprawled onto the ground, her legs still barely functioning. She did not understand why any of this was happening, but she was not going to question her freedom. She stood, a naked figure whose chameleon-like skin camouflaged her in the darkness, and began limping from the fortress. With every step away from the despised prison, her legs felt stronger, and soon she was walking, then running. The cool night air was decadent on her skin, and for the briefest of moments, pleasure pierced the veil of pain that covered her unceasingly.

Lia fled into the night without the slightest idea of where she was going, overcome by an almost rapacious exuberance.

Edward and Susan met Victor in the courtyard. Susan gasped. Edward was more restrained, but even he could not restrict his commentary.

"Oh my," he murmured.

Victor was carrying Ryan, who appeared to be sick or injured as well as unconscious. Both were disheveled and dirty, and their clothing was torn. Angry welts and bruises were visible on their skin. Because of the nearly unmatched power of each, it was not hard to guess how their conditions came about.

"Yes, yes," Victor sighed, "we did this to each other."

This was less shocking to Edward than to Susan, who was still getting used to the casual violence that permeated Victor and Ryan's relationship. Edward, for his part, wasn't even really surprised although he was concerned about his master's current condition.

"Shall I dare ask how this came about?" he prompted, examining Ryan's limp form.

"Let's get her settled," Victor said.

Within minutes, Ryan was back in her bed. Staff members materialized and under Susan's guidance, cleaned the wounds that were already healing. Ryan shifted fitfully at the attention but did not awaken. Jason entered, leading Drake by the hand. For once Drake did not run forward but pressed close to his friend.

Victor watched the ministrations silently. He had no idea what had happened although it was clear that Ryan had suffered another bout of amnesia. But this one was dramatically different from the one before. Whereas previously she had seemed almost vulnerable, this time she was recklessly out-of-control. And she had exhibited strength that was stunning.

Victor's expression grew grim. And that was not even what had made her so dangerous. She had also exhibited a rash abandon coupled with a wicked sense of humor, a combination that would make her irresistible to their Kind. Even he had difficulty controlling his passion when attempting to subdue her because she was appealing to, and in fact reveling in, their most primal instincts.

Victor sighed, and Edward turned to him expectantly.

"I'm going to need some help."

# CHAPTER 6

RYAN OPENED HER EYES. Drake was no longer sleeping with her, but that was not surprising because it felt like she had been asleep a while. She was surprised to see Victor at the foot of her bed who, aware of her awakening, was examining her warily. Her eyes shifted to the fading bruise on his cheek, then drifted downward to the welts on his arms.

"Well, what happened to you?" she asked.

Victor said nothing but cast his own eyes downward, and Ryan followed his gaze. She, too, had welts and bruises covering her arms.

Ryan's tone filled with self-recrimination and resignation. "What did I do now?"

"You don't remember?" Victor asked.

Ryan shook her head. "The last thing I recall is Drake reading to me."

Susan walked in as Victor responded.

"It seems you went out for a walk, then were a little resistant when I tried to bring you back."

Ryan felt the stirrings of despair and more than a little frustration. "What exactly did I do?"

Victor was uncertain, but because of his own fierce predatory nature could not help but find a degree of humor in the events. "I'm not completely sure, but I think you were going to try and eat me."

"Oh dear god," Ryan said, hiding her face in her hands, "I thought I'd gotten that out of my system."

"How are you feeling now?" Susan asked, moving to her side. She placed her hand on Ryan's forehead, noting that Ryan's skin temperature had returned to normal. She also noted that her iris color had returned to a more typical hazel. Ryan's eyes often shifted color with her mood, but Susan had never seen them maroon before.

"I feel fine," Ryan said. "Still a little tired, but nothing extreme."

"Hmm," Susan said. "Your blood work is coming back completely routine." She stopped and clarified. "Well, routine for you. And Victor doesn't seem to have had any ill effects from your contact."

Ryan sat upright. "What contact?"

"One of your blows split the skin here," Victor said, fingering his collar bone, "causing me to bleed."

The implication was obvious to Ryan, especially if she had been as out-of-control as described. "I took your blood?"

"Barely," Victor said, thinking back to the strange encounter. "The minute your lips touched my blood, you jerked back as if you had been electrocuted."

As he said that, a disjointed series of visions rushed through Ryan's head. The deformed creatures standing in the shadows watching her, the monstrous tentacles clutching her torso and pulling her downward, the shower of blood that blocked out all light then ran down her throat, suffocating her with pleasure. There seemed to be something else there, some other story she couldn't quite remember, but she returned to the series of images that rushed through her mind with such force they caused physical pain.

"I…" Ryan said slowly, "I actually remember some of that."

This seemed significant to Susan. "What do you remember?"

Ryan struggled to sort the images. "Nothing before that. Nothing after that. But I remember the moment Victor's blood touched my lips." She turned to Victor. "And somehow it seems my reaction to the connection was mental, not physical."

Susan felt her own sense of frustration. None of this made any sense. When Victor told her of the contact, she had swabbed the wound but found nothing more unusual than traces of thrombolin. Although this would have been abnormal in a human, it was normal for Ryan because Susan had previously discovered the anticoagulant in the saliva of their Kind. And although Ryan may have taken a small amount of Victor's blood, Victor had taken none from Ryan.

Ryan settled back into the pillows, her exhaustion returning full force. She was clearly distressed by this turn of events. One last thought kept her from sleep.

"Is Drake alright?" she asked Victor.

"Yes," Victor said. "He's fine. Would you like to see him?"

"No," Ryan said, rolling over onto her side and turning her back to her father. "He should not be near me right now."

Victor clenched his jaw at the pain in his child's voice, and at the knowledge that she was right.

Susan watched the handsome dark-haired man from the hallway and Edward appeared at her side. Both were moved by Victor's emotions. Edward could sense Susan's emotions as well.

"Ryan has been through worse," Edward said, somehow doubting the truth of his own words. They were not exactly an untruth because he had no idea what Ryan was going through right now.

"I'm going back to my lab," Susan said, pushing her sadness aside. She needed to focus on her work. "Will he stay with her?"

Edward nodded. "Victor will not leave her side. I doubt she will be able to wander off again."

"I would take my turn keeping watch," Susan said, "but if she wakes in her amnesiac form, there is nothing I can do to stop her."

Edward pondered her words. "I doubt there's anything I could do to stop her. Which is why," he continued, "it's good that Victor has taken additional precautions."

Susan turned to him, curious. Despite the seriousness of the situation, Edward smiled.

"His lordship has taken it upon himself to summon the elemental forces of fire and ice."

Susan assessed the odd statement, then took a quick breath as she grasped its meaning.

"Both of them?"

"Yes," said Edward said, "they should be arriving today, in fact." Despite his usual misgivings directed at the incoming visitors, his approval for this course of action was unequivocal. Desperate times required desperate measures.

For Susan's part, this pronouncement brought an odd mixture of anxiety, relief, and pure exhilaration.

# CHAPTER 7

THE MID-SIZED JETS ARRIVED ALMOST simultaneously, quite a feat considering they had departed from different continents. The flurry of activity at the private landing strip was at a level normally associated with the arrival of royalty. The subsequent entourage from the runway to the mansion exceeded even that bloated standard. The long caravan wound its way about the circular drive and then the two central limousines stopped at the bottom of the stairs.

Outwardly, Edward was a picture of efficient servitude, his patrician features calm and composed. Inwardly, he was steeling himself for the coming onslaught.

The first door opened and a ravishing, dark-haired woman stepped out. Her dark eyes sparkled with wicked mirth as glanced up at Edward, instantly assessing his internal state. She tossed her head to the side, placing her hand on her hip and tilting her chin with sultry nonchalance. Power and desire emanated from her in equal parts like heat emanating from an inferno. Edward struggled to maintain his composure.

The second door opened and another woman stepped out. Older in physical appearance and fairer in coloring than the first, she was just as stunningly gorgeous. Icily elegant, she carried herself with a regal and forbidding poise. Her power, unlike that of her fiery companion, was carefully contained and controlled, but just as unmistakable. Her eyes were filled with cool amusement as she greeted the raven-haired woman.

"Hello my dear," Abigail said, "it feels like we were just here."

"Bonjour, Ma Cherie," Marilyn responded, kissing the cheek Abigail proffered. "I believe that we were." She glanced up at Edward. "I'm quite curious why Victor has summoned us in such short order."

Abigail extended her hand and Marilyn took it, giving the outward appearance of assisting the matriarch up the stairs. But Marilyn knew as well as any that Abigail required no assistance, rather this was one of the forms of subtle and sensual influence that Abigail exerted. Marilyn participated in the charade without hesitation or reservation, partially because she enjoyed it, and partially because that was how Marilyn approached everything.

Edward watched the two, noting the physical and non-physical contact in the greeting. There had always been a delicate balance of competition and cooperation between these two Old Ones, and Edward felt that a tilt towards the latter would be far more dangerous than the former. He did his best to hide his thoughts, but he knew that the she-dragon approaching him sensed the theme if not the entire content of his concerns. Her cool gaze and slow smile told him as much. The twitch of Marilyn's full lips told him she knew as well.

Edward sighed and bowed deeply from the waist. "His lordship is extremely grateful that you have responded with such haste."

"We live to serve him," Abigail said. "Which brings to question, why does his lordship not greet us himself?"

"Yes," Marilyn added, "where is Victor?"

Edward chose his words carefully. "He sends his most fervent apologies and has said he will greet you properly once you're settled."

Abigail's examination was acute and Edward would have felt no less exposed had he been standing there naked. The silence stretched for a long moment while Edward waited for the question he knew would follow.

"And where is Ryan?" Abigail asked, her gaze penetrating.

Edward again chose his words carefully. "She has not completely recovered from her ordeal and is spending a great deal of time resting."

This comment brought intense scrutiny from both women. Edward sighed, and again bowed deeply, doing his best to imply that he was simply the hired help. Neither woman bought the act for a moment.

"Then why don't you get us settled in our chambers," Abigail said, "so that we can meet with Victor."

Marilyn spent no time in her quarters but immediately went to Abigail's suite. She entered without knocking, causing Abigail's staff to attempt looks of disapproval. But the raven-haired beauty was simply too infectious to inspire even the mildest ire in them, so they quickly disappeared lest they more successfully elicit that emotion from their mistress.

"Please come in," Abigail said drily.

Marilyn glanced about the room. Whereas her chambers were decorated in warm, bold colors with plush, modern furnishings, Abigail's were a study in timeless luxury; all pale, cool colors, antique furniture, and classic works of art. The decor had been a nod of respect from Ryan and both suites suited their occupants perfectly.

Marilyn settled onto the couch across from Abigail and opened her mouth to speak. But before she could utter a word, the door opened once more.

"I see I have another interloper," Abigail said, unable to disguise her pleasure.

Drake peeked around the door. Then, without hesitation, he raced into the room and into Marilyn's open arms. She lifted him from the ground onto her lap, facing her.

"Mon Dieu," Marilyn said under her breath. The child was gorgeous. She had just seen him weeks before, but at this age he was growing so quickly he had already changed. He was getting taller and leaner, losing what little baby fat he had. His black hair was thick and luxurious, just like his grandfather's, and his deep blue eyes sparkled. He laughed, clapped his hands on Marilyn's cheeks, and planted a giant kiss on her lips. He leaned back, quite satisfied with himself.

"Oh my," Marilyn said, feeling such a powerful mix of tenderness and desire for the boy. "You can't grow up fast enough."

The boy sensed both emotions from the beautiful woman and was alarmed by neither. He instinctively understood the tenderness because he was a child, and the desire because he was Ryan's child. Marilyn ran her fingers through his hair.

"I know why Victor kept Ryan from us when she was this young," she murmured, kissing his forehead.

Drake turned his attention to Abigail and suddenly grew shy. Abigail stared at him for what seemed an eternity, and his small body visibly trembled with anticipation. Finally, with the smile she could no longer contain, she gave him permission to approach.

"Come here, little one."

Drake climbed from Marilyn's lap and approached Abigail in a far more circumspect manner. She, too, pulled him onto her lap to face her and he sat patiently as she examined him. She noted his fine features, the chiseled cheek bones, the perfect mouth.

"You," she said to the small boy, "look exactly like your mother."

This pleased Drake greatly and he blushed, smiling shyly. He very slowly leaned forward and touched his lips to Abigail's, the kiss utterly gentle and chaste, but extending just that fraction of a second longer than a truly chaste kiss would. He leaned back to assess the results of his experiment.

Abigail was amused. "You," she said, "also act exactly like your mother."

He again smiled shyly, showing no indication that he truly understood what he had just done. Abigail wondered what the boy would be like around the sight of blood.

"Drake?" came the uncertain voice from the doorway. Jason leaned inside, a look of trepidation on his face. He caught sight of his young companion and stepped inside, clearly apologetic.

"I was supposed to be watching him, but he disappeared on me."

Marilyn eyed the young man appreciatively. She had not seen much of him lately, and he, too, was undergoing dramatic changes. She estimated he was on the verge of adolescence and although he also strongly favored his mother, his father's genetic influence could be seen. Jason was already as tall as Susan with a strong and sturdy build.

Jason grew flush under Marilyn's scrutiny. The dark-haired woman already played a large role in his fantasies and her dancing eyes told him that she knew it.

"Come here, Jason," Marilyn commanded playfully. Although her tone was teasing, refusal was not an option. Abigail glanced over at Marilyn, and Drake shifted to get a better view. His friend seemed quite out of sorts at the moment.

Jason stepped closer and Marilyn's examination continued. His mop of red hair from childhood was turning bronze, much like Susan's, and he shared her coloring. He also shared her penchant for uncontrolled blushing as his cheeks went to a deep red. Marilyn thought it quite fetching.

Abigail watched Marilyn toy with the young man, and watched as Drake seemed quite intrigued by the whole situation. It would be most interesting to watch these dynamics as the boys grew older.

"Jason."

Jason started at his mother's voice. Susan was standing in the door, aware of her son's discomfort and dilemma. She would do her best to rescue him, although she herself wanted to run from the staggering power that was in this room.

"Why don't you go give Edward a hand?" she suggested, having no idea what Edward was doing at the moment.

Jason was torn. Torn between wanting to run away, wanting to retrieve Drake, and wanting to simply stay right where he was. Drake seemed to sense his friend's quandary and took it upon himself to rescue him. He smiled conspiratorially at Abigail, then let himself to the ground. He ran over to Jason, grabbed his hand, then pulled him from the room. Susan sought to follow them but was arrested by Marilyn's voice.

"Hello, Dr. Ryerson," she said smoothly. It was clear from the tone of her voice that since Susan had removed the source of her entertainment, she was required to take its place.

"Marilyn," Susan said, "Abigail," she said, turning to the older woman.

"Dr. Ryerson," Abigail said.

Marilyn let her eyes drift over Susan, noting the same deep flush as her son. Her offspring had been a beautiful human, a beauty that had only been enhanced by her Change. Marilyn had been unable to Change Susan directly because she was far too powerful and her blood would have killed Susan. But Ryan had chosen a young man from Marilyn's lineage to initiate the transition and Susan clearly bore Marilyn's mark. Marilyn wondered idly if Susan was strong enough now to survive Sharing with her, and thought she would perhaps explore that option sometime soon.

Susan turned a deep crimson and Abigail smiled to herself. Although Susan was not yet powerful enough to read the thoughts of others, it wasn't difficult to tell what Marilyn was thinking. She wore everything on her sleeve, especially her desire.

"Dr. Ryerson," Abigail continued, "perhaps you can tell us more of Ryan's condition since Edward was less than forthcoming."

Susan's senses returned to her. "That's actually why I'm here. I'm meeting Victor in the great room to update him on my latest progress, and he's asked that you be there."

Abigail entered the great room and Victor turned from the fireplace to greet her. He took the hand she presented and kissed it. She bowed slightly in response.

"My king, it's good to see you."

Victor knew Abigail's misuse of the title was intentional. "Technically," he said, "Ryan is still king until she chooses to relinquish the position."

"Ah," said Abigail smoothly, "but it's my understanding that if the king is indisposed, another must be appointed, if even on an interim basis."

"I see we're going to get right to the point," Victor said, his jaw clenching.

Marilyn flowed into the room. "And what is the point, Mon Cher?" She did not offer her hand but rather leaned forward and kissed him fully on the mouth. Susan and Edward followed Marilyn in. Edward was unmoved by the open display but Susan blushed profusely. The desire and interplay between the Old Ones always overwhelmed her.

Aeron's subsequent entrance surprised both Abigail and Marilyn, not because they had not sensed him, but because it was rare for him and Victor to occupy the same space without violence. Victor glanced at him coldly, but nodded. He opened his mouth to reply to Marilyn's question, but was stopped.

"And would you hold such a reunion without me?" Ryan said drily, her tone of voice indicating she knew full well the reason for such a gathering. She was dressed casually but was no less striking for the simplicity of her clothing.

Abigail's expression remained neutral. She had become aware of the girl's presence, but only as Ryan entered the room. It was apparent that none of the Others, not even Victor, had sensed her approach. It also did not appear that Ryan was making any effort at disguising her aura, it just was not visible. Abigail's eyes narrowed. This was a gift that would bear watching.

Ryan approached Victor, taking his hand and kissing him on the cheek. It was at that moment Abigail noted the injuries to both that indicated mutual combat.

"How are you feeling?" Victor asked, assessing her carefully. She seemed fine.

"I feel normal," Ryan said. "But," she added, "that seems subject to a moment's change."

Victor smiled grimly as Ryan moved to Susan. In an unusually

55

affectionate gesture, Ryan kissed Susan on the forehead. It was a very gentle acknowledgment that bespoke of Ryan's current mood. She moved to Aeron, giving him a once-over that bespoke more of their past relationship than her mood.

"My love," she said, gently sarcastic. She gave him a chaste kiss on the lips and he struggled with the desire that ignited within him. The girl was absolutely ruthless with her sparse affection toward him, causing him endless torment. At one time, he would have taken her to the ground for trifling with him in such a way, or at least wound up in hand-to-hand combat. But now he was not certain of the wisdom of either course of action, although had the Others not been in the room he probably would have pursued one or the other anyway.

Ryan moved on to Edward, taking his hand and bowing slightly. "My friend," she said simply.

Edward was deeply moved, but he would not presume any familiarity in a public setting. "My lord," he said firmly. Edward always addressed Ryan in formal masculine form, which somehow did not seem incongruous.

Ryan smiled, and moved on to Marilyn. Although Ryan was exceptionally tall, she was still slightly shy of Marilyn's height. Ryan also appeared younger than Marilyn, even though physical appearance was no indication of age or power amongst their Kind. This did not stop Marilyn from continually taking advantage of these psychological edges.

"Hello, little one," Marilyn said, her pleasure evident. She leaned down and gave Ryan a long, languorous kiss. Marilyn's influence on her was so powerful, Ryan felt her head swim even after centuries of such treatment. Edward finally cleared his throat and Marilyn reluctantly finished the kiss.

Ryan's jaw clenched, one of the many mannerisms she and Victor shared. She had agreed with Susan that she should not Share with anyone until it was determined safe. But it was already difficult enough being around Victor and Aeron. Adding Marilyn's constant flirtation to the mix was highly volatile. Ryan turned to the last person in the room.

And then there was Abigail.

The matriarch examined the girl. Outwardly Ryan appeared fine, perhaps just a touch pale. As always, she appeared androgynous as a Renaissance angel, an impossibly ideal physical specimen regardless of sex. The youthfulness of her appearance added to this androgyny because Ryan had been Changed exceedingly young, long before she had matured into an adult woman. The fact that she had lived most of the first 400 years of her life as a man probably added to the illusion.

Inwardly, Ryan's current state was an entirely different matter. Abigail had seen Ryan in chaotic states before, particularly when she was battling the virus that Aeron had unleashed. She had watched Ryan become the physical manifestation of rage. She had seen her act with reckless abandon and a total lack of self-regard. She had seen the girl exhibit power and gifts that no one thought possible

But this, Abigail thought, this was something different. Underlying all her magnetism, all her strength, all her composure, one thing was quite clear to Abigail...

Ryan was filled with uncertainty. She was so uncertain in fact it seemed for the moment she had given up trying to make sense of things. She was uncertain of herself, uncertain of those around her, and indeed, uncertain of reality itself.

Abigail smiled. Now this was something she could work with.

Ryan felt the subtle probing of her psyche, and knew that whatever had been discovered pleased the elegant woman in front of her greatly. She stepped forward, not completely voluntarily, and grasped Abigail's outstretched hands. Abigail pulled the girl gently to her, leaned forward, and very slowly touched her lips to the side of her neck, brushing the carotid artery that jumped to life beneath the kiss. The touch staggered Ryan, and Abigail held her for a moment so that she would not fall.

The near-imperceptible act was greeted with various reactions about the room. Edward was unsurprised; it was typical of the she-dragon. Marilyn was completely amused. Aeron's bloodlust was aroused and Susan felt her insides flutter and twist inside her. Victor was resigned, as Abigail had always toyed with Ryan in such a manner.

"Perhaps we can start now?" Victor said caustically.

57

Ryan sat at the head of one end of the table, flanked by Edward and Susan. Victor sat at the other end, Abigail at his right and Marilyn at his left. Aeron sat in the middle of the table. For a long moment, no one said anything, and Ryan and Victor just stared at one another. Ryan finally spoke.

"It seems," she said, humor in her voice, "that I've not been myself lately."

She turned to Susan as she continued. "I'm sure that Dr. Ryerson can offer more insight than I have, but I've been passing through some interesting phases, most of which I don't remember at all."

This caught everyone's attention and Ryan seemed at a loss as how to continue. Susan, though the youngest at the table by centuries, came to her aid.

"When Ryan first returned from captivity, she slept for almost three weeks." Susan's voice was hesitant, but grew stronger as she settled into her element. "I monitored her condition and it seemed almost cyclical in nature as she passed through periods of deep sleep, then transitioned into shorter, more fitful bouts, then returned to the deep sleep. It seemed similar to REM and non-REM sleep, but more extreme. I use the term 'sleep' loosely because Ryan's brain waves never indicate a true sleeping state but are more akin to deep meditation."

Susan glanced at Ryan, who was staring at the table in front of her, her chin resting on her fist. "When Ryan first awoke, she experienced a period of retrograde amnesia, which quickly passed."

This intrigued Abigail. "Amnesia? Can you describe that, Ryan?"

Ryan removed her chin from her hand and thought back to the strange episode. "I saw a man, and I understood that it was a man, but I had no understanding of how I came to possess that knowledge. I also had no memory of any man other than the one sitting in front of me."

Ryan nodded to Victor. "That man was my father." She gave a nod to Susan as well. "When Dr. Ryerson entered the room, I didn't recognize her either, having that same sense of extreme disassociation. I didn't recognize anything in the room, or in fact, anything at all until Drake came in."

"And you recognized your son?" Abigail prompted.

"Yes," Ryan said thoughtfully. "Not immediately. But when he climbed onto my lap and looked into my eyes, suddenly everything I knew came crashing back."

Ryan winced at the memory, wordlessly communicating how painful the experience had been. Abigail watched her for a long moment, then turned her attention back to Dr. Ryerson.

"There were other phases?"

Susan nodded. "Yes, a short time later, Ryan described feeling profoundly weak."

"She actually fainted and collapsed in my arms," Victor added. "I carried her to the lab."

Ryan gazed at her father, then took up the story line. "I came to and just felt extremely tired. I could barely hold up my head."

Abigail, ever astute, caught the shift of expression on Susan's face, interpreting it correctly. "You have seen this behavior before," she said.

Susan felt as if she was somehow betraying Ryan, but she could not resist Abigail's probing.

"When we were in captivity," Susan said, "Madelyn would bleed Ryan completely, and it would take days if not weeks for her to recover."

Ryan stared at the table in front of her and began tracing a strange geometric pattern with her finger. Abigail watched the odd, repetitive behavior, then turned her attention to Victor.

"And what happened after this most recent bout of weakness?"

Ryan's cheeks colored slightly as she continued tracing the pattern. Marilyn noted the blush and leaned forward. This would be interesting.

"Ryan disappeared," Victor said, "and I went to look for her." He stared down the table at his offspring, seeking to explain the inexplicable. "When I found her, she very clearly did not recognize me again."

"But this was different from her earlier memory loss?" Abigail prompted.

Victor was still searching for words to explain. "She wasn't herself."

Ryan stopped tracing the pattern. "Apparently I was completely out-of-control," Ryan said with self-recrimination. "I attacked him."

Victor slowly shook his head. "No, I don't think you were out-of-control at all," he said slowly. "I initially had the same impression. But after some thought, I realized you were on the verge, but your mannerisms were very calculating." He turned to Susan as if seeking support, "Her physical strength was astounding, and her body temperature was very high."

Susan nodded. "I didn't see Ryan until Victor brought her back. But the physiological changes were still present. Ryan's body temperature was far above even her extremes. And the color of her eyes had changed to a deep maroon which faded as her body temperature returned to normal."

"And she experienced both retrograde and anterograde amnesia in this instance?"

All eyes turned to Marilyn, who quite stunningly had trotted out that bit of technical jargon. It even brought a smile to Ryan's face. She could not let this pass without comment.

"And all those years ago when I taught you to read," Ryan said wryly, "I assumed those lessons were just a ruse to keep me under your thumb."

Marilyn smiled wickedly. "Oh, Ma Cherie, they most certainly were. I assure you any learning that occurred was purely accidental."

Those pleasant memories occupied Ryan for a moment but as they faded, she again began tracing the strange geometric pattern on the table.

Susan watched the behavior and it stirred some sort of memory in her, something she couldn't quite place. Ryan was clearly distracted and paying little attention to what she was doing, and the inadvertent actions were borderline obsessive.

With a start, Susan recognized the pattern and stiffened. Simultaneously, whether she had recalled the pattern on her own or gleaned recognition from Susan, Ryan's finger stopped and she grew very pale. She abruptly stood.

"I must take my leave. My apologies."

And with that, she was gone, startling everyone in the room. The unexpected departure was greeted with silence until finally, Susan stood. She intended to leave but first would answer Marilyn's question.

"Ryan experienced both retrograde and anterograde amnesia. She had no recall of who or what she was during the spell, then had no memory of the spell after the fact. But once the spell was over, it seemed her overall memory was intact." Susan looked toward the doorway. "I'm going to make certain she's alright."

Victor swallowed hard and nodded. He could feel Abigail's gaze upon him. Edward also stood, bowing low.

"I'm going to see to my master as well."

The silence remained a while longer as the four Old Ones contemplated Ryan's strange reaction and abrupt disappearance. Marilyn spoke and for once was quite serious.

"Dr. Ryerson didn't quite get around to it, but I'm assuming she has found nothing thus far?"

Victor shook his head. "She's found nothing unusual and nothing that would explain any of this."

Abigail's gaze had not left Victor. "So now why don't you share with us what you would not say in front of Ryan."

Victor made a derisive noise. "She could be at the far end of the mansion and still hear me."

"Yes," Abigail agreed without relenting, "and she can also read your thoughts. So you might as well speak them."

Victor yielded, his frustration palpable. "Ryan has yet to share with me any of what happened to her, so other than her cryptic comment about my 'mother,' and what Dr. Ryerson has told me, I have no idea what she's been through."

"You haven't Shared with her?" Abigail asked.

"It was my intent," Victor said, then admitted, "for many reasons, not all of them altruistic. But Ryan has not been well since her return, and even though I thought my blood might strengthen her, Dr. Ryerson expressed concerns."

"Dr. Ryerson was correct in her concern," Abigail said, "if Ryan

Shared with this creature Madelyn, contact with her might not be safe. We can't risk the both of you."

"Ryan and I did have brief contact," Victor said, thinking back to the end of their battle, "she took a small amount of my blood and it seemed a great shock to her system. But it also seemed to break her from the spell she was under."

"But you said Dr. Ryerson has found nothing wrong with Ryan," Marilyn interjected.

"That's true," Victor said, "but that doesn't explain her odd behavior, nor the phases she has passed through." Victor grew thoughtful. "When she awoke without memory, she was almost like a child again, vulnerable because she didn't know who or what she was, yet still possessing an extraordinary power she seemed unaware of."

"I wish to babysit her during that phase," Marilyn murmured.

Victor continued. "When she described feeling overcome by weakness, none of us could detect any weakness in her. She was just as powerful as she's always been."

Marilyn pondered that situation. "I will take that shift as well."

"But when she was in her 'wild' phase," Victor said, disliking the term but having none better, "she was unlike anything I've ever seen." He thought back to the creature he had fought in the forest. "She was like an animal, her movements feral, like some great panther. Her manner was controlled savagery, calculating, as if she were stalking me. She seemed amused by the situation, as if it brought her great joy. Her strength was enormous, and I think it was only her own recklessness that kept us equals. I don't know what she's capable of in that mode."

"Hmm," Marilyn said thoughtfully, "a close call. But I will yield that shift to Aeron."

Aeron cast an icy glance in her direction. "Why thank you," he said sarcastically

"Yes," Victor agreed, "that might be appropriate since I had the distinct impression that Ryan wanted to eat me."

Aeron looked to Abigail, who merely smiled enigmatically. He was never going to live that down.

"Anyway," Victor said, tiring of the conversation, "her weakness concerns me, but it's transitory. The memory loss when she's normal is disturbing, but doesn't appear dangerous. But when she's in the savage phase," he paused, searching for the right words, "she's unstoppable."

Something in his tone caught Abigail's attention, and she focused on it with sharp precision. "Is she unstoppable because of her brute force? Or unstoppable because you don't wish to stop her?"

"I'm certain it's a little of both," Victor said coldly. "Her strength is enormous. But her manner is primal in a most attractive way, one that would be hard for any of us to resist, even if it meant our destruction."

Abigail bowed her head to him, indirectly drawing attention to his fierce response. "I meant no disrespect, my lord."

Victor softened. "I apologize. This has been most difficult for me."

"There is no apology necessary," Abigail said graciously, "I think it would be good for you to spend some time with your grandson. We will help you watch Ryan."

"Then you have my thanks," Victor said. He bowed to each, even Aeron, then took his leave.

Abigail watched the dark-haired man stalk from the room. She turned her attention to Aeron.

"And do you think you will be able to exercise self-restraint if you're faced with Ryan in that condition?"

A sharp retort was on Aeron's lips, but instead he let out his breath in what was a half-sigh, half-snort. "I don't have a good record when it comes to self-control with that girl."

It was a surprising admission from the arrogant aristocrat, and seemed too much for him. He, too, pushed away from the table and stalked from the room.

Marilyn sat across from Abigail, a devilish glint in her eyes. "So let me guess how this is going to play out. You will manipulate one of us into sacrificing ourselves so that you can determine if Sharing with Ryan is safe. Then, if this little experiment is successful, you will move to pull the girl back into your gravitational field."

Abigail was not insulted, only amused. "I don't know that the girl has escaped my gravitational field. And I'm certain that with the combined lust present in this room only minutes ago, little if any manipulation on my part will be necessary for that experiment to take place."

Abigail stood gracefully, taking her leave with a parting comment.

"And don't worry, my dear," Abigail said over her shoulder, "I would throw Aeron off that cliff long before I would sacrifice you."

Susan wandered down the dark hallway with a Diet Coke in her hand. Although she no longer required or even desired food or drink, for whatever reason she still craved Diet Coke. The bifurcations, connections, and realignment of her digestive tract and circulatory system had fascinated her and she had documented them at length as her body transitioned from its human form. She had also documented the sudden withdrawal of the physical need for food as well as the slower withdrawal from the psychological habit of eating.

But she had not given up Diet Coke. Ryan had found this profoundly funny, but also understandable. She herself had consumed wine and ale prior to her Change when she was a child in the 14th century. The alcoholic beverages carried no stigma for children at that time and were even considered a good source of cheap calories for the poor. Ryan still drank wine, albeit of much higher quality than when she was a peasant, simply because she liked the taste.

Susan took a sip of the beverage then gently pushed open the door to check on Ryan. Edward was seated at the foot of her bed and Drake was reading aloud from one of his many books. Ryan was fast asleep. Susan closed the door quietly and moved two doors down to her own chambers. She pushed open one of the double doors, entered, and the door whispered closed behind her.

She removed her clothing and pulled an oversized silk shirt over her head, luxuriating in the feel of the soft material against her skin. She turned from her closet and stifled a scream when she saw Abigail seated in the easy chair next to her bed.

"Oh, I assure you my dear, I've seen it all before."

"Abigail," Susan stammered, feeling greatly exposed, "what–, what can I do for you?"

Abigail stood and with deadly grace moved toward Susan, towering over her and causing her to take a step backward and press against the closet door. She was completely overwhelmed by the older woman's magnetism even though Abigail was tightly controlling the manifestation of her power. She was here for a very specific reason.

Susan felt the mixture of terror and desire that all Young Ones feel when confronted with someone so much greater than themselves. Few of Susan's age would ever come face-to-face with one such as Abigail, and all would throw themselves at her feet. Abigail was impressed with Susan's attempt at composure, as ineffectual as it was.

"Relax, Dr. Ryerson," Abigail gently commanded, and Susan relaxed with marked obedience. Abigail took a moment to examine Susan quite thoroughly and could hear the young woman's heart pounding, a throw-back to her human autonomic nervous system. "Hmm," she said, "you actually are quite attractive. But I doubt that even bleeding you to death would satisfy me. Not to mention," she said, half to herself, "that Ryan would never forgive me."

Abigail's gaze returned to the blue-green eyes. "No, I'm here only for information, and although I can very nearly read your thoughts, this will help."

Abigail leaned forward and brushed her razor-sharp teeth across the throbbing artery in Susan's neck, placing her mouth fully on the wound so that not a drop of blood escaped. The shock caused Susan to press against the woman holding her, her senses swimming at the intensity of the contact.

Edward frowned and sat upright in the room down the hall. He glanced at Ryan, who shifted fitfully in the bed but did not awaken. Fortunately Drake had fallen asleep as well, and he merely curled his form to fit his mother tighter.

Aeron was outside in a far part of the courtyard, but he tilted his head at the sensation then smiled his shark's smile. Abigail was a model

65

of efficiency.

Marilyn examined the feeling, unsurprised. She had sensed Abigail's intent prior to the act. She was only mildly perturbed, and that was mostly because she was going to have to undo the dysfunctionality this was likely to cause in her already uptight offspring.

The contact did surprise Victor, but only because he was so lost in his own thoughts. He quickly assessed the situation and determined he would not intervene. He knew what Abigail was doing and wondered why he had not done it himself.

Abigail tasted the blood and although it provided none of the intense passion and near-sexual ecstasy of her equals, it was still decidedly pleasant. Dr. Ryerson was going to grow interesting with age and perhaps it was time to begin pairing her with those stronger than her to accelerate that rate of growth. Abigail pushed this thought away and withdrew from Susan's neck.

Susan felt drugged, struggling to maintain any semblance of control. She had no idea how Ryan had survived around these people when she had been young.

"Ah," Abigail whispered, having full access to Susan's mind. "Ryan is very special. But you know that," Abigail said, considering one of Susan's memories that Abigail could now see, "because you've tasted her blood."

And the scene came fully to life before Abigail, an exhausted Ryan in captivity, Susan offering her blood to Ryan to try and help her, Ryan's teasing response and then ultimate acceptance. Abigail saw Ryan bleed Susan, then give her the tiniest drop of her own blood to strengthen Susan and keep her from passing into death. The infinitesimal drop tore through Susan's system, causing destruction but also having the desired effect of saving her.

Susan's memories were unclear and chaotic and Abigail knew she would have to focus the woman to obtain the information she wanted.

"I want to see from the beginning, when you first arrived at the compound where Ryan was held."

The hazy memories came into sharp focus at the guidance. Abigail could see the creature Madelyn, cold, beautiful, and terrifying. She watched as Madelyn took Ryan away again and again, returning her broken and spent. She saw Madelyn treat Ryan with contempt, then angry respect, then growing desire and outright possessiveness.

"Where did she take her?" Abigail whispered into Susan's ear, pressing her cheek to Susan's temple.

Abigail listened to the conversations between Susan and Ryan, and those between Susan and the creature's servant. There were two rooms, the first an inner chamber and then an inner sanctuary, and apparently, at least according to the servant, Ryan should not have been allowed in either. Abigail watched the memories play out, absorbing every detail. She felt she had almost everything she wanted, with one exception.

"The pattern that Ryan was tracing on the table today," she whispered, "what is that from?"

Abigail saw a series of images: the hieroglyphic-like figures on the doors to the rooms where Ryan was taken, and the fractal-like, geometric patterns of the bricks of the walls themselves. It was these latter patterns that Ryan stood before for hours, then days, then weeks, tracing the outlines of the geometric bricks, weakening the structure of the wall until at the very end, she pushed a section of the fortress outward in exactly the shape she had traced for months. Susan had thought the behavior random and obsessive, not realizing the hidden purpose in what Ryan was doing.

Abigail mentally released Susan, who collapsed into her arms.

"Are you quite finished with her, Madame?" Edward asked from the doorway, his manner tightly controlled.

"Yes," Abigail said smoothly. She released the young woman physically when Edward approached and he gathered the limp form into his arms. He carried Susan to her bed as Abigail left the room without a backward glance.

"Aeron is right," Victor commented upon Abigail's entrance, "you are brutally efficient."

"I wonder, my lord, why you did not think of it yourself."

Victor glanced at her sharply since her words were so close to his own thoughts. But it appeared she was merely using her formidable intuition and not actually invading his mind.

"I haven't been at my best since Ryan's return," he admitted. "I'm questioning my judgment in a lot of things." He walked to the window, looking out but focusing on nothing.

"Then perhaps Ryan's uncertainty is catching."

Victor turned back to Abigail, who had settled gracefully onto the lounge. "What do you mean by that?"

"I sense an overwhelming uncertainty in Ryan right now," Abigail said, "as if she feels her grip on reality is very tenuous."

Victor sat down next to Abigail. "That's not surprising given what she's told me, especially about Ravlen."

Abigail could not hide her flair of interest. "The creature she described as your mother?"

"Yes," Victor said. "She has actually told me very little. But she did say that the woman was 'not of this world' and 'not human.'"

Abigail considered this. "I don't know that the statement is really that outlandish. We have no explanation for our origin, and it's as good as any. And given what I've now seen of Madelyn, she wasn't human, nor our Kind." She turned to the dark-haired man. "I know we've spoken of this before, but do you have any recollection of your life before your Change?"

Victor shook his head. "No, I remember nothing. In fact some of my very first memories are of you."

This admission touched the glacial queen although she tried to disguise that fact. She stood and sought to excuse herself. Victor's hand on her arm stayed her movement, as well as sent an electrical shock that traveled the length of her arm, then the length of her spine, arriving most pleasantly at both its extremes.

He stood and his words were simple. "Stay with me." His eyes swept her form, so gracefully concealed yet tastefully accentuated by her clothing. He more than anyone knew of the flawless body beneath that dress, the curve of her hip, the fullness of her breasts, the taut stomach. If Ryan had achieved ideal beauty by freezing time prior to feeling its touch, Abigail had achieved it by abusing Time itself, maturing to full ripeness, than refusing to let the rot of it touch her.

"Is that a command or a request, my lord?" Abigail said, softly mocking, "because as you reminded me earlier, Ryan is still king."

Victor pressed his body to hers. "Then it is, of course, a request."

"I see," she said, "and will you be so 'brutally efficient' as you were last time?"

Victor smiled, both at the words she tossed back to him and to what she referred. When he had awakened from his illness to find Ryan missing, he had taken her blood in a cold manner with the utilitarian motive of gaining information, much like she had just done with Susan.

"No," he said simply. "It's not information that I want right now."

"Ah," Abigail said, taking his hand and leading him toward the bed, "then I get to be on top."

"Hmm," Victor said, "so business as usual."

# CHAPTER 8

LIA WANDERED THROUGH THE FOREST. There was a hare ahead of her, perhaps a hundred yards or so, attempting to hide in the undergrowth. She thought about hunting it but she wasn't really hungry, then thought about killing it just because she could.

As if aware of her intent, the hare bounded off and disappeared into a burrow. It was of no matter, Lia thought, continuing on her way. She had grown less and less hungry and was hardly eating at all now. In fact, her last dinner had ended most strangely when she had stalked and brought down an elk with nothing more than her hands. She had pounced upon the beast, ripping its skin from its body in the ravenous way that no longer disturbed her. But she did not seem to want the flesh this time, but rather the blood, and fastened on the beast's neck, draining it dry. She pulled away, her actions having long since lost any ability to horrify her, and instead was occupied by how dissatisfying the act had been.

She turned her attention to the forest around her. She could hear everything, the insects scratching on the leaves, the drip of dew as it fell from flowers, the scrape of small rodents in the gnarled tree roots. She could smell everything as well, and it was this ability that told her she was approaching yet another burned-out village. She pushed her way through the brush, ignoring the thorns that tried and failed to pierce her hardened skin. Even when one snagged deeply and was able to prick the surface, the sensation barely registered as it was so beneath the threshold of pain that she lived with constantly.

The sight that greeted her as she exited from the forest was familiar. Smoke rose from gutted dwellings, bodies were strewn about, dogs fed on carcasses and flies were omnipresent. She strolled into town, unaffected by the atrocities, and glanced about with interest. She was always amazed at the number of ways in which humans could die, the number of ways in which their bodies could be mutilated and contorted. She searched through the rubble, curious to see if there was anyone who looked like her.

There never was.

Something moved ahead of her, catching her eye. It was a man, bent over a child, tears streaming from his eyes. He appeared to be engaged in some great internal struggle, cursing himself as he took bites from the child's corpse. Lia moved closer to him, unmoved by his plight. She gazed down at him without pity and he turned upward, his face blanching at the sight of her. Although he did not quite comprehend what stood before him, he would ask for mercy all the same.

"Please kill me," he whimpered.

Lia's jaw tightened. It was the one mercy she would always deliver, the one request which she would never again refuse. She leaned down and with the inhuman strength she now possessed, snapped his neck cleanly at the base of his skull. He fell on top of the child, his misshapen face relaxing into an expression of peace.

A scuttling noise behind her attracted her attention and she became aware of another survivor. This man was attempting to crawl away from her, but none too quietly. When she approached, he curled up, shielding his head with his arms.

"Don't kill me!" he pleaded.

The back-to-back requests amused her. She had become quite the arbiter of death. This creature before her was pathetic, great lumps protruding from his arms like tumors, each with hair sprouting from their rounded surfaces. He had lumps on his head as well, and lumps on those

71

lumps. It gave his head an almost pyramidal shape.

The man peered out from between the lumps on his upraised arms. He had seen horrible, horrible things in the last few days, but even so, the woman before him gave him pause. She had horns on the side of her head and her skin had a scaly appearance that shifted in color with the light. At the moment, the skin had a greenish brown tint that magnified her startling green eyes. She wore animal skins about her waist and breasts, but beyond that, nothing. He wondered if she was a demi-goddess, so exotic and frightening was her appearance.

The man would take no chances; he shifted himself with effort into a kneeling position. Lia noted the strained exertion.

"Are you in pain?" she asked.

The man gritted his teeth. "It is like fire that burns me constantly."

"And yet you do not wish for death?"

The man shook his head.

Lia contemplated her victim. He did not seem to have any of the mental defects of the others, no madness or stupor. In fact, it seemed only his physical appearance was affected by the plague.

Just like her.

"Very well," Lia said, turning away from him. She started back down the street in her original direction of travel.

The man watched the goddess stroll away, the sinewy form growing smaller as he sat indecisively. It hurt him to rise to his feet, and hurt him more to walk, but nonetheless he gritted his teeth and hurried down the street after her.

Ryan awoke with the unnerving thought that something important was rapidly slipping away from her.

But it was gone.

She looked about, finding herself alone without a guardian at the foot of the bed. Perhaps Victor and Edward had determined there were enough Old Ones in the mansion that she did not need a full time babysitter. Edward materialized in the doorway and Ryan revised that opinion. Perhaps they just thought they were of sufficient numbers that they were willing to give her a head start.

The mental picture of the ensuing chase was humorous to her and it brought a smile to her face that pleased Edward.

"How are you feeling, my lord?"

"Well," Ryan said, stretching her neck. "I recognize you and don't wish to tear your head off, so those are both good things."

"Excellent. Your father and Abigail are down in the study. Drake and Jason are with Susan in the lab. Aeron, as usual, keeps his own council and I'm certain Marilyn will appear since you have awakened."

Ryan took a quick shower, put on fresh clothes, and started down the stairs toward the study. She actually felt surprisingly good, better than she had in a very long time. The disquiet she felt on awakening had disappeared.

Abigail and Victor glanced up at her entry, both thoroughly assessing her and both pleased at the results of the assessment. Ryan seemed almost normal. She picked up a copy of the newspaper and sprawled in one of the oversized chairs across from her father. As Edward predicted, Marilyn entered, tousled Ryan's hair, and sat adjacent to her. Ryan was just about to speak to Marilyn when something sensory began pulling at her mental peripheral vision.

She turned her attention to Victor, examining him closely. His expression was benign and neutral. She then turned her attention to Abigail who also gazed at her with an impassive expression. Ryan's eyes shifted back to her father, then slid back to the matriarch once more. Ryan raised an eyebrow and cleared her throat. There was quite an aura of contentment about the two.

A shadow of a smile played about Victor's lips, but he returned to his paper. Abigail remained perfectly expressionless and returned to her stitchery.

"Hmm," was all Ryan said. It did not bother her in the least that the two Old Ones had satisfied one another's blood thirst. It felt appropriate. Although Abigail engaged in unions for a multitude of reasons, political and otherwise, Ryan knew she Shared with Victor for only one: she enjoyed it.

Ryan again turned to Marilyn to engage her in conversation when Susan appeared in the doorway. Ryan's gaze was immediately attracted to the fading bruise on Susan's neck, and to the mild flush on her cheeks when she saw that Ryan had noticed it. It wasn't so much the bruise that bothered Ryan, but rather the discomfiture with which Susan displayed it.

Ryan's eyes drifted back to Marilyn, who was entertained by the subtle detective work in which Ryan was engaged but whose expression communicated she was not the prime suspect. Ryan glanced back over at Victor, who looked up at her from his own paper then returned, unconcerned, to his reading. Ryan's eyes moved to Abigail, who was gazing at her steadily with the unblinking gaze of their Kind, quite unrepentant. Ryan glanced at Susan then back to Abigail, and Susan shifted uncomfortably.

"You will not do that again without my permission," Ryan said coldly, addressing Abigail.

It was quite an astonishing statement and the silence in the room extended and became pronounced. Victor looked over the top of his paper at Ryan and Marilyn made an elaborate show of plucking some non-existent lint from the armrest of her chair. Abigail continued to stare at Ryan, unblinking. When she finally spoke, her tone could not have been drier.

"Should I provide a dowry beforehand in the future?"

Marilyn burst out laughing and Victor studiously returned to his paper, his mouth twitching. Susan fled the room, adding to Ryan's consternation. She turned a black look on Marilyn, who was unrepentant in her own way.

"Oh come, Ma Cherie, you have to admit that was funny."

Much to her dismay, Ryan did have to admit it was funny, and it had quite deflated her fury. She tried to generate even mild anger but had to settle for minor annoyance. Her annoyed look deflected off the Teflon of Abigail's demeanor and the matriarch returned to her needlework. Ryan sighed.

"I'm going to find Dr. Ryerson."

This task was remarkably easy as Susan had made it only as far as the stables before Ryan caught her.

"Susan," Ryan said, stopping the red-haired woman as she entered the barn. Ryan turned her around to face her. "Did she hurt you?"

Susan shook her head, embarrassed. "No, no, it was nothing like that. She simply wanted information."

"So she took your Memories," Ryan deduced.

"Yes, my Memories of you, of course. She wanted to know about our captivity, and about Madelyn."

Ryan's jaw tightened and Susan continued. "I'm sorry. I showed her everything."

Ryan shook her head. "It's not your fault. There is no way you could have resisted her. I can't even resist her," Ryan admitted.

Two arms encircled Ryan's waist as Marilyn appeared behind her. "Yes," the dark-haired woman said, laughing, "even now she twists you about her finger like a piece of tattered twine. I thought you would grow out of it, little one."

"Right," Ryan said wryly, "just as I was able to grow out of you."

"Ah," Marilyn said teasingly, "I'm so happy to know you still care. But I didn't come out to the stables to discuss our relationship, but rather to discuss the state of my offspring here."

As she said this, Marilyn turned the full force of her attention to Susan as she leaned against Ryan, peering over her shoulder. Susan nearly wilted under the seductive onslaught.

"When," Marilyn asked, "is the last time you Shared with anyone?"

Susan's cheeks were the color of her hair. "Well, there was just Abigail."

"That doesn't count," Marilyn said emphatically, "and you didn't take any of her blood."

Susan tried to think back. "Well, Ryan gave me a drop of her blood several months ago."

Marilyn glanced to Ryan with interest. "Really? Well, that always counts. But that isn't what I'm talking about."

Ryan was growing concerned, understanding Marilyn's line of questioning. "Susan, when is the last time you Shared with someone?"

Susan could not really remember. "Maybe when I last saw Raphael?"

Raphael was the young man Ryan had chosen from Marilyn's line to initiate Susan's Change. Susan had spent some time with him after her transition, but Ryan calculated the gap in time and realized that had been quite a while ago. And there was no one about the mansion she could successfully pair with because all were so powerful that even Edward's blood would most likely kill Susan.

"I've been selfish," Ryan said with recrimination.

"Oh yes, little one," Marilyn said, exasperated, "you were entirely too caught up in your own petty affairs, the illness of your father, your assumption of command of the hierarchy, your battle to the death with that hideous creature. Mon Dieu, how could you be so selfish?"

It was Ryan's turn to blush at the sarcasm. "Okay, maybe I've been a little busy. But we have to rectify this."

"I agree," Marilyn said, and Susan tried to pretend they were not discussing her like a piece of meat. "We could invite that young man here."

Ryan was thoughtful. "No," she said slowly, "that might be awkward for Raphael. He seems uncomfortable around Victor and Abigail."

"I can't imagine why," Marilyn said. There was nothing like meeting the pillars of your Kind while still an infant.

"No," Ryan said, more certain, "we should take Susan to them."

"What is this 'we?'" Marilyn said, glancing down at Ryan in surprise. "You're not going anywhere. I'm quite certain your father will not approve of this. And I know," Marilyn said with emphasis, "that your taskmaster will not approve."

Ryan turned to Marilyn and, raising herself to her full height, looked her directly in the eye. "I'm still the leader of our Kind, and unless Victor or Abigail wishes to challenge me, I haven't yet relinquished the position."

Marilyn smiled. Only she could rile Ryan into such a rash action.

"And," Ryan said, nodding toward Susan, "if I receive her medical permission, I will be traveling in the company of my physician."

"And finally," Ryan said, "although I can't believe these words are coming out of my mouth, you will be there to keep an eye on me."

Marilyn glanced over at Susan, then back at Ryan. "Very well," she said as if capitulating, "if that's your plan." She winked at Susan, then disappeared as if she had never been there at all.

Ryan stared at the empty space in front of her that had so recently been occupied by the dark-haired temptress. She turned to Susan with a sigh.

"How does that woman always get exactly what she wants, and yet somehow it's always my idea?"

# CHAPTER 9

"ARE YOU REALLY CONVINCED OF the wisdom of this journey?" Abigail said to Victor at her side. The two watched as the private jet taxied the runway, gained speed, then lifted off.

"Of course I'm not," Victor said, "I think it's a terrible idea. But when Ryan agreed to a three-week waiting period, I assumed she would suffer some sort of relapse that would eliminate the possibility. And you know how stubborn she is."

Abigail watched as the plane grew smaller. "And she will not have Edward's steadying influence."

"No," Victor agreed. Edward would be watching the boys. "She has only Marilyn."

"I assume," Abigail said mildly, "that you will have transportation ready at a moment's notice?"

"I left explicit instructions. The cars are prepared, the plane is waiting on the runway. Our total response time is under an hour."

"That may not be enough if something goes wrong," Abigail said, her tone still entirely conversational. They could have been discussing the weather.

"Yes, I know. Which is why I've sent for reinforcements."

The plane was now out of sight. Abigail turned to him, assessing his last statement. She understood.

"He may not be able to stop her if she enters a 'savage' phase."

Victor watched the sky where the plane had disappeared. "Yes, but I think he will have more luck than I."

Susan was excited in spite of herself. Perhaps it was because she had been working non-stop, at first documenting her own Change, then attempting to diagnose what was wrong with Ryan. Perhaps she was still feeling the after effects of her prolonged captivity. Perhaps she was looking forward to being in the company of her Kind who did not completely overwhelm her. Or, Susan admitted to herself, maybe she was looking forward to the possibility of Sharing with someone in a union that would not end in her death.

Marilyn examined the high color of her progeny. This was a very good idea. Dr. Ryerson's development had been neglected thus far. Most Young Ones spent their time in the company of other Young Ones, or at least with those of the middle ground. It allowed for exploration and growth. It also allowed for a great deal of collateral death as Young Ones were routinely killed in the act of Sharing due to the lack of control of the more powerful in the union. Sharing to the point of death was the greatest ecstasy of their Kind, and it was in fact a powerful check on their population numbers.

Marilyn's eyes shifted to Ryan, who sat gazing out the window of the plane. It was unlikely that anyone would dare harm Dr. Ryerson, or even attempt to.

Ryan was lost in her own thoughts, but they were not on the pleasantness of Sharing. They were on the last few times she had been on a jet. The time prior had been when she had returned from her captivity, rescued by her father and the army he had assembled. But prior to that, she had been on a jet several times, bound, blind-folded, and drugged as Madelyn had carted her back-and-forth across the planet. A muscle in her cheek tightened as she recalled the helplessness and despair she had felt.

79

"Ah, little one, I would do anything to banish that look from your eyes."

Ryan turned to Marilyn and she could not have maintained the dark mood even had she wanted to. "Anything?" she asked, her mood turning distinctly playful.

"Oh yes," Marilyn assured her.

"You forget, I'm still under quarantine. Although," Ryan continued thoughtfully, "I seem to have taken Victor's blood with no ill effects for him, so perhaps I could take yours."

Marilyn was amenable to that plan. "You know I like giving as much as receiving."

Susan put a stop to the dangerous flirtation. "There will be none of that."

Marilyn cast a baleful eye in Susan's direction. "You're quite domineering for a Young One. Perhaps you're actually of Abigail's line."

Ryan muffled laughter at this comment as Susan tried to maintain her dignity.

"Until I have medically cleared Ryan it's too dangerous for anyone to have contact with her blood."

"Of course," Marilyn said, "because lord knows that Sharing is so inherently safe."

This again brought a smile to Ryan's face. Susan was thankful that the plane began making a quick descent.

It was several hours before they were to meet Raphael at the library and Ryan wanted to go for a walk. The limousine dropped them off at the gate to the local park, a beautiful recreational facility surrounded by greenery and teeming with urban wildlife. Doves, crows, pigeons, swallows and robins were all abundant. Fat brown squirrels dove for cover as the occasional peregrine falcon appeared, then came boldly back out in hopes that the visitors would ignore the signs that forbid their feeding. Ducks and geese glided across the various water features of the park.

The three made quite a sight as they progressed through the park, the fair-haired, the dark-haired, and the red-haired. Susan was surprised that they were not attracting more attention. Ryan was striking and Marilyn stunning and the two of them together were simply overwhelming. But she herself seemed to be the only one attracting any notice, and that ranged from looks of polite appreciation to outright leering.

Ryan stopped at a fountain to examine a family of ducklings that had taken up occupancy. Susan watched as one duckling made a beeline toward Ryan, swimming right into the hand she placed in the water. Ryan gently lifted the duckling from the water and her eyes lit up at the tiny water fowl.

"Interesting, isn't it," Marilyn said, "how that miniature ball of fluff feels safe with what is probably the most powerful creature on this planet?"

Ryan gently returned the duckling to its worried mother. "Yes," Susan said, watching Ryan move with her usual deadly grace, "and I'm always struck with how oblivious Ryan is to the attention she generates."

"Well, none of these people can actually see her right now," Marilyn said, then with a knowing glance down at Susan, "except you."

Susan blushed, realizing she had been staring at her friend. Marilyn did not let the reaction pass without comment.

"You're going to have loosen up a bit, my dear. You remind me of those from the Victorian era. Although," Marilyn admitted, "they are only puritanical on the outside. Inside, those are some of the most deviant people I've ever met."

Marilyn made this statement sound like a compliment, and Susan was thankful it did not require a response.

Ryan was aware of the conversation between her two companions but she found her surrounding so visually interesting she did not wish to engage. Even the people here were interesting, which was surprising because humans generally attracted no attention from her. But these humans reminded her of the carnival-like characters from her childhood. There was the freakishly thin bald man with his numerous piercings, eating the glass of a light bulb to the cheers of those surrounding him.

There was the gray-haired woman who looked twice her actual age, carrying her life's belongings and a mangy calico cat in a dirty designer hand-bag. There was the drug addict couple, euphoric and intensely in love, at least for the moment. And the preacher in his tattered black dress pants, scuffed patent leather shoes, and wrinkled white shirt with the sleeves rolled up, complete with a clip-on tie, preaching loudly from the Bible he had stolen from his rat-infested motel room.

Ryan's perusal of the crowd stopped abruptly on one figure. Now this one was very strange. He was utterly deformed, a freak even amongst this crowd. His skin was pock-marked with scars and he had a large tumor-like growth on the side of his head, so large it seemed almost a second head. The features of his face sagged, not as if from normal aging but as if all of the connective tissue of his skin had given way at once. His mouth sagged open, his nose draped downward, his cheeks were jowls, and his lower eyelids drooped open, revealing the wet redness beneath his eyes. But it was not even his hideous appearance that so attracted Ryan's attention, but something far more significant.

She was quite certain he was one of her Kind.

His eyes were locked on her, which was somewhat surprising because she was currently blocking her aura and should not have been visible to him. But if she was surprised, he was absolutely astonished that she could see him. In fact, his look went beyond astonishment into utter disbelief, as if he still was not certain what was occurring. He moved to his left, as if testing her ability to see him, and a look of horror spread onto his features when her eyes followed him.

"Ryan, what's wrong?"

Susan joined her, and Ryan nodded to the man in the crowd. "Do you see that man?"

Susan glanced in the general direction that Ryan was indicating. "Which one?"

"The one with two heads," Ryan said, exasperated, "which one do you think I'm talking about?"

Susan looked again in the direction that Ryan was indicating. She didn't see anything unusual. "I'm afraid I don't see what man you're talking about."

Marilyn sensed Ryan's consternation and joined them.

"Marilyn," Ryan said, "do you see that—?"

She stopped. The man was gone.

"Do I see what?'

Ryan's jaw shut with an audible snap. She quickly canvassed the entire area, including all exit routes, and could not see the man anywhere.

"Are you okay, Ryan?" Susan asked with concern. "If you're not feeling well…"

Ryan gave one last look around the park, then shook her head vehemently, dismissing the incident. "No, no," she said, "I'm fine. I just thought I saw something."

Susan glanced at Marilyn, who was examining the fine features of her companion closely. She seemed minimally satisfied with her assessment.

"Let us continue on, then," Marilyn said, "we have an appointment for Dr. Ryerson to keep."

The bouncer at the door evaluated the trio before him. Two barely registered on him, but the red-haired one, now she was luminous. As the gate-keeper to this establishment, it was his responsibility to screen the entrants, ensuring that only the most desirable of his Kind were given entrance. He lifted the velvet rope, allowing the trio to enter.

As they entered the dark hallway leading into the establishment, Ryan expressed her reservations.

"This doesn't look like a library," she said doubtfully.

As they entered the dance hall, the booming base resolved itself into crashing music. The entire room was mirrored, adding to the assault of the flashing lights and writhing bodies on the dance floor. The room was full of Young Ones in the throes of joy and blood lust, the latter expressing itself in the contortionist, irrelevantly sexual movements of the participants.

"Oh dear god," Ryan said.

Marilyn laughed at Ryan's reaction. She herself was largely unmoved by the spectacle. Once you had seen the debaucheries of the Borgia court or in fact anything associated with Papal Rome, this was quite tame by comparison. And Marilyn knew it was that tameness that stoked Ryan's disgust, not the debauchery. It was the utter banality of the scene that inspired her irritation. Susan seemed unaware of Ryan's horrified reaction.

"I don't see Raphael anywhere."

"I thought we were going to a library," Ryan said.

"Not a library," Susan corrected, "The Library. That's the name of this club." She looked at Ryan curiously. "Did you really think we were going to a library?"

"Yes," Ryan said, "that's where I met Raphael. I was hunting during the cleansing and I came across him and his companions at an actual library. I spared them," she said, turning her attention to the debacle in front of her, "this, on the other hand, I completely destroyed."

"Now, now," Marilyn said soothingly, "we can return and destroy the place if you wish when Dr. Ryerson is finished."

"No!" Susan exclaimed, appalled. She was never quite certain when these two were joking.

"Fine, fine," Marilyn said, "just go find your little friend and we will find a corner to hide in."

Susan left and Marilyn guided Ryan to a spot at the bar. The two attracted no attention, which was really quite anomalous since they were taller than everyone in the room, moved with an unnatural flowing grace and seemed bound together by some web of sensuality that shut everyone else out. Ryan leaned against the bar and Marilyn leaned against Ryan.

The bartender approached the two. Generally, he could guess someone's age and the date they had been Changed within a decade. It was a good skill to possess as a bartender. The crowd in this club was decidedly young and of little interest to even those of the middle ground.

Every once in awhile, someone would come in who was a few centuries old, but there was little to attract such a being to this place.

Oddly, he could not get a fix on either of these two. The dark-haired one glanced at him casually and the fair-haired one ignored him entirely. For some reason he felt the need to please them.

"We have some very fine 'spirits' tonight, if you wish." He extended a wine glass filled with red liquid that Ryan could smell without any need to get closer.

"No thank you," she said graciously, politely hiding her disdain. When he departed she turned to Marilyn.

"Now where is the fun in that," she said, "why in heaven would you drink blood from a glass when you could drink from a vein?"

"Hmm," Marilyn speculated, "perhaps it gives them the opportunity to drink the blood of one more powerful without risking death."

"I repeat," Ryan said emphatically, "where is the fun in that?"

Marilyn smiled her agreement as Susan approached with Raphael and a few of his companions. The handsome black man was unaware of their presence.

"Raphael," Susan said, introducing her friend, "you remember Ryan."

At that moment, Ryan lifted the perceptual veil she was maintaining, allowing Raphael to see her. His eyes widened and, if possible given his skin color, he blanched. "My lord," he stuttered, "I mean your majesty…"

To Ryan's dismay, Raphael went to one knee.

"Oh dear god," she said under her breath. Like lightning, she grasped him by his collar and with one hand hauled him upward so forcefully that for a second he dangled several inches of the ground. She gently set him on his feet, brushing him off.

"Let's have none of that," she said uncomfortably, "we're trying to present a low profile here."

"Who is we?" Raphael asked, uncertain.

Marilyn lifted her own perceptual veil and Raphael again began to go to one knee. Ryan anticipated the maneuver and caught him halfway

85

down, hauling him upright once more.

"Low profile," she reminded him.

Raphael was embarrassed. But to be greeted by both the mother of his line and the ruler of their Kind was overwhelming.

A few of Raphael's companions were becoming aware of them as well. Ryan thought she recognized one from their previous meeting.

"Courtney, is it not?" Ryan said politely.

Courtney was thunderstruck and could not get a word out, so she simply nodded. Finally her voice returned. "Why can't anyone see you here?"

"I'm blocking their perception" Ryan said, smiling, "something not so difficult with Young Ones but quite a trick with Old Ones."

"Oh, I get it," Courtney said. She waved her hand across her face. "These aren't the droids you're looking for."

Ryan looked at her blankly then turned to Marilyn for assistance, who merely shrugged while Susan hid a smile.

"Why don't we go find a table?" Susan said to Raphael, leading him away by the elbow while glancing over her shoulder at a grateful Ryan.

"It's a wonder that the Change of 'Courtney' was ever consummated," Marilyn mused.

"Be nice," Ryan said, also wondering the same thing.

They stood there for awhile, but Ryan was clearly restless.

"Why don't we go for another walk?" Marilyn suggested. She, too, was bored.

"Very well," Ryan said with relief. "I'll go tell Susan we'll be gone for a short time."

Ryan started across the room, the crowd parting as some invisible force moved through their midst. She was about halfway there when she slowed, then stopped, turning to her right. There in the crowd, standing with his back to the wall, was another very strange man. This one seemed to ooze some sort of secretion as he breathed out of the gill-like structure on the side of his neck, and several teeth protruded from his left cheek as if a second mouth had been randomly placed there. He had

86

an indentation on his forehead in the shape of a brick. He was staring at her with slit-like eyes that widened in shock as she turned and looked directly at him. He, like the previous man she had seen, seemed stunned that she could see him.

Ryan looked around at those near him. No one else seemed aware of his presence, although once again, he was clearly one of her Kind. She glanced back at Marilyn, who had been watching her and was trying to ascertain what had attracted Ryan's attention. But Marilyn, too, seemed not to see the odd creature. And when Ryan turned back to him, he was gone.

She stood there, uncertainly, then shrugged.

Well, she thought to herself, then stopped.

Susan felt the wave of power wash over her and braced herself. With the exception of Marilyn, she was probably the only one present who understood what was happening and steeled herself for the tidal wave. Those around her were not as fortunate as they staggered at the blow. Susan turned to Ryan in surprise. She had no idea why Ryan would reveal the full extent of her power so casually.

Ryan was standing in the center of the room, completely unveiled to those around her. Reaction ranged from total confusion to sheer terror as the Young Ones sought to understand what was in their midst. Most did not have the senses to even grasp the extent of this One, only that it was beyond anything that they had felt before. Fear and desire were at war and the impulse to move closer canceled that of wanting to flee, so everyone just froze in place.

"Oh no," Susan said.

The girl was completely bemused. She had no idea who any of these people were, nor any idea of where she was. She could not remember anything about herself and the sensation was unnerving and frustrating, frustration being something she understood but could not recall ever having experienced. She looked around, wondering if one of these people could help her, but language seemed just out of her grasp at the moment. She did not recognize this place

Marilyn appeared behind Susan, startling her companions because no one had seen her move.

"So," she said, her eyes glued to the girl standing in the center of the room, "which Ryan is this?"

"Her eyes aren't maroon, thank god," Susan said, "and she hasn't collapsed. So I'm guessing that she has lost her memory."

"Really," said Marilyn and Susan glanced at her sharply. Marilyn's tone of voice indicated her fascination with Ryan's condition was not entirely motivated by concern for Ryan's well-being.

The Young Ones milled about the startling creature uncertainly, keeping a careful distance. The young woman was strikingly beautiful, tall, lithe, graceful, and they wondered how they could have missed this being they couldn't take their eyes from. They began to murmur amongst themselves, wondering if this was an "Old One," and the girl wondered why they were bothering to whisper when she could clearly hear them, although she had no idea what an "Old One" was. A very attractive red-haired woman was approaching, and the girl mused upon the meaning of red for a moment because it was not quite an accurate description but it seemed the appropriate usage.

"Ryan?" Susan said uncertainly.

The girl considered the word, realized that it was a name, but felt no connection to it as her name. She could come up with no other name, however. She examined the red-haired woman quite thoroughly and others in the crowd began to examine Susan as well, wondering what the connection between the two could be. They still could not grasp the very elemental power that stood before them.

They could less grasp when a second staggering power manifested in the room, this time belonging to the ravishing dark-haired beauty who slowly sauntered across the floor. Now there were two Old Ones in their midst, similar yet distinctly different.

The girl was completely confused, but her attention was abruptly drawn to the raven-haired woman. She could not assess the feeling because it had no context; she only knew that there was an instant, magnetic attraction to this one. And because she possessed no cultural cues of subtlety or reservation, her admiration was quite overt. Somehow, the unabashed openness came across as incredibly innocent.

"Oh my," Marilyn murmured to herself. The last time she had seen such a combination of power and naiveté was when this girl was a child. Victor had stopped her from taking advantage of that situation.

But Victor wasn't here right now.

"Hello, little one." Marilyn said.

The girl assessed the greeting. It was odd because she was not little, but the dark-haired woman was one of the only people in the room actually taller than her, so perhaps it was a relative appraisal.

"Hello," she said uncertainly, trying out the unfamiliar word.

A smile played about Marilyn's lips. What an extraordinary opportunity. To be allowed a second chance at the seduction of this innocent, this time with no threat of interruption and with a far greater return. Ryan's power had exponentially increased over time, yet now she was at a greater disadvantage than when she had been an infant in Abigail's drawing room those centuries ago.

"Marilyn," Susan said warningly. It was not difficult to see where this was going.

Marilyn ignored her and slipped her arm about Ryan's waist. "Would you like to go for a walk with me?"

The girl contemplated the question. "Yes, I think I would like that."

"Marilyn!" Susan said firmly.

Marilyn turned her gaze on Susan, and although she was never as cold as Abigail she could be just as intimidating. "I will be fine, Dr. Ryerson. You stay here with your friends and enjoy yourself."

Susan was deeply unhappy about this turn of events for a multitude of reasons. "Victor should know about this."

If the statement was meant to be a threat, Marilyn ignored that aspect of it. "Give me five hours."

Susan crossed her arms over her chest. "Three," she said stubbornly.

"Four," Marilyn bargained, and Susan knew that was the best she would do.

89

"Very well," Susan said, "you have four hours. And then I call her father."

The girl glanced at the pretty red-haired woman, wondering who they were talking about. But she was enjoying the closeness of the raven-haired one, which somehow made her think of standing next to an open fire, which then forced her to try and remember what fire was. Susan watched the two leave with great qualms.

The bouncer's jaw dropped when two of the most amazing creatures he had ever seen walked from the club. How in the world had he missed them? The dark-haired one sent him a sultry smile that turned his insides to liquid, the kind of look that indicated her companion was in for quite a night.

Marilyn led Ryan to the limousine that pulled to the curb in front of them.

The girl examined the vehicle, searching for anything in her memory that would register. "This is a nice car," she said at last with child-like admiration.

"Yes, it is," Marilyn said, highly amused since it belonged to Ryan. She held her hand and helped Ryan into the car, mostly to expedite their exit. Once settled across from the girl, she rapped the window. "To my property on 4th and Main."

The limousine pulled smoothly away from the curb and the girl examined the interior of the car, then settled her gaze on the dark-haired woman across from her. The expression on the woman's face was hard to decipher with her current limited mental vocabulary.

"Are you hungry?" the girl asked.

Marilyn actually caught her breath, a human gesture she thought she had lost centuries ago. "Yes," she said, "you might say that."

"Yeah," the girl said, "me too." She paused for a beat, then said, "I think."

Marilyn rapped the window again. "Get us there quickly."

The unseen chauffeur exercised his preternatural skills and pushed the vehicle to its limits, arriving at the hotel within minutes, parking in a sideways skid that sent bellhops flying. He exited as fast as he could, but Marilyn was already out of the vehicle.

The girl exited the limousine and looked upward at the high rise luxury hotel. "This is really nice," she said.

"Yes, yes," Marilyn said with complete distraction. Of course it was nice, she had owned it for a hundred and fifty years and it was now worth more than the GDP of most countries. But none of that mattered to her right now.

The concierge glanced up at some sort of commotion at the front entrance, then went white. The majority of his guests were human, but the one moving full steam toward him clearly was not. He grew even paler when he realized who exactly was approaching him.

"Madame de Fontesque," he said, bowing so low he nearly prostrated himself before her, "I beg your forgiveness, we were not expecting your arrival."

Marilyn dismissed him with a wave. "It's a spontaneous visit, Ferdinand," she said. "I assume my quarters are ready?"

"Of course," Ferdinand said, "your quarters are always prepared."

"Good," Marilyn said, still distracted. She stepped sideways to reveal her companion. "I'm not to be disturbed."

If possible, the concierge grew even whiter. He was almost certain the one accompanying his mistress was Ryan Alexander, the undisputed leader of all their Kind. Her majesty seemed quite enamored with the exquisite architecture of the lobby.

"Of course, Madame," Ferdinand said, again bowing low.

Marilyn led Ryan to the elevator that was rarely used because it had only one stop at the top floor. Ryan settled with her back on one wall facing Marilyn, her casual stance nearly her undoing as Marilyn thought of taking her to the floor of the elevator. The speed of the mechanical lift delayed her fate, however, as the ascension took no time at all. The doors opened and Marilyn gestured for Ryan to exit.

The girl entered the elaborate penthouse suite, again openly admiring the furnishings. Marilyn calmed herself. It was likely she would not ever be presented a similar opportunity, no sense in rushing it.

"Would you like to see the view?" Marilyn asked.

The girl nodded. "I think I would like that very much."

Marilyn pressed a button and two huge curtains parted, displaying immense floor-to-ceiling windows that revealed not only the city skyline but the full night sky. The girl moved to the windows, gazing out at the view. Marilyn moved behind her, wrapping her arms about her waist. The girl evaluated the position, deciding that it was quite pleasant. And when the dark-haired woman guided her backward to a chaise lounge, it was even more pleasant.

Marilyn held the girl in front of her, gazing out at the skyline. She would not be able to prolong this much longer. The girl sensed something from the dark-haired woman and could not interpret it beyond discomfort or vague unease.

"Is something wrong?" she asked, concerned.

"No, little one," Marilyn said, placing her lips on the side of the girl's neck, producing an instantaneous arch of the girl's back.

An avalanche of feelings thundered through the girl, not one of which she understood. She herself felt uneasy, uncertain, inadequate. "I'm afraid I don't really know what to do," she said hesitantly.

This was finally too much for Marilyn. "I'm sure I can provide you some instruction," she said, and sliced into Ryan's neck.

The sensations that tore through the girl were beyond intense, and the accompanying mental explosion of images only added to the intensity. She could make sense of none of the images, although oddly many of them contained someone that looked a great deal like her. The dark-haired woman was taking her blood and she had no sense of whether this was an anomalous act or totally normal, only that it felt extraordinary. Her heart, an organ absent until this moment, beat powerfully in her chest, matching the pace of the organ seeking to dominate it. Waves and waves of pleasure flooded her mind and body and she had two conflicting yet complementary thoughts: one, that she could not stand a single second more of the intensity, and two, that she could in fact do this forever.

Marilyn finally broke free, sated but with her veins bursting with pressure. She felt out-of-breath, an oddity for someone who did not require oxygen.

"There is something I should be doing," the girl said uncertainly, causing Marilyn to grit her teeth with anticipation.

"Yes my dear," she said, "I'm sure it will come to you in a moment."

The girl glanced up at the beautiful dark-haired woman, and her eyes were drawn to the vein throbbing in her neck. "Yes," Marilyn said approvingly, "that's it."

The girl brushed her lips against the vein, then brushed her razor-sharp teeth against the skin. It split under the gentle contact and the dark liquid poured into her mouth, down her throat, then spread throughout her body to every extremity. The rhythm of their pairing was gentle, incessant, softly and inexorably dominant, a seduction that was all the more powerful because of its subtlety, a subtlety so complete that the seducer had little concept of the torturous pleasure she was inflicting.

As it continued, death was near, but merely flirted rather than threatened. The innocence of the powerful creature controlling the act forbid dancing too near that cliff, and when the precipice appeared, the naïve concern of the omnipotent one took over, pulling both participants from danger.

Marilyn lay with the girl in her arms. Just when she thought it impossible that she experience anything new, this girl proved her wrong. When young, Sharing was primarily a physical act, the sensations stimulating all of the nerve endings newly acquired after the Change. As one grew older, Sharing more and more occurred in the realm of the mind, the sensations stimulated there far superior to anything occurring in the physical realm.

Marilyn ran her finger through Ryan's hair and had one last thought before she joined the girl in sleep: many could master the physical realm, but few could master the mental, and this one was ruler of both.

Marilyn's eyes opened slowly and she glanced down at the girl sleeping in her arms. At some point in time, they had made it to the bed and Marilyn was now curled about Ryan's back. The position was wondrously warm and comfortable, and Marilyn's eyes drifted closed again as she began to go back to sleep.

Her eyes popped back open again. No, something was definitely wrong. She lifted her head off the pillow to look down at the foot of the bed.

Victor sat there in an armchair, his arms crossed over his chest, one long leg crossed over the other. Abigail sat next to him, her hands crossed on her lap. Both were looking at her with the unblinking gaze of their Kind.

"The two of you look like my parents," Marilyn said without the slightest embarrassment or repentance.

"I am her parent," Victor reminded her, nodding to the still-sleeping Ryan. He uncrossed his arm and pulled a thin pocketbook from his breast pocket. He pulled out a thousand dollar bill and handed it to Abigail. "I was quite certain it would be Aeron who would be first to engage in such a foolish act."

Abigail took the bill, her eyes still on Marilyn. "Whereas I had my money on you, my dear, simply because you're so predictably reckless."

The sound of the voices began to register on Ryan and she stirred. She opened her eyes, becoming aware of her intimate and compromising position with Marilyn. And although she could not remember anything, it wasn't difficult to figure out what had happened. Ryan glanced down at the foot of the bed, taking in Victor and Abigail. She sighed aloud.

"And, of course, now my memory chooses to return." She was not entirely familiar with the concept, but this scene had all the earmarks of a Spring Break gone bad.

Victor stood and Abigail followed suit. "We'll be leaving in about ten minutes," Victor said, then lest there be any misunderstanding, "All of us." The two disappeared.

The minute they were gone, Marilyn rolled over onto Ryan and pinned her to the bed. "Do you hear that, Ma Cherie? We have ten more minutes."

Ryan's expression was angry.

"How could you do that?" she said accusingly.

"Do what?" Marilyn said, surprised that Ryan was upset that she had taken advantage of the situation when it was so like her.

"How could you risk yourself like that?"

Marilyn realized Ryan's anger was out of concern for her.

"I wasn't in any danger, little one."

"But you could not know that," Ryan insisted, her anxiety evident in her eyes, "it would kill me if something happened to you, especially if it were my fault."

Their relationship had always been playful and this rare heartfelt admission touched Marilyn deeply. She grew serious, and her words were spoken with great gravity.

"Abigail plans," she explained, "she schemes, she maneuvers, she manipulates. I, on the other hand, operate on pure, raw instinct." Marilyn paused. "And it might surprise you to know that I'm right at least as often as she is, possibly more." She rolled over onto her back, then rose gracefully from the bed.

"I was never in any danger," she said over her shoulder as she left the room.

Ryan stared up at the ceiling, trying to remember anything that had occurred. The last thing she recalled was being in the club and going to find Susan to tell her they were going for a walk. No, she stopped herself, that wasn't the last thing. She remembered seeing another strange man, the one with the gills and the second mouth on his cheek, the one that no one else seemed to notice. The last thing she remembered was him disappearing.

Ryan gazed at the elaborate ceiling tiles in frustration. Was she imagining things? Or was she seeing things that no one else could see? She could understand if Susan and the other Young Ones could not see him, but surely Marilyn should have been able to. And why the hell was she losing her memory?

Ryan sat up in the bed. The whole "hallucination" thing, if that was in fact what it was, reminded her uncomfortably of her captivity. It was there she had seen creepy, crawling things out of her peripheral vision, things that seemed to be real but were just on the edge of her perception. She still didn't know if those things had been real or just a symptom of the extraordinary stress she had been subjected to.

The thought of her captivity angered her, and she picked up a pillow and threw it across the room. It landed with a dissatisfyingly soft thump. Ryan gazed at the pillow for a very long moment.

Why the hell was she so hot?


Abigail and Victor stood out on the sidewalk in front of the hotel and both looked upward at the same moment. Marilyn was exiting the front of the hotel, shadowed by the concierge attempting to attend to her every need. She slowed her pace abruptly, causing the concierge to nearly collide with her, and she, too, looked upward.

Susan was already seated in the limousine. She had felt mildly apprehensive about seeing Marilyn, even though she had given her the full four hours, but when she saw the three Old Ones look upward to the 40th floor, her apprehension spiked for a completely different reason.

"Is that what I think it is?" Abigail murmured.

"I'm afraid so," Victor said.


The girl stood on the edge of the balcony, enjoying the cool breeze that caressed her burning skin. She knew nothing about anything and cared for the same. She could hear and feel the hundreds of insignificant little creatures that scurried about the building below her, picking out their conversations yet understanding nothing of what they said. She could hear their hearts beat, their lungs expand with each breath, the ligature of their joints pop and snap as they moved. They meant nothing to her, trivial in a microscopic way.

The beings on the street below, however, now those were interesting to her. At least three in number, they drew her attention and she tracked them with startling visual acuity. She smiled. She sensed them and they sensed her. She stepped off the ledge.

Victor watched as the figure plummeted toward them, picking up speed with every floor. It seemed a controlled descent, no flailing arms or wind-milling legs, but rather a tight, feet-first aerial movement, like someone leaping lightly off a porch, but in this case doing so for forty floors.

And, like someone leaping off the porch, the figure landed on its feet, crouching lightly at the landing, right before the impact blew a thirty foot crater in the middle of the street and dust and debris obstructed everything. The sound of the impact was enormous, as was the shattering of glass that accompanied the resultant shock wave.

Several cars wrecked in a screech of tires and the crunch of metal. A small fire started in one of the smashed storefronts. Pedestrians began screaming and fleeing in all directions. The dust began to settle, and slowly, inexorably, the figure rose from its crouched position.

Victor gazed at his daughter, feeling both fear and resignation. He noted that her eyes were once again a deep maroon. She moved with the same predatory grace that she had in the woods, tilting her head and sniffing the air in an almost feral movement. Her gaze held the same mixture of reckless amusement and careless savagery. She moved closer, then slightly sideways, as if stalking her prey as she examined Victor at length. She turned her attention to Marilyn and examined her with the same exhaustive intensity.

"I may not be interpreting the body language correctly," Marilyn said under her breath, "but I think she wants to eat us, or possibly rape us."

"Or perhaps some unfortunate combination of the two," Victor murmured back. It seemed ridiculous that with all the commotion they were whispering to one another, but neither wanted to startle the creature in front of them.

The girl's attention shifted to the third of the group and her eyes narrowed. This one was of great interest to her, but she could not pinpoint why. The older woman returned her gaze with an equal degree of interest and intensity, and unlike her companions, there was no fear in her eyes. The girl stepped toward the matriarch, and Abigail tilted her head, intrigued to see where this was going. To her great disappointment, it seemed it would go nowhere as something distracted the girl from behind and she turned around. The girl stopped, utterly still, and stared down the street through the dust and debris.

A figure was moving toward her, lithely stepping through the destruction, maneuvering effortlessly through the smoke and fire. It was an incredibly handsome Asian man, his chiseled features impassive, his gait measured and controlled. His broad shoulders and powerful chest bespoke his considerable physical prowess, and the grace of his movement bespoke of ancient technical skills.

Kusunoki stared at Ryan and he slowed his approach. Victor had warned him of Ryan's condition but he was having a hard time grasping that the creature in front of him was his beloved student. He could see the heat emanating off her in waves, could see the fire burning in her maroon colored eyes, could feel the tensile strength coiled within her like some great serpent ready to strike.

Victor had made a broad sweep around Ryan and now joined Kusunoki. "Thank you for coming, old friend," he said.

Kusunoki glanced over to return the greeting, but that was a mistake. A huge object landed directly in front of him and then took a serendipitous bounce, traveling over and just clearing his head, then crashing into the buildings behind him.

Kusunoki looked back at the girl in the street, who appeared to be laughing.

"Did she just throw a car at me?" he asked in disbelief.

"Yes," Victor said with resignation, "she did."

Kusunoki extended his senses. As Victor had indicated, he felt no recognition from Ryan. The creature before him was indeed a savage, but one that was highly intelligent and extremely skilled, a veritable killing machine. It was Kusunoki himself who had trained Ryan centuries earlier, teaching her to control her formidable power and giving her the fighting skills to match her preternatural abilities. He knew how deadly she was under normal circumstances, but this thing…

This thing was unconquerable.

The girl's attention was now entirely on the Asian man with a single-minded focus that was alarming. It was as if everyone else on the street had ceased to exist. Kusunoki was very aware of this focus and determined that he would use it.

"If I run," he said, "she will follow me, just like a predator will follow its prey."

"I don't know if that's such a good idea," Victor said, "if she catches you, I'm certain she will treat you just like prey."

Kusunoki began moving slowly to his left because Ryan had begun to casually circle him in a classic flanking maneuver. It was as if he were dealing with a piranha that operated according to the precepts of Sun Tzu. "That may be," he said, "so my only hope is to avoid her until this phase passes." Kusunoki tensed, preparing to bolt because he sensed that Ryan was doing the same.

"The length of the phases seems random," Victor warned, "so I can't tell you how long you will need to outrun her."

Kusunoki smiled grimly. "It's not as if I'm going to stop."

Ryan sprang and, in a flash, the samurai was gone. In a second flash, she was gone.

Victor stared up the street in the direction they had taken flight. He hoped this phase was no longer than the last because even under normal circumstances, Ryan was by far the fastest of their Kind.

But Kusunoki was not going to rely entirely on speed. He was going to resort to trickery, subterfuge, and whatever advantage he could find in an urban environment. His first act was to kick over a fire hydrant, which sheared at the base and exploded into a fountain of water that caught Ryan squarely in the chest and shot her up into the air. She landed with a graceful tumble and was on her feet in an instant, but it had bought Kusunoki a few crucial seconds. He scaled a fire escape ladder, then snapped it off at the top, shoving the heavy metal contraption down onto Ryan. She caught it and tossed it to the side like it was a toy, then began to pull herself upward with force powerful enough it allowed her to go from level to level on arm strength alone.

Again, it bought Kusunoki a little time and space as he began running across the rooftops. He jumped from building to building in leaps so improbably long he seemed to be flying. Ryan was right beyond him and rapidly closing the gap between them. He searched ahead and found what he was looking for, and he leaped onto a power line, sliding across the wire as sparks flew everywhere. He landed on the open deck, and grasped the brick chimney, which fortunately came off in one large piece. He turned, timing his release perfectly, and threw the massive structure at Ryan right as her feet left the adjacent rooftop in a great leap forward.

As powerful as the creature was, Kusunoki surmised that she couldn't violate the laws of physics. And once airborne, she had no leverage to apply that great strength. Ryan caught the chimney easily, but its size was too large for her to twist around, and its mass was so great relative to hers it redirected her flight almost backwards. That momentum shift would have crushed any normal being but it merely slammed her into the building, then dropped her four stories onto a metro bus.

Kusunoki stared down into the indentation in the metal of the roof of the transport, unsurprised to see the figure get to its feet. Ryan looked up directly into his eyes and he could swear that she was laughing. The bus turned right and disappeared.

Kusunoki did not fool himself into thinking he was safe. He began running again and saw a multilevel parking structure in front of him. This might be advantageous ground for him because of the many twists, turns, and obstructions that would slow her down. He made one more great leap and landed on the top level of the parking lot. He could sense that she was again approaching, but he could not get more than a general idea of her direction.

A car drove past him and the occupants gaped as he started down the concrete ramp. He would be safer inside than out in the open. The level that he was on now was about half-full and there were no pedestrians around at the moment. He had a sudden sense of danger, but it was imprecise and he could not diagnose the threat or direction.

The wall next to him exploded in a spray of concrete chunks, rebar steel, and dust. The car that came hurtling through the wall caught him solidly at the waist and carried him a hundred feet before it pinned him against another wall. Ryan came through the opening after the car, having successfully negated any advantage of twist, turn, or obstruction. Kusunoki was able to free himself from his pinned position, but Ryan moved to block his exit and he realized she had easily corralled him.

Kusunoki knew that he was trapped and now had little choice but to fight. He took a deep breath to calm and center himself, then gracefully moved into a martial arts position of attack.

The girl paused. Something about the movement was familiar and it gave her pleasure. Slowly, with no mental memory but pure muscle memory, she moved into the counter-position for the attack, utterly stilling herself. Kusunoki knew that what he was doing was sheer suicide, but he was out of options. In an explosion of movement, he leaped forward and began his assault.

Ryan met each blow effortlessly with perfect technique. Kusunoki was surprised that he got in even five strikes before he was swept off his feet and thrown hard to the pavement. In a flash, Ryan was atop him, straddling his waist. She did not seek to pin his arms, however, merely sat on top of him, arms crossed, as if she were the winner of the great game they were playing.

The handsome Asian stared up at his pupil. The maroon eyes were frightening, yet beautiful. Her skin was flushed with the heat that poured out of her, which made her high cheek bones even more defined than normal. Her manner was entirely casual, and she presented the face of a terrifying, charismatic, irresistible monster.

The girl examined the man she had pinned to the ground, and her eyes traveled to his bare skin. His shirt was torn from his body, bunched about his waist, and she sat atop his bare torso. The pectoral muscles of his chest were extraordinary and she could not help but run her fingers over them. Her eyes and fingers traveled lower, following the diagonal line of the serratus anterior down to the oblique muscle, then tracing the square outlines of the ridged abdominal muscles. She brushed her fingertips over the opposite oblique, then back up to the serratus, then down the center of his abdominals to just above his groin where she sat perched.

It took all of Kusunoki's willpower to remain still. The girl's touch was like fire, utterly primitive and erotic, a casual exploration that made him grit his teeth with desire. She was like an animal, no morals, no reservations, no hesitation, only instinct.

And it was in fact instinct that took over as she bent down and sliced into his neck. Kusunoki moaned at the assault, both because of the unmatched pleasure it brought him and because he knew it would kill him. She drew his blood quickly and there was no bonding or mental connection; it was a purely brutal, physical act. His vision began to darken as she drained him, and it was nearly black when she stopped.

Kusunoki opened his eyes. The creature was sitting atop him, perplexed. His vision swam as he sought to focus on her. She seemed thoughtful, as if perhaps she wished to experiment with him prior to dispatching him from the mortal realm. This theory was given credence as she lifted her forearm to her face and lightly gashed her own wrist. She held the wound inches from his lips, allowing the blood to drip down into his mouth.

The effect was instant and Kusunoki felt strength flow through his system. More importantly was the effect it had on Ryan because Kusunoki, master of all things mental, was able to create an instant psychic connection with her.

Ryan flew backward as if struck, the return of her memory crushingly painful. She curled into a ball, trying to shut out the avalanche of images that buried her. It was like white light burning a hole through her brain tissue, and she writhed about in an attempt to escape the inescapable.

Kusunoki half-held, half-pinned her, trying to control her movement because he feared she would injure herself. It was almost as if she was having a seizure, so violent and involuntary was her thrashing. Her body temperature was dropping rapidly, and was in fact heading in the opposite direction as it was now far below normal. With a last gasp, Ryan opened hazel eyes filled with despair that were focused on nothing, then went unconscious.

Kusunoki was greatly saddened. It almost seemed his beloved pupil was possessed by Oni, or in fact had become one herself. He lifted her into his arms and began his long trek back.

# CHAPTER 10

SHE WATCHED THE YOUNG MAN on the horse with her glittering green eyes. She had heard rumors of his birth for almost two decades, yet none of her spies had seen him in the presence of the hated one. In fact, it seemed the dark-haired man whom she despised had gone out of his way to keep this one isolated, even from his own kind.

It was very strange, she thought to herself. At first she suspected that the hated one had become aware of her, or perhaps aware of some of her minions. Although she tried to keep him under constant watch, she also kept her distance because his strength and senses were daunting. She knew that the time had not yet come for action, that her forces would have to outnumber his by thousands, if not tens of thousands, in order to have any hope of victory. Her people were strong and brave, but they were no match for him.

This one, however, she thought as she eyed the youth, now this one she could easily destroy. Maybe that was the reason the dark- haired man kept him a secret even from his own kind: the boy was too vulnerable.

Lia easily kept pace with the young man even though he was on horseback. She moved through the forest like a monstrous, graceful beast. Several times the young man stopped and looked back as if he sensed he was being followed, but each time he shook his head in consternation, as if he were simply imagining things. On one such stop and cautious perusal of the forest, Lia was close enough to finally get a good look at him. The beauty of his features enraged her, the golden hair, the sensual mouth, the dark eyelashes framing eyes of an indeterminate color. But something else caught her attention and she had to look closer. With a shock, she realized that the young man was actually a girl. Her shock transitioned to intrigue, staying her hand once again from what probably would have been an effortless attack.

She continued to follow the girl and became aware that a few of the dark-haired man's kind were some distance ahead of them. The girl was oblivious, or at least was until the smoke from the burning village became more apparent. The girl's concern was evident and she kicked her horse into a sprint while Lia easily kept pace behind.

Those in the village had meant something to the girl, and the acts perpetrated upon them reminded Lia of the death and destruction that had given birth to her current form. Perhaps it was this stab of empathy that again caused her to pause, paralyzing her so that she did little more than watch as the girl buried her dead. She inwardly cursed as the girl set out after the band that had left such carnage in their wake. She had just passed up a prime opportunity to kill the brat.

The girl had surprising stamina, requiring little in terms of food and rest, which again made Lia wonder if there could be any truth to the rumors regarding this one. None of her people were capable of reproducing; they could only infect one another through blood. It brought her bitter delight that none of the dark-haired man's kind could reproduce, either, although it did seem they got a great deal more joy from biting one another than her people. It was odd to her that this man had infected no one.

Years ago, her scouts began reporting rumors that the man had finally transformed someone, although it seemed to be a child, which made no sense to Lia. Children did not survive the transformation, not within her people and not amongst the dark-haired man's kind. Which is why the rumor grew that the man had actually fathered the child.

Lia had dismissed the rumors, but now that she was following this one, she began to have doubts. The girl did not seem to be transformed, but nor did she appear to be human. She was far too fast and too strong for a human, especially a human female. And although she did not appear to have preternatural senses, she did appear to have some extrasensory abilities. And when she caught up to the band of men who had destroyed her village, she unleashed a bloodbath that was a joy to behold.

The green-eyed woman blended into the forest, watching the girl slaughter the men one after the other. A few of the band were actually transformed, young no doubt, but they should have been more than a match for the girl. She cut them down in her fury, even the last who was very strong, the one who told the girl that hell would wait for her anyway.

When it was over, the girl was exhausted and Lia knew it was time for her to strike. But just when she was moving into position, she felt another presence in the forest, one that was rapidly approaching, one that was immensely powerful, and one that would discover her existence if she attacked. Lia cursed herself, knowing that her opportunity had just passed.

What she could not know is that it would be centuries before she would have another chance. The girl might have been human or might not have been, but within days that issue would become moot as the girl would move beyond the realm of mortality forever.

Susan entered a very somber scene. Victor sat before the fire, his elbow propped on the armrest and his chin resting on his fist. Kusunoki stood a short distance away near the mantle, and Abigail and Marilyn sat on the overstuffed couch. A large screen television was tuned to a newscast that was describing a terrorist attack in a nearby city. Aeron entered from the opposite side of the room about the same time as Susan. All eyes turned to her.

"Ryan is resting," Susan said, "her memory seems normal right now although she remembers nothing after awakening in Marilyn's penthouse. She's describing a pronounced feeling of weakness, but nothing physically seems abnormal with her other than the fact that her body temperature is very low."

"She doesn't feel weak to me," Abigail commented, "she feels just as powerful as always."

"That's the same as before," Victor said. "She could barely hold her head up, yet you could feel the power flow from her."

"Yes," Susan agreed, "she continues to pass through these phases. But they don't seem to have any pattern in terms of length or frequency, or even in terms of what might be a triggering event. It's all very frustrating and random."

The room grew quiet as the various members contemplated Ryan's condition. Susan's attention was drawn to the television screen in which a reporter was standing in front of Marilyn's hotel and describing in great detail the terrorist attack that had occurred. The devastation across the city that Ryan left in her wake was attributed to several incidents unrelated to the terrorist attack, including a drunk driver who smashed full speed through a wall in a parking structure.

"Odd that they're not even close to what really happened," Susan said, more to herself than anyone in the room.

"Not so odd," Victor said with a pointed look at Abigail, and Marilyn glanced her way as well.

Abigail smiled her serene smile. "It's not so difficult to control the media when you own it."

This did not surprise Susan, although in this day and age of polarized politics she wondered what side Abigail had come down on.

"So do you favor conservative or liberal media outlets?" Susan asked.

"You misunderstand, my dear," Abigail replied, "I own all of them."

This was a rather stunning assertion, although somehow from Abigail, not that stunning.

"An amateur could create a news empire, then use it to espouse

107

a particular rigid point of view," Abigail explained, "but a far more sophisticated approach would be to buy opposing networks, then pit them against one another in a constant battle of extremism." She smoothed her skirt, "and when you own all of them, it's a simple matter to keep the world in a perpetual state of confusion and misdirection through the elevation of irrelevant and petty matters. There's a reason public discourse is now no more than a constant stream of ambiguous assertions, tautologies, and 'straw man' arguments."

"And that reason is?" Susan asked, appalled at her cynicism.

"Well, primarily," Abigail said without a hint of remorse, "because I like it that way. But it also allows our Kind to hide in plain sight. Which normally isn't necessary, but occasionally," she said, glancing at the havoc on the television screen, "becomes an issue."

"And I apologize for that," Ryan said, "it seems I'm once again at fault in drawing unwanted attention."

All eyes turned to the figure in the doorway. Ryan looked pale but was otherwise steady on her feet. Edward was respectfully behind her but within arm's reach if need be.

"Should you be out of bed?" Victor asked.

"This will only take a minute," Ryan said stiffly. She turned to Kusunoki. "Are you still my Second?"

Kusunoki bowed low. "Of course, my lord. I live to serve you."

The gesture touched Ryan. She did not know exactly what had transpired during her latest blackout, but she knew it had not been good and that her mentor had borne the brunt of it. She returned his bow.

"Then I wish you to assemble the Grand Council in ten days' time."

Kusunoki glanced around the room, his expression saying what he would not. Ryan understood perfectly.

"I realize all but Ala are already present, but I wish a formal gathering in the Council chambers."

Abigail watched the girl closely. "And the reason for this assembly?"

Ryan had begun to slump a little due to fatigue, but at this question she straightened to her full height.

"It's clear that I'm no longer fit to serve as King. In ten days' time, the Grand Council will meet and I will relinquish the throne to Victor."

It was not an unexpected pronouncement but it still weighed heavily on everyone in the room, and most heavily on Victor.

"Are you sure?" he asked. "Because I'm willing to assume command of the hierarchy on an interim basis until you recover."

"No," Ryan said firmly, "you will be King again." She again turned to Kusunoki.

"I have a secondary purpose for wishing to travel to the Grand Council chambers. My last act as ruler will be to confine myself to my quarters there. My first choice would have been my island in the Atlantic," she said, looking pointedly at Aeron, "but I blew that up."

Aeron shifted uncomfortably. She had destroyed the island in a retaliatory attempt to kill him.

"Nevertheless," Ryan continued, "the Grand Council chambers are a perfect location for incarceration. Ten stories underground, a limited number of exits, and walls that are ten feet thick. If that can't hold me when I," she paused, searching for words, "when I'm out of control, then I'm not sure what will."

"I will begin moving my medical equipment there immediately," Susan said without hesitation.

The red-head's forceful response caught Ryan off-guard, and Susan pressed the matter before she could object.

"Jason enjoyed the time he spent there and I'm sure he'll look forward to going back. And I'm not stopping my research until I can figure out what's going on with you."

"Drake and I will join you as well, of course," Victor added. "If you're 'indisposed'," he said, phrasing the condition delicately, "then I will care for him."

"I'm sure you will have lots of company, Ma Cherie," Marilyn said, "I kind of like you with maroon eyes."

For some reason, this description made Ryan look at Abigail, who merely smiled her enigmatic smile. Ryan had the strangest feeling that

Abigail, too, liked her with maroon eyes, but for far different reasons than Marilyn. But she did not have the strength right now to decipher Abigail's ever-mysterious motives.

"If this is acceptable," Ryan said to Kusunoki, "then I will leave the arrangements to you." Ryan's fatigue was obvious. "And I will take my leave."

Ryan left with Edward at her side.

The room was quiet for a moment, then Susan started toward the door, wishing to check on her patient.

"A moment, Dr. Ryerson," Abigail said with her gentle, steely authority.

Susan turned back.

"Have you found anything in your examination of Ryan to explain any of this?" Abigail asked.

"No," Susan said, her disappointment evident, "Ryan had some memory loss when she was fighting off that virus. But that was different. While she was in the phase, she still remembered who she was and acted accordingly, she just couldn't remember what she did after the fact. That's not that unusual and can result from injury, illness, traumatic events, etc. And later, Ryan did recall most of what she did during those time periods, which again is consistent with temporary, short-term memory loss. But for her to lose all memory completely and have no sense of even who she is, that's far different."

"And the 'savage' phase?" Abigail pressed.

"I'm at a loss," Susan admitted. "Obviously I've been unable to examine her in this phase, so I'm not certain if there are physiological changes taking place that revert when she returns to normal. But I've found no permanent changes in her after the fact."

Susan's phrasing caught Abigail's attention. She considered it for a moment, turning the phrase over and over in her mind. She reached out and mentally touched Susan, probing and assessing. She spoke at last.

"There is something you're not saying, Dr. Ryerson."

Susan was instantly the focus of everyone's attention.

"Well," she began reluctantly, "there is something I've noticed."

"I implore you, please speak freely, Dr. Ryerson," Victor said.

"I assure you," Susan replied, "my hesitation is due only to the fact that I have no proof, only speculation, and what I'm proposing seems so outlandish."

"Go ahead, dear," Abigail prompted her, both verbally and with a subtle mental influence.

"Perhaps it's only because I've been documenting my own Change so exhaustively, but something occurred to me while watching Ryan struggle with these cyclical phases."

Susan continued, choosing her words very carefully. "Clearly this is just a theory. Madelyn was not our Kind, but she was something similar. It's possible that exposing Ryan to her blood could initiate another cascade of genetic mutations since Ryan's blood is so malleable."

Victor stared at the young woman very hard. "What exactly are you saying, Dr. Ryerson?"

Susan stopped herself, and there seemed to be a collective holding of breath even though these creatures did not breathe. Susan mentally sought medical terms, technical phrases, anything that would make her pronouncement sound less demented. But in the end, there was only way to say what she needed to say.

"Ryan may be undergoing a second Change."

Victor stared at the young woman, stunned. He had thought in terms of infection, of disease. This possibility had not occurred to him.

"Into what?" Marilyn asked, interjecting at last.

"I don't know," Susan said, "after all, it's just a theory, an untested possibility."

The room settled into silence, each occupant mulling this potential outcome. Victor realized that Susan was still standing there, and released her.

"Thank you, Dr. Ryerson," Victor said. "Please continue your work and keep me informed."

"I don't know if I want her to Change," Marilyn said at last, "I kind of like her the way she is."

Victor stood, his unease translating into motion that he could no longer contain. Abigail watched him closely.

"What if Dr. Ryerson is correct?" she asked. "What if contact with Madelyn's blood has initiated another Change in Ryan? Neither you or I can remember anything before our Change, so it's possible that Ryan is in the early stages of something similar."

Victor turned to Abigail and he could not hide the anguish in his eyes. As concerned as he was about this scenario, there was one that was even worse. The monstrously powerful creature that had saved Ryan at the end had dwarfed Madelyn's abilities. What if it was contact with this creature's blood that was initiating a Change in Ryan? The question resolved itself into its simplest, most brutal form.

What would happen to Ryan from Sharing with his mother?

# CHAPTER 11

RYAN SAT IN HER SUITE, extending her senses throughout the compound. The chambers of the Grand Council were a marvel of engineering, deep beneath the surface of the earth with thick, solid rock walls. It was the thickness of the walls that made it an ideal location for the members of the Grand Council as no one, not even those with such exceptional hearing could hear through them. The isolation of the location, as well as the near impossibility of accessing the facility without permission, also made it ideal for the chambers of the Old Ones.

Those characteristics made it an ideal prison as well, Ryan thought grimly. With proper precautions, it was unlikely she would be able to escape from here even in her most uncontrolled state. And she certainly wouldn't be able to wander out when her memory slipped away.

She glanced around the room. The furnishings were simple but luxurious and she wanted for nothing. Still, she could not help but compare her current lodging with her captivity. She had been imprisoned in a rock fortress high in the mountains and her furnishings there, although odd and alien, had been fairly luxurious as well.

She stood, struggling with the feelings that threatened to overwhelm her. She reminded herself that this was by her own edict, her own choice, and that no one had imprisoned her here. She could probably convince the others to let her leave if she truly wanted to.

"Ah, little one, I've never seen you like this."

There was no need to turn at the presence. She had sensed Ala's arrival, and that low, melodic voice flowed over her like warm water, soothing, caressing, healing. Ryan closed her eyes at the sensation for a moment, enjoying the power emanating from the earth mother. She opened her eyes and turned to the last member of the Grand Council.

Ala smiled and her teeth were brilliant against her ebony skin. She was gorgeous in a most earthy way, her beauty formed at a time in the world when famine ruled and those who were wise worshiped generous, fertile curves. She was an African goddess, her grace and elegance moving past all cultural and temporal norms. She was an immortal archetype, the child of Egyptian royalty.

Ryan interacted with each of the Old Ones in a unique way specific to her relationship and orientation to them. She moved to the beautiful black woman and without hesitation fell into her arms, embracing her in almost desperation. Ala pulled the youngster to her ample breast, her heart wide open to the girl. At last, Ryan regained control and stepped back.

"Thank you for coming, Ala," she said, "I know that you were just here, and that there's much that you face on your continent right now."

"Shush girl," Ala said, settling herself onto a couch and patting the space next to her. "Kokumuo loves to be in charge when I'm gone. Although," she said, "when I told him I was coming to see you he was quite despondent he would miss the opportunity. He has had quite the crush since he attempted to crucify you."

The memory made Ryan smile as she settled next to Ala. She quickly sobered. "I really am not myself right now," she said, "I'll just warn you ahead of time."

"Yes, yes," Ala said dismissively, "Victor has told me of your phases, and you know how close Kusunoki and I are."

Ryan sighed. Ala and Kusunoki were very close, almost like lovers. It was likely Ala knew more of her actions than she herself did. She had not spoken much to anyone since she had ordered the assembly of the Grand Council, and other than spending time with Drake, she had

114

chosen to spend her time alone.

"That's not good for you," Ala said disapprovingly, Ryan's thoughts so open to her. "It pains your father to be apart from you."

"Yes," Ryan said, "and it pains me to have attacked him, and Kusunoki as well. It pains me to be a threat to everyone and everything that I hold dear. It pains me to be so out of control that I don't know if I'll wake up remembering who I am or if I'll be wandering about throwing cars at people."

Motion became imperative and Ryan jumped up and began stalking about the room. "I seem to have made a devil's bargain," she said, "time never held much meaning to me. When I was human, life was short, hard, brutal. When I became immortal, centuries passed quickly. But now my son is aging before my eyes and time has become so incredibly precious again. Yet I'm missing so much of his life, which is ironic because it's the only reason why I stayed here."

"What do you mean 'the only reason you stayed here?'" Ala asked slowly.

The muscles on the side of Ryan's jaw worked spasmodically. "The creature, not Madelyn, but the one who took me at the end. She wanted me to stay with her." The tension in Ryan's body mirrored that which she was attempting to communicate. "And I wanted to stay with her, more than anything. But I could not leave my son. I could not let him grow up without a mother."

Ryan whirled around, continuing her stalking. "And so I made an agreement. I would be allowed to stay until my son was grown and safely Changed."

"And then?" Ala asked, not wanting to know the answer.

Ryan turned to her and stopped. "Then I have to leave," she said simply. "I promised to return to Ravlen."

"And Ravlen is Victor's mother, your grandmother?"

Ryan nodded. "Yes, I believe so."

Ala did not like this conversation. "And if you choose to break your promise?"

Her expression transitioned from sad to utterly fatalistic. Ryan's tone was unequivocal. "You don't understand. There is no breaking of this promise. There is no choice at all involved in this. Ravlen and her Kind are almost incomprehensible to us, and I'm here only because she allows it."

Ala felt a coldness deep inside of her. "Have you told your father this?"

Ryan shook her head. "I haven't told anyone." She began stalking again, her restlessness overcoming her. "It was my intent to Share with Victor at the first opportunity, to pass on what I've seen. But then it became obvious that something was wrong with me." She sprawled, almost violently, into a chair opposite Ala. "I had brief contact with him, but nothing significant. I Shared completely with Marilyn," then added under her breath, "from what I understand, but I had no memory at the time and therefore passed on nothing. And my connection with Kusunoki was so violent there was no mental connection at all."

Motion again took control and Ryan leaped to her feet. "And it's not as if I can relay all of this in a simple conversation. I didn't receive it verbally and could never communicate it that way. All I have are images, emotions, implicit understandings of things that are not understandable to us. I have an alien world flitting about in my head, one that's burying me, crushing me, and one I just can't comprehend."

Ala was silent for a moment as she watched the girl stalk about the room, the energy in her threatening to overwhelm them both.

"And you don't wish to relive it."

Ryan stopped, and Ala feared the corporeal form in front of her would explode with the energy that threatened to erupt. But instead, Ryan just stood there considering her words. At long last she spoke.

"You're right," she said simply, "I don't want to relive it."

"Then why don't you tell your father what you can?" Ala said gently. "He needs to know, and you need to share your burden."

Ryan sat on the couch across from Victor. She had chosen this room because of its informal comfort, and for the fact that all could sit in the circular arrangement of the cushioned seats. Ala was settled next to Victor, and Kusunoki was on her other side. Susan sat adjacent to Ryan and Edward next to her. Marilyn, Abigail, and Aeron were not expected for another day or so, but Ryan knew that Victor would communicate whatever she had to say to them as well. She did not want to wait for their arrival because she had little faith in the stability of her mental and physical condition. Jason was entertaining Drake off in the corner, out of ear-shot of the conversation. But Ryan was very aware that her son could hear her. He glanced up uneasily every once in awhile, as if to assure himself that she was still there.

"Go ahead, Ryan," Ala said encouragingly.

The words seemed trapped. Ryan stared at her father, uncertain how to begin. She started to speak, stopped, then slowly but surely began forcing the words from her mouth.

"I can't explain much, but I can tell you what I've seen. It started when I began to see a young boy. I think he was Roman, but I can't be certain. The time period seems sixth or seventh century, it's hard to tell. His parents were killed by barbarian invaders when he was very young, but he was able to flee the sacked city."

"Do you know the name of the city?" Victor asked.

"No," Ryan said, "but I think it was in England before it was England, and I think the barbarians were Saxons." She combed her memory. "The boy's name was Ambrosius and he fled to the countryside. He was a very skilled hunter and so he was able to survive even though he was very young. He made friends with the tribes in the forest and often saved them from the barbarians. When he was still young, maybe fifteen or sixteen, he came across a woman in the forest."

Ryan stopped. She could see the perfect goddess standing in the water as she spoke, feeling the awe and desire of the young man who stumbled across her. The visions became clearer and clearer to her as she spoke, and her voice took on a mesmerizing quality.

"She was stunningly beautiful: dark-haired, dark-eyed, moved with an inhuman grace. She seemed almost amused by the boy and she

117

seduced him." Ryan watched the scene play out in her head, the ferocious passion of the two causing her to pause in her recount. "Then the woman left and Ambrosius was devastated. He became a great warrior, even a king, and most thought it was the horror of his parents' death that drove him. But it was really the pain of the loss of this woman that molded him because he was dead without her."

The sorrow weighed on Ryan for a moment, the burden as great as if the sorrow were her own. And as she began to fully experience and be absorbed into this life of another, she exhibited a gift that none of her Kind had ever exhibited before, one that she herself had manifested only once.

The Others could see what she was seeing, feel what she was feeling, see it displayed out before them as an extraordinary movie in holographic form. Both Susan and Victor recognized the sensation because Ryan had accomplished the feat at her trial, showing those present the life and death of her mother.

Ryan felt the connection and knew she had only to narrate what she was now seeing. "Many years later, on the eve of what was supposed to be a hopeless battle, the woman returned to Ambrosius. He was now a man, tall, strong, fearless, but the minute she appeared, he was lost to her."

Victor could clearly see the man Ambrosius, but he could not get a clear picture of the woman and wondered why. He wondered if it was something Ryan was doing on purpose, or if it was completely involuntary. She continued her story.

"They had only a single night together and Ambrosius knew he would never see the woman again. He went out to battle the next day, and he drove the Saxon invaders back into the sea. They would not conquer the British Isle in his lifetime." She raised her eyes to Victor.

"The man's name was Ambrosius Aurelanius."

Victor cocked his head to one side, as did Ala. Both were great scholars of history, having lived through so much of it themselves. Ryan nodded her affirmation.

"Your father was likely the inspiration for the legend of King Arthur."

The room had been silent already but now the silence seemed to deepen. Ala mulled this revelation and it pleased her greatly. Edward and Susan were astonished. Kusunoki, as always, kept his emotions tightly controlled, but he, too, seemed startled and pleased. Victor, however, had not taken his eyes from Ryan.

"And the woman you're describing, she was my mother?"

All eyes returned to Ryan and it was apparent she was struggling, uncertain what to say. She had to move forward in her story before she could move backward. "At the end of my battle with Madelyn, she revealed that she was not human, and not our Kind."

It was clear that Ryan was significantly editing this version of events and Victor was not certain he wanted to know exactly how Madelyn had made this revelation. These images Ryan did not share.

"Madelyn struck a mortal blow," Ryan continued, "and I knew I wasn't going to survive. But I suddenly realized that something was coming for me, something I had sensed for years, something I had feared and dreaded and thought was coming to destroy me."

"But it didn't come to destroy me," Ryan said, "it—, I mean she, came to save me."

Ryan turned her gaze upon her father. "The woman from Ambrosius' memories, your mother, returned to save me from Madelyn."

"And she wasn't human either," Kusunoki said quietly.

"No," Ryan said, "I've never felt or seen anything like her. She destroyed Madelyn effortlessly. I can't even describe her power."

"How much were you able to learn from her?" Ala asked, "we felt your near-death and sudden absence, but you returned almost immediately."

Ryan nodded, "Yes, but it felt as if I'd been gone for weeks." Again, Ryan did not think she had any words to describe the experience. She was trying to concentrate but the images began flitting through her head so quickly it made her nauseated. Her vision blurred and she tried to focus. She could feel the creature holding her, the warm, smothering claustrophobic, ecstatic feeling. Ryan forced herself to continue speaking, enunciating her words very slowly.

"Ravlen is from an ancient race, a species of predators that makes us look like infants. They are a violent, matriarchal society, a plague that spreads across galaxies, destroying, assimilating, or enslaving everything that crosses their path." Ryan turned to her father, her tone half disbelief and half bitter amusement.

"Your mother, my grandmother, is over a hundred thousand years old and the undisputed ruler of this species. She came here because they were going to harvest this planet and the only reason they did not was because that boy, Ambrosius, intrigued her."

"So how did I come about?" Victor asked quietly, trying to contain the horror that was growing within him.

"I can't even describe the multitude of ways in which this species is capable of reproducing. Ravlen didn't think humans capable of mating with her kind, and she had no idea that her final night with him had produced a child. Her gestation period was so long that you were born years after your father's death, and he lived to be a very old man."

Ryan was struggling with her own horror and was speaking as much to herself as to those in the room. "Apparently, early 'experiments' with humans yielded only monstrosities, so she was quite surprised to have such a child as you. But when you were born, she wanted you to stay here where you would be a king as opposed to staying with her kind, where you would be a slave."

"And so how were the Others created?" Susan asked, finally breaking her silence.

"Ravlen, in her brutally benign way, did not wish Victor to be alone. So she sent others of her species to transform or 'Change' some companions for him. The attrition rate was catastrophic, and the vast majority of the attempts were monstrous failures, resulting in millions of deaths. Out of that campaign, the first generation of our Kind was born, and I believe that Abigail and Aeron are the only two out of that generation that remain. You," she said, nodding to Kusunoki and Ala, "as well as Marilyn are second generation, transformed by one of the originals. I imagine that all of the others are dead. We are, after all,"

Ryan said, mildly sarcastic, "the children of an extraterrestrial killing machine."

Those in the room sought to digest these dumbfounding facts, unbelievable were it not that they were presented with such reluctant persuasion.

"And so what does this Ravlen want from you?" Ala said at last.

Victor looked sharply at Ala, then turned back to Ryan. "What is she talking about?"

"I didn't think Ravlen was going to let me leave," Ryan said, "but she sensed my desire to raise my son until he could be safely transformed."

"And what then?" Victor asked.

"And then I am to return to her."

Victor stared at his child. "I will not let you go."

Ryan gazed at her father, and with the flexing of a mental muscle, allowed him at last to see what she would not previously reveal. Victor, as well as everyone in the room, had a sudden mental picture of Ravlen as Ryan saw her. Stunning. Terrifying. Beautiful. Cold. Reptilian. Unstoppable. Brutal. Omnipotent.

"There is no resistance in this matter. I don't know what's worse, father," Ryan said, emphasizing the appellation, "the fact that I have no choice, or the reality that I would probably choose to join her even if I did."

# CHAPTER 12

RYAN LAY ON HER BED staring up at the stone ceiling. The recount she had provided to Victor and the Others had left her drained, and she could tell that it had horrified them, most pointedly her father. It was one thing to be a semi-controlled predatory species that preyed primarily on itself. It was another thing to be the offspring of the destroyer of worlds.

A noise in the adjacent room attracted Ryan's attention and she rose from her bed. She thought it might have been Edward come to check on her, or perhaps Susan. Either way, she felt she would have enjoyed the company.

It was neither.

"Well, well, well."

Ryan stared at the creature who was seated in her anteroom, baffled. He immediately reminded her of the two deformed creatures she had seen previously. He was mildly hideous by human standards, with a mouth that did not quite close properly, a nose that was slightly pig-like and nostrils that were a little too large. His skin was stretched tight in places it should not be, yet loose and hanging in others. His left arm was misshapen, and he had tumors sprouting from various places on his personage, not unlike the "Elephant Man." His voice was throaty, full of mucous, and he spit as he talked.

"So you're Ryan Alexander."

"Okay," Ryan said uncertainly, "and you are?"

"My name is Petrus," the creature said phlegmatically. With immense fanfare, he hawked a great wad of mucous and spat it upon Ryan. Ryan gazed at the blob of spit on her torso, still uncertain.

"Was that an insult or a greeting?" she asked.

The creature stopped, stunned. "And if I said it was a greeting?"

Ryan matched the creature in the crudeness of his hawking and spit back on him, skillfully landing the missile.

"Then hello," she said.

Petrus stopped. This was the last thing that he had expected, and Ryan successfully interpreted his expression.

"You have to remember," she said, "I was born in the Dark Ages. It's almost impossible to offend me unless intended."

The creature simply gazed at her.

"How did you get in here?" Ryan asked. "This facility is impenetrable."

"Well who's to say I'm even here?"

Ryan's eyes narrowed. "And what exactly is that supposed to mean?"

The creature glanced around him with interest. "Seems to me you've been having some mental problems lately."

"And how would you know about that?" Ryan asked suspiciously.

"Yes," the creature said shrewdly, "how would I know about that? Maybe I'm just a figment of your imagination."

"Well that should be determined easily enough," Ryan said, unperturbed. She reached out mentally to Edward, gently touching him and requesting his presence. Within seconds he strode through the door.

"Is there something you require, master?"

Ryan glanced at Edward, then over at the strange man in the corner. Edward followed her gaze with no reaction. He turned back to her. "Is something wrong?"

"You," Ryan said slowly, "you don't see anything odd in this room?"

Edward glanced about, again passing by the deformed man without pause. "No," he responded, just as slowly, "is there something I'm missing?"

Petrus laughed raucously, which again failed to produce any response in Edward. Ryan gave him a dirty look, then spoke to Edward.

"Could you check the security cameras, see if you can identify anything out of the ordinary?"

Edward was uneasy. "Of course, however, they are constantly monitored right now, so I would think anything unusual would have provoked an immediate response."

"Very well," Ryan said uncertainly, "that will be all. Thank you."

Edward bowed low, and with one last apprehensive look, exited the room.

"See, girly?" Petrus said. "You are a complete lunatic."

"Really?" Ryan said, "'Girly?' I'm almost 700 years old. I hardly think 'girly' is an appropriate moniker. And certainly nothing my own mind would come up with." She propped her chin on her palm, somehow darkly amused by the whole situation. "So are you my id, ego, or super ego?"

"Freud was an ass," Petrus said bluntly, "someone far too interested in excrement to be taken seriously."

"Ah, so we agree on something," Ryan said. Strangely, she felt no danger at the creature's presence. In a way, she found him invigorating, something new and interesting in her self-imposed confinement. This thought did give her a little pause, however, as she recognized the possibility that maybe she had created him just to entertain herself.

"So why exactly are you here?" Ryan asked.

"Well," Petrus said, "I see two options. Either I'm real and here for reasons unknown, oddly and impossibly undetectable by your colleagues, or I'm some mental construct you have created for some therapeutic reason."

"Ah," Ryan said, nodding, "so either you're here for nefarious purposes, or I'm losing my mind."

"Let's go with option number two," Petrus said, "I don't see your pal Edward running back here with camera footage."

"Alright," Ryan said agreeably, "so why would I manifest you in such form?"

Petrus' tone was bitter. "You mean so hideous?"

The response was mild. "Actually, no. Although humans probably would cringe from you, my perception goes a bit deeper. I'm far more concerned with the fact that I can't get a fix on you at all."

Petrus would not let this go. "Wait. You mean you're not appalled and disgusted by the way I look?"

Ryan shrugged. "No, not really. When I was a child, physical abnormality wasn't that abnormal. No real medical care, lots of inbreeding, horrible hygiene. The church always tried to make any 'defect', for lack of a better term, a judgment from god. But the church and I parted ways very young."

Petrus leaped to his feet and stormed towards her. "This isn't right!" he practically screamed, "you're supposed to be disgusted with me. Why the fuck are all your kind so beautiful?"

Ryan's demeanor was still perfectly calm. "I hardly think profanity is necessary," she said, more sarcastic than serious, "and I don't have the slightest idea why we're drawn to beauty. Perhaps it's a human thing, but 'beauty' changes from generation to generation. I'm guessing it's more an evolutionary bias towards survival of the species. A lot of times what is considered beautiful also serves some subtle genetic purpose."

Petrus stood before her, practically trembling in fury, angered as much by her lack of reaction as by the position she was taking.

"Then how is it that I'm as old as your father!" he raged, spittle flying from his lips.

Ryan cocked her head to one side. "Now that's interesting," she said, "how is it that you're as old as my father? Or, going with option number two, that I would create you the same age?"

With that comment, Ryan leaned forward to touch the creature, and her hand passed right through him. Very slowly, she withdrew the appendage and sat back.

"I really am losing it," she murmured.

Petrus spun on his heel and went back to his corner. He sat there in silence for a few moments, glowering at her. The click of the door lock release was loud in the quiet that hung heavy between them. Susan strode into the room. She glanced into the empty corner to see what Ryan was staring at, then turned back to her.

"Edward said I should come and check on you. Is there something wrong?"

Ryan stared at Petrus while addressing Susan. "I'm going to ask you a question and I want you to answer it as objectively as possible."

"Okay," Susan said.

"Is there anyone else in this room right now?"

Susan glanced about, assessing every corner of the room. She had no idea what Ryan was getting at.

"I don't see anyone else in here," she said slowly.

"Fine," Ryan said, resignation in her voice. "That's all I needed to know."

Susan was concerned. "Are you okay, Ryan?"

"No, I don't believe so. But apparently everything is happening in my mind right now."

The comment struck a chord with Susan. She turned it over and over, assessing it, analyzing it, devising a hypothesis, a potential theory, and methods of testing it.

"You know what, Ryan? You may actually be right," Susan said, the excitement in her voice evident. "You just gave me a great idea."

Susan rushed from the room, the lock clicking loudly in the returning silence. The comment was small consolation to Ryan as she stared at the glowering creature that clearly did not exist.

Susan rushed into the surveillance control room. Victor and Edward sat gazing at the screen, concern evident on both their features. Victor was having difficulty viewing the picture, but he had seen enough.

"Edward," Susan began, "I'm going to need some additional

equipment. I want to run full CT and PET scans on Ryan's brain. It's the one avenue I haven't really explored, and it might be the answer to what's going on with her right now."

Victor was very pale as he sat watching the video of his daughter, and he did not respond. Edward, ever the faithful servant, pulled himself together and acknowledged Susan's request.

"I will have the equipment shipped immediately," he replied, "and I think that's a very good idea."

Susan was taken aback at his tone of voice, and turned to the footage they were reviewing. Ryan was seated in her room having what appeared to be a very animated conversation with an empty corner.

"So," Ryan said, "if I've created you then why did I give you this form?"

"You mean why do I look like a pig mated with a chimpanzee then was hit by a bus?" Petrus said sarcastically.

"Well, not exactly in those words, but yes."

"Not a clue," Petrus said with unhelpful enthusiasm, "maybe Grandma did a number on you."

Ryan's eyes narrowed. "What do you know about my grandmother?"

"I know what you know," Petrus said, "we share the same mind, remember?"

"I'm still not buying that scenario," Ryan said.

Petrus moved closer and plopped himself blob-like down in front of Ryan. "Then let's try this on for size."

"For the first time in your life, you're really afraid."

Ryan was noncommittal. "And what am I afraid of?"

"Well, short-term, I think you're afraid of what you might turn into. You might start sprouting tentacles or perhaps grow a claw or two."

The color drained from Ryan's face. The creature was remarkably accurate.

127

"Second, you don't have a lot of control right now and I think you're afraid you're going to kill someone close to you, maybe that hotty Marilyn or your Asian boyfriend, or perhaps that handsome father of yours, or maybe even your son."

Ryan gritted her teeth, but did not deny it.

"And finally, I think you're pretty afraid of grandma in general."

Ryan made a derisive noise. "That's not exactly a revelation. Only a fool would not fear that one."

Petrus' tone grew calculating. "I think there's more to it than that. I think you're afraid of what grandma's ultimate intentions toward you are."

Ryan was growing increasingly uneasy. "What are you blathering about now?"

Petrus shrugged expansively. "Let's face it. This is a race that fucks and kills just about everything that moves. What if grandma wants to—"

Ryan did not let him finish but leaped towards him, arms outstretched to choke the life from him. Unfortunately she passed right through him and went full speed into the rock wall, nearly breaking both her arms. The collision stunned her and she slumped to the ground while the creature cavorted about the room, chortling mercilessly. The door slammed open and Ryan could hear her father.

"Ryan!'"

Petrus winked at her with a rheumy eye. "Got to go!" he said, and disappeared. Ryan stared at the empty spot on the floor.

Victor, Edward, and Susan all entered her chambers. Ryan sat leaning against the wall, despondent.

"I don't suppose any of you saw that creature."

Victor looked around the room and saw nothing. Susan knelt down at Ryan's side. They had all seen the massive collision with the wall on camera, but it did not appear that Ryan had suffered any injuries, none physical, at any rate.

Ryan sighed. "Of course you didn't."

On the fourth try, Susan was able to inject Ryan with the radionuclide, but only after Ryan had split her own skin to facilitate the process. Susan felt a pang of guilt at the stirring of desire the blood elicited. But Ryan was oblivious, lost in some private hell she did not wish to share with anyone. They had already conducted the CT scan which Susan had analyzed to assess the structural integrity of the brain. Although Ryan's brain was abnormal for a human with far too many ganglia and too many neural connections, the structure appeared normal for her. This result had been disappointing to Susan, but she had hope that the PET scan would show her something relevant and significant.

Victor stood leaning against the wall. He stood upright as Ryan bent over as if in pain.

"Are you all right?" he asked, moving to her side. He was relieved that her eyes were not maroon. He was also relieved to see that she still recognized him.

"Yes, I think so," she responded, "I think I'm having one of those weak spells."

Susan grasped her under one arm while Victor took the other. "As terrible as this sounds, I'm actually glad," she said, "we couldn't hope for better timing. And if I had to pick one of the phases to examine, this is probably the one I would choose because at least you're in control."

They led her to the scanner and Ryan reclined onto the surface. She did not feel in control right now, in fact, all she wanted to do was sleep. From what Susan had explained to her about the PET process, she did not think this would be a successful test at all. The scanner was designed for functional imaging, meaning it would measure the metabolic output of her organs, in this specific case, her brain. The scan would translate the glucose consumption of her brain into a color-coded image, revealing what portions of her brain were currently most active. The inactive portions would show up as black or blue and the highly active portions would show up as yellow or even red hot spots. As lethargic as she felt right now, Ryan was quite certain the image would show up entirely black.

Susan waited impatiently while the machine recorded the images.

It was the very latest technology and probably the fastest available in the world, but it still seemed glacial. She was particularly interested in the activity surrounding the hippocampus, which had a direct role in memory retention and retrieval. She was also interested in the amygdala, part of the limbic system responsible for emotions and the flight or fight response, and the pre-frontal cortex, the seat of logic. Overall, however, she just wanted to see what parts of the brain currently had the most blood flow and were burning the most oxygen.

After about forty-five minutes, the machine finally finished and Susan was disappointed to see that Ryan appeared to be sleeping when the tray slid silently outward from the scanning tube. That would affect the results, especially if Ryan was in normal sleep versus REM sleep. REM sleep would have a few more red areas where the brain was strengthening memories and processing new experiences and information. Normal sleep would be very fairly inactive. In either case, the pre-frontal cortex, unless Ryan was lucid dreaming, was probably offline entirely.

Victor went to Ryan's side and gently shook her, relieved that she still appeared to recognize him when she awoke. He picked her up despite her protest and carried her to a nearby chair. The two waited while Susan pulled the results up on the computer. In a normal hospital, this process might have taken two or three days while a technician read the results then prepared a report for the doctor, but Susan was able to cut to the chase. In a matter of minutes, she had the results on the screen in front of her.

"Oh my god," she murmured to herself.

Victor helped Ryan to her feet and the two joined Susan, looking over her shoulder at the screen.

"That doesn't seem right," Victor said uncertainly, "at least based on what you explained to me."

"No," Ryan agreed, leaning against her father, "that doesn't seem right at all."

Susan stared at the screen, astonished. The three dimensional depiction of the brain was accurate, and the color coding should have represented the metabolic processes occurring in the tissue during the scan, with inactivity express in darker colors and extreme activity expressed in the brighter hues. Although Susan had hoped to identify the areas most active to determine what exactly was going on in Ryan's head, this was one result she had not anticipated.

The scan of Ryan's brain was entirely red.

Drake was curled up in Ryan's arms as she sat before the fireplace. Clever engineering allowed fire far beneath the surface of the earth, providing oxygen for it to burn and the ventilation for the smoke and fumes to exit. The heat felt good on her skin because she still felt cold from her weakness. Drake sensed her need for warmth and pressed against her, causing her to smile. She marveled at how quickly he was growing. Victor watched the two, feeling profoundly sad.

"I don't really have an explanation for this." Susan said, entering the chambers. "I tested the machine and it appears to be working fine."

"So let's assume that the results were correct," Ryan said tiredly, "what would that indicate?"

Susan shook her head, thinking aloud. "I don't know. It could be simply that the machine is designed to scan humans and therefore the parameters aren't applicable to you." She continued to think aloud. "The problem with that scenario is that I've done these scans on you before. Although I found extreme results in visual and spatial memory, not to mention the number of different parts of the brain accessed for any given task, I've never seen anything like this."

Susan marveled at what she was about to say. "Theoretically, what the scan indicates is that 100% of your brain is 100% active."

"Would that make me hallucinate?" Ryan asked.

Susan could not help but think of Ryan's bizarre actions on the camera. "Yes," she said slowly, "it could make you hallucinate. But that's not really surprising given what I've learned about memory versus Memories. I can't imagine what impact it has on the brain to inherit the experiences of another as one's own."

"I didn't seem to have much problem with it until the Memories belonged to another species," Ryan said, a tinge of sarcasm in her voice.

Susan did not quite know how to respond to this. "Your mind has never been normal in a human sense. Even your sleep patterns are closer to meditative states than actual sleep. It's possible that the extreme mental activity is a result of your brain adapting to the stress by building new neural connections, new visual and spatial relationships."

"So is this the 'Change' you were proposing?"

"No," Susan said thoughtfully, "I would think if you were undergoing a second Change, there would be more physiological changes, but I've found nothing."

Victor had kept silent but spoke at last. "I'm sensing another theory here, Dr. Ryerson."

Susan turned to him. "These phases that Ryan is passing through, especially the one where she is normal but has no memory, remind me of your reaction to Aeron's virus. Your body basically shut down to protect itself, going into a deep stasis to prevent damage, not unlike inducing hypothermia in spinal cord and brain injuries." Susan turned and addressed Ryan directly.

"The first phase, in which you simply have no memory, might be a form of mental stasis. The second phase, where you're extremely strong and violent, odd as it sounds, might be a form of physical stasis. And the third phase, like now, where you feel weak but where we feel no difference in you, might be a self-imposed recovery period. And when I say self-imposed, I don't mean that any of this is under your control. This is probably an instinctive reaction of your system, much like Victor's hibernation."

"So you don't think these phases are part of a second Change?" Ryan asked.

"No," Susan said, her conviction growing, "I think they're your mind's attempt to fight it off."

Several hours later, Ryan sat alone in her chambers before the dying fire. Susan had taken Drake and put him to bed with Jason. Victor went to make arrangements for the upcoming council meeting. Abigail, Aeron, and Marilyn would be arriving soon.

Because her thoughts were still full of Susan's recent conversation, she was not surprised to see the creature Petrus reappear.

"So it's true," Ryan said, "you're officially my imaginary friend."

Petrus cocked his head to one side, surprised at the phrase. "You would consider me a friend?" he wheezed.

"Sure, why not," Ryan said, "you haven't tried to kill me or hurt anyone I love. I mean, look at Aeron. He did both those things and I had sex with him."

"So do you want to have sex with me?" the creature said slyly, a bit of drool hanging from his mouth.

Ryan turned a dispassionate gaze on him and to his enormous surprise, there was no disgust or loathing at the question. "Do you think we would be genetically compatible?" she asked doubtfully, "I seem to have a very narrow range of reproductive options, at least on this planet."

The creature stood there, mouth agape at the casual, matter-of-fact response. He sought any sort of come-back, then settled for a snorted reply accompanied by a black look.

"You're an odd creature, Ryan Alexander."

"Then I seem to be in good company," she said, leaning back in her chair.

Petrus moved closer and plopped down in the chair across from her. He seemed to have a filmy, sebaceous substance on his skin that should have stained the fabric but appeared to be doing no such thing. Ryan examined the phenomenon. "I'm still not certain of the significance of your current form, if you are in fact a figment of my imagination."

"You mean why am I so goddamned ugly?"

"You seem to have some issues with that, maybe we should discuss them."

Petrus leaned forward. "You mean to tell me that you wouldn't have any problem looking like me, or if you had a son that looked like me instead of that perfect little replica of you."

"No," Ryan said honestly, "I can't say that. I, like everyone else, am a product of my genes, my environment, my experiences, my culture. I think I'm perhaps a bit more flexible than most because I've seen and experienced so much, including things that never actually happened to me. But now that I'm considering the possibility of growing tentacles or claws, or some appendage that does god-knows-what, I begin to understand the relativity of it all."

"Oh, so now you've obtained perfect enlightenment," Petrus said caustically.

"Not even close," Ryan admitted, "but I do wonder if I'd been born a member of this other species, would I be proud of my tentacles? Would I look forward to growing a claw? Would I be boasting that my claw is bigger than your claw?"

Ryan sighed. "That still doesn't explain why I've chosen you in this form as opposed to a 'perfect little replica' of me."

"Why do you think?" Petrus asked, leaning forward expectantly. Evidently her imaginary friend was greatly interested in this topic.

Ryan gazed at him, the sagging skin, the rows of uneven teeth that poked through the slit-like mouth, the reddened, knobby protrusions that erupted upward on his skin like permanent boils.

"I think it has something to do with what happened here when my father was born."

"Ah," Petrus said, settling in. "So grandma did do a number on you."

Ryan would not rise to his baiting. "I'm not certain what bothers me. I've killed a lot of people in my life, probably tens of thousands. I've killed for a multitude of reasons. I've killed in war, I've killed in peace. I've killed humans and thousands of my own Kind. I even attempted to kill my own father."

"And eat him," Petrus reminded her.

"Yes, and eat him," Ryan agreed. "So I have very few moral qualms about killing."

"But—?" Petrus prompted.

"I keep thinking," Ryan said, her gaze distant, "about the humans that were experimented upon by Ravlen's kind. The ones they attempted reproduction with, the ones they genetically modified and mutated, the ones they tortured and killed trying to find companions for my father."

"The abominations," Petrus finished for her.

"Well," Ryan said, her gaze still in a far off place, reliving memories that pre-dated her birth by 700 years. "I don't know if I would call them that. And it wasn't their appearance that gives me such pause," she said, searching for the words to describe what she was feeling, "it was their suffering."

"And where did you get that insight from? Whose memories are those?" Petrus said bitterly, "Was that from Madelyn's blood or Grandma's?"

Ryan clenched her fists, controlling the flare of anger. She did not want more camera footage of her, this time tackling an empty chair.

"You look like them, you know, the ones who didn't make it." Ryan said simply.

"I hate you, Ryan Alexander," the creature said, coughing on a secretion.

The comment should have wounded her, or angered her, or engendered any sort of emotion at all. But she was beginning to understand what was happening to her mind as it attempted to adapt to the unspeakable.

"I know," she said without judgment, and the creature disappeared.

# CHAPTER 13

THE MEMBERS OF THE GRAND COUNCIL sat in the great hall waiting for their leader. Abigail was seated in the middle with Ala and Kusunoki on one side and Marilyn and Aeron on the other. They did not wait very long as Ryan strode into the room, followed by Victor and Edward. Ryan appeared quite normal and was in a relatively good mood.

Both Abigail and Ala reached out to mentally touch the girl, and both received the same impression. Ryan's mood was genuine, a combination of pleasure and relief to be returning command of the hierarchy to Victor. But there was also a mild underlying sense of melancholy. Ryan began without hesitation.

"When I assumed command of the hierarchy, it was my right to dissolve the Grand Council and it was my choice to request its continuation, a request that was graciously granted by the members before me."

"I stand before you today with another request. That you accept my resignation from the position and return the crown to its rightful possessor, Victor Alexander."

"And your reason for this request?" Abigail asked out of formality. There were very few acceptable reasons for the transfer.

"My health has made me currently unsuitable for the position, and I don't feel I can effectively serve."

Abigail nodded. It was one of the acceptable reasons. "And are there any challenges to this transfer of power?" she asked rhetorically.

Ryan cast a glance in Aeron's direction, as did Victor and Edward. He seemed amused by the attention.

"Not at this time," he replied.

"Are there any objections to this transfer of power?" Abigail asked. She glanced down the table.

"I approve," Ala said.

"As do I," Kusunoki said.

"And I," Marilyn added.

There was a slight pause as Aeron cleared his throat, apparently having some difficult getting the words out. "I agree as well," he said stiffly.

Abigail turned her attention back to Ryan. "As do I," she said. "Then it's decided by unanimous decree that Victor Alexander assume the throne once more."

This was a far different scene than the triumphant coronation in which Ryan had assumed the throne, but no one wished for that type of pomp under the current circumstances, least of all Victor.

"And now there is the matter of naming your Second, Victor," Abigail said, moving to the final piece of business.

Victor turned to Ryan but as he knew she would, she shook her head. "I'm not fit to serve in that capacity, either."

They had already discussed this at length and Victor knew she would not yield. He turned back to the Council. "I ask Kusunoki Masahige to act as my Second."

Kusunoki stood and bowed low. "I accept this great honor with respect and humility," he said, pausing, "but only on an interim basis." His gaze was on Ryan. "Once the crown prince is fit again, I expect her to assume her place as Second."

Ryan bowed. "I will do as you wish." She then turned to Victor, bowing again. "My king."

Victor smiled and brushed her hair from her eyes. "My prince."

And for the briefest of moments, everything was as it should be.

137

Ryan was back in her chambers, locked in by choice although she felt perfectly fine at the moment. Susan was still searching for a pattern in the occurrence of the phases, recording their onset and termination as precisely as possible, but they still seemed frustratingly random.

That did not appear to deter certain individuals, however, and the locks on her door were designed to keep her in, not others out.

"You're awfully brave at the moment," Ryan said over her shoulder.

Aeron moved into her line of sight. "And you seem almost normal. And in a far better mood than I've seen you in awhile."

"That's funny coming from you who are known for your sunny disposition."

Ryan reached for the glass of wine at her elbow and took a drink. Aeron watched the graceful movement, noting the unintended sensuality that permeated every gesture this girl made. "Would you like a drink?" Ryan asked.

"What are you offering?"

Ryan smiled. "You're brave tonight," she commented, "I'm not certain of the wisdom of Sharing with me right now."

"Marilyn didn't seem to have any ill effects," Aeron replied, a trace of jealousy in his voice.

"I'll have to take your word on that," Ryan said, "as I have no memory of that encounter." She handed him a glass of wine.

Something caught Aeron's eye. He placed the wine on the table and went to a nearby shelf, returning with a chess set.

"Would you like to play?" he asked.

"I don't know, our last game took over four hundred years and ended quite badly, if I remember."

Aeron set the board down and began arranging the pieces. "I thought it ended quite well, with the two of us in bed."

Ryan began setting up her own pieces. "You have a selective memory. That was several moves before it ended. The game was actually over when I put you in checkmate and then blew up my island."

"Ah yes," Aeron said in his clipped, aristocratic accent, "it's all coming back to me now."

Ryan could not help but smile. In terms of dysfunctional family dynamics, she had to be in some class all her own. The game board was prepared.

"We normally have some sort of wager at this point," Aeron said.

Ryan allowed her eyes to drift down his perfect male form.

"And what exactly is it that you want?"

"We could try for a girl this time," Aeron said.

"You," Ryan said pointedly, "have no concept of what a bad idea that is. Besides, I have a feeling that I'm rarely capable of reproduction. Susan's friend, that 'Courtney' character, likened it to something called 'Pon Far,' but I have no idea what that is. My general understanding is that it means mating happens only once in a great while."

Aeron stared at the artery visible in her throat. "There are other things we could do that are just as enjoyable."

"You have never been one for subtlety," Ryan said, moving the Queen's pawn forward, "speak your terms."

Aeron moved his pawn to counter the classic opening. "I want your blood, of course. And what is it you want if you win?"

Ryan stopped, suddenly deadly serious. "I want you to take care of Drake. If something happens to me, regardless of how you feel about Victor or the Others, I want you to protect our son."

Aeron also stopped, perhaps even more serious than her. "You ask in wager for something you already possess."

Ryan assessed him at length, then returned her attention to the board. "So do you," she said, smiling. She moved her bishop into an attack position.

Aeron stared at the girl in front of him for a long moment. Although he had known her and probably been in love with her for centuries, she never ceased to surprise him. He moved his piece to defend against the "Queen's Gambit."

"This is probably unwise."

Victor analyzed Abigail's statement. "If Ryan wishes to dally with Aeron, I will not interfere."

"You mean you have no qualms sacrificing him should she lose control."

"No," Victor said, "that's not what I mean although it's a true statement. If Aeron wishes to play with fire and burns himself, I cannot prevent that. But even if Ryan transitions to her most vulnerable state, where she has no memory of who she is, she is still more powerful than him."

Abigail was mildly surprised at the response. Victor was normally adamantly opposed to any contact between Aeron and Ryan.

"This is about Drake," she said.

"Of course it's about Drake," Victor replied. "Aeron may be many things, most inspiring nothing but disgust in me. But he is a surprisingly good father, and an unyielding protector of the boy. In some ways, I'm not sure Ryan could have chosen a better mate."

Victor really could not believe he was speaking these words. "There will come a time when it will take all of my strength to protect Ryan, and when that happens, it will be Aeron's job to protect Drake."

"Well this is going far quicker than our last game."

Ryan glanced at the ancient timepiece mounted on the wall. Aeron was right; they had been at it a mere six hours.

"You say that as if you sense the end is near."

Aeron examined the pieces on the board. "You are the most amazing opponent I've ever faced. It's difficult to tell if you play by logic or intuition. There are times when I feel you have calculated out every move, then others when I feel you make the most marvelously absurd move on pure instinct."

"And what's your feeling now?" Ryan asked.

"Well," Aeron said, examining the board, "I have two choices. I can attack your Queen, whose apparent vulnerability is an illusion and will result in my loss of the game. Or I can take a defensive position, which will ultimately result in a draw."

"I notice that 'winning' is not one of your choices."

Aeron smiled his shark's smile. "Yes, somehow that option is rarely available with you."

"And yet I always offer a draw," Ryan said.

Aeron turned his attention away from the board to the stunning creature across from him. "Yes," he said, "something I've always found curious but am beginning to understand."

Ryan moved a piece on the board, one move away from solidifying the "draw" ending. "That's something I learned from Kusunoki."

Aeron winced. "I see you're not above low blows."

Ryan smiled as he moved his piece into the position that ensured the draw. He turned his gaze once again upon her. "So does a draw mean that we both lose?"

"Possibly. Or it could mean that we both keep our part of the bargain."

Aeron's gaze returned to the artery in her throat. "I would accept that interpretation of the rules."

Ryan gazed at him steadily with an unblinking gaze. "Then you will protect our son at all costs."

"Of course I will," Aeron said, his blue eyes dark with multiple emotions. His eyes appeared more like his son's than Ryan had ever seen them.

Ryan glanced around. "So were you just going to take me on the floor, should I bend over the table or what?"

Aeron uncharacteristically caught his breath. "I particularly like the bending over the table option."

"I don't think so," Ryan said, and disappeared.

Aeron caught her, just barely, in the hallway. He lifted her off her feet to keep her from fleeing because she was so much faster than he was. He kissed her as he removed her clothing, and she returned his kiss, laughing.

"I hardly think it's necessary for you to remove my clothing to bite my neck," she said, amused.

He began removing his own clothing with urgency, desperate to feel her skin against his. He half-carried her into the bedroom where they collapsed in a pile on the bed.

"Not everything has to be 'necessary' to be enjoyable," Aeron said.

Ryan had to concur because the hardness of his body against the firmness of hers was luxurious. And although that particular sensation was irrelevant to the upcoming act, it was still pleasurable. Aeron's teeth on her neck, however, wiped that minor pleasure from her perception as the most powerful of pleasures took hold.

Ryan arched upward, feeling the ecstasy of the union. She could feel the blood rush from her system, giving her the familiar light-headed euphoria and the rhythmic pulsing through her veins. She could see Aeron's life unfold before her, see his Memories, see his disbelief and joy at the first sight of his son. She watched the experience change him, fundamentally alter the immortal, unbending, rigid creature that he had become.

Aeron pulled away from her, almost unable to do so. "Are you able to take my blood?"

The vein in his throat was tantalizingly close but Ryan forced herself to focus, forced herself to remain in control. "I think so," she said.

She rolled over on top of him and fastened on his neck. Aeron moaned aloud as his blood poured into her. Ryan could feel the dark place beckon, the inner sanctum where she danced with death and brought all her paramours to the edge of time. But she resisted the siren call, knowing that an ancient race beckoned her there, wishing her to wreak destruction on all who would dare accompany her to that blood red world

Ryan did not enter that mental space, knowing what awaited her there. But Aeron was still sated, as was she, at least physically, and the two fell into an exhausted sleep, their bodies entwined.

The bodies were stacked by the hundreds. Rats fed upon the rotten remains, and flies blanketed the corpses in black. The boy stepped carefully, quietly, terrified that he might disturb the rats or the flies. The insects, if rousted, would take to the sky in a smothering angry swarm of stinging hell. The rodents were even worse. If agitated, they would attack him en mass. Only yesterday he had seen a woman stumble upon a cadre of the beasts and within seconds go down in a filthy sea of lashing tails and wriggling bodies. In shame he had fled as the woman's agonized screams chased him down the alleyway.

His only consolation was that the rats and the flies would be dead before tomorrow. Everything that touched the corpses died. His blue eyes darkened. He had fled even from his own mother when her hands blackened with necrosis as the flesh began dying on the bone. He had stayed with her as long as he could, even when she began coughing the bloody sputum. But when the fingernails turned black and the tissue on her knuckles began to rot, he could not stand it anymore.

His mother had been the last of his family alive. His father had returned from the war, pale and ashen-faced at what he had seen. But the boy knew it was not the horrors of war that had so diminished and debilitated his father. His papa had been a proud soldier, a fierce fighter who had risen in station because of his skills on the battlefield. No, it had been something else that had changed his father into a shadow of his former self, but it was something the boy did not know because not long after his father returned he grew terribly sick and died.

Many other soldiers grew sick and died soon after their homecoming. Then after that, their families began to sicken. The boy watched his two younger sisters and brother die painful but blessedly quick deaths. His mother had been strong and had not sickened right away. And even when she began to display the initial symptoms, some force of will seemed to hold off the disease. But eventually even she crumbled before its hideous onslaught, her fortitude resulting in only prolonging her suffering.

The boy was all that was left, not only of his family but of his entire town. He was going to leave soon, he just didn't have any idea where to go. He had heard that the army was still conscripting and was so desperate it might even take someone as young as him. The losses had been enormous but many whispered it wasn't battle that had taken the majority.

He was almost to the shanty he had been staying in. Most of the homes in his town were now vacant; it had just been a matter of finding one that wasn't filled with death. He rounded the corner, then quickly ducked back into the shadows. He peered around the corner, careful to keep hidden.

Some sort of creature was sitting on its haunches, crouched over a dead body. The thing appeared to be eating the diseased flesh and it took the boy a moment to realize that the creature was a woman. The filthy thing jerked her head upward, sniffing the air like a wild animal, her yellowed eyes flitting about furtively. She had open lesions on her skin and her lips were split and bleeding. The boy pressed backwards into the shadows, his heart beating wildly. The woman was frozen in place, only the eyes moving about, and the boy was certain she would see him.

Suddenly, a beam of light split the air behind her, the woman opened her mouth to scream as she caught fire, then she disappeared into a pile of ash. The boy was so startled at the instant vaporization that he, too, nearly screamed, but instead clambered under a nearby wagon filled with hay. He peered out from beneath his cover.

Three figures walked into the street, two men and a woman. They were dressed strangely in garb the boy had never seen before and could not even describe. One of the men had a scar on his face and held an odd item in his hand, an item that appeared to be the source of fire that had turned the woman to ash. They spoke to one another in a harsh, rasping tongue that the boy could not understand. Their manner, however, was easily translatable, filled with menace and disdain. The man pointed the weapon at a nearby wooden structure and it exploded into a cloud of splinters.

It was all he could do to keep from starting in terror from his position, but he knew he would not get far from these three. Instead he calmed himself, then inched his way over the wagon's edge and into the pile of hay. With as little movement as possible, he wormed his way down into the deepest part of the grassy stalks, then willed himself to stay completely still.

The three continued to talk in their unknown tongue and there were additional sounds of massive destruction as the weapon was discharged. The smell of smoke was thick and the boy was afraid he would burn to death in the wagon, but he was far more afraid of the strangers. The sound of voices and destruction faded into the distance as the three moved away. Finally, the boy could stand the smoke no longer and burst from his hiding place. He fled the burning town as fast his he could run, his eyes tearing at the fumes and his lungs burning from the smoke. He ran and he ran and he ran, thinking he might never stop running again.

Ryan opened her eyes and stared up at the ceiling. Although the dream was vivid in her mind, she could not shake the feeling that there was some other dream she was forgetting. For the briefest instance she saw a pair of glittering green eyes, but the vision slipped away.

She looked down at Aeron's naked form draped around hers, his head next to hers on the pillow. She examined the dark eyelashes resting against his cheekbones, noting how they contrasted with his fair hair. He opened his eyes, and although his pale blue eyes could never be described as warm, they were less like ice at the moment than cool blue water.

"What?" he asked.

Ryan turned to him, slightly adjusting her position in his arms. "Do you remember anything about your childhood?"

"No," he said. "I remember nothing before my Change. And I don't believe Victor or Abigail does either."

"I always wondered why," Ryan said.

Aeron noticed that she used the past tense. "Do you know something from my past?"

"I'm not certain," Ryan said, "I'm seeing visions of a young boy during an ancient time. There's a lot of death and destruction, and some sort of disease, but it's difficult to tell what's happening." She shook her head and rolled over. "The visions come to me like dreams, and right now I don't trust my mind. I can't say what might be your Memories and what I'm simply making up."

Aeron settled in behind her, content just to lay with her. Ryan could be notoriously reserved when she felt like it.

Ryan took comfort in the presence of her lover and enemy, and was not certain which role comforted her more: the lover for obvious reasons, or the enemy because it was so soothingly familiar. Either way, it helped temper the disquiet the dream caused.

She had not been completely honest with Aeron. Although she genuinely was not certain the boy was him, she had a much better idea of what was happening than she described. In fact, she recognized more from the dream than the boy who had lived through it. The odd garb of the three "strangers" was something she instantly recognized; Madelyn's men had worn something very similar. The strangers themselves felt familiar, as if she had seen them before, but she could not place them. And she was very certain that the "disease" was nothing of the kind, but rather the results of an intentional biological experiment on the people of the time.

Ryan again considered the possibility that the dream had been just that, something her mind had concocted, trying to reconcile and encode the Memories she had received from so many different sources, perhaps even an attempt to reconcile the guilt and grief that were beginning to surface in her. The possibility gave her a brief flare of hope, one that was just as quickly extinguished.

One facet of the dream gave it an overwhelming sense of reality. The boy in the dream understood nothing of what the strangers were saying, but Ryan understood everything. Just as Drake had acquired her language, having assimilated it wholly in content, context, meaning, idiom, and expression, Ryan had assimilated an alien language so richly structured around complex personal and political relationships imbued with violence, it presented itself to her in its entirety. Although fluent in multiple human languages, there were certain things she could not even begin to translate, yet still somehow understood.

The strangers in the dream spoke the language of Ravlen, words that Ryan herself could not yet formulate because she had never heard them before, yet words she could translate because the template resided in her blood.

The man with the pale blue eyes led the scouting team to the edge of the city. It was not their primary target, but it was in the path of their army and of strategic importance. Its importance was emphasized by the fact that the Tribune was assigned to lead the reconnaissance; normally such tasks were far below his rank and abilities.

The men were terrified of the Tribune. Tall and broad-shouldered, his temper was as legendary as his battlefield heroics. He was fearless and expected all around him to be the same. He had no patience for coddling and rumor was he had joined the military as little more than a child. He was unbelievably strong and skilled with a sword, but most of all he was ruthless, giving absolutely no quarter. Those who ranked above him knew not to send him into a battle and expect survivors.

The man's eyes narrowed. Something was wrong. Other than a few fires burning, there were no signs of life he would expect from a city this size. It was obviously a trap, the women and children already moved to safety and the men waiting in ambush. It was what he would have done to protect a city such as this, had he known an attack was imminent. It brought a flush of anger to his cheeks to realize he must have a traitor in his ranks. He would deal with that later.

He motioned for his party to follow his lead and moved quietly along the wall to the drawbridge that was open before them. This was more evidence that this was a trap. Who would leave the primary entrance to the city open wide before them, unprotected? The man stood at the corner edge, then carefully peered around into the entry courtyard. He froze.

It was not the bodies strewn about the courtyard, nor the smell of burning flesh which a slight breeze brought to his nostrils. It was not the rats or the flies or the dogs or the ravens feeding on the corpses. It was not the blood that splattered the walls in uneven patterns that bespoke violent contact. He had seen all of these things in twenty-five years of battle, and they did not faze him.

Rather it was the figure crouching down on its haunches in the middle of the courtyard, the creature unrecognizable as male or female but undeniably human, the figure with the yellowed eyes that darted furtively about as it munched on the entrails of the corpse it had just disemboweled.

The man jerked back. "We must leave."

The men were startled. This was not what they had been ordered to do, but they would not disobey the Tribune.

"I said move!" the Tribune shouted, and the men responded with alacrity, nearly fleeing back to their camp.

The argument in the tent was quite loud and could be heard throughout the campsite. The Legate was castigating the Tribune for failing to obey orders, and the Tribune was uncharacteristically on the defensive.

"This is an act of utter cowardice!" the Legate screamed, "and if not for your exemplary performance to this point, you would be facing death for dereliction of duty, if not treason."

"You don't understand what is in that city," the Tribune said, "you don't know what will happen when we take it."

"We have seen the plague before," the Legate said, shoving some scrolls from the table onto the ground, "it rears its head like a snake every decade. We may lose a few to sickness, but we will not lose this war because you fear a few corpses."

The Tribune nearly lost control, desperately wanting to put his fingers about the Legate's throat and squeeze the life out of him.

"I have left thousands of corpses in my wake," the Tribune said through gritted teeth, "and I fear no sickness. But this is not the plague and you cannot defeat what is in that city."

The Legate's pudgy jaw firmed. Although not as skilled on the battlefield as his Tribune, in his own way he was just as ruthless.

"You will take the city tomorrow, or you will be crucified by noon. It's your choice."

The blue-eyed man led his forces into the city. He anticipated little resistance and was not surprised when they met no opposition. He marched through the courtyard, keeping his eyes forward and his pace steady. It was his men who slowed, their jaws dropping at what awaited them. For seasoned troops they showed a remarkable lack of discipline as some slowed to a stop, stunned, mouths agape.

The dead lay about in contorted forms, their limbs and expressions twisted in pain. The bodies were all deformed, many with additional arms or legs or even occasionally a complete second head. There were tumors and protrusions, eyeballs on the sides and backs of heads and torsos. One woman had an entire second face, eyes, nose, and a mouth just below her three breasts, the expression on the second face one of uncompromising horror and agony. One man sat on the ground, slumped over, gazing downward with lifeless eyes at four complete sets of bulbous genitalia. The children were perhaps the worse, with additional appendages that did not even resemble anything human, more like tentacles or claws.

These men had seen deformity before. Birth defects were not uncommon, with cleft palates and extra fingers or toes frequently seen. But those infants rarely survived and were often drowned or smothered. Few lived to adulthood with such mutations.

The blue-eyed man came upon a woman who, other than the fact that she was bent over in pain, looked fairly normal. When she stood upright, however, the right half of her face appeared melted, the skin

149

flowing downward in a disgusting river of fluids. The man drew his sword and without hesitation beheaded her.

"Anything you find that still lives, destroy it," he ordered without emotion.

It took a few hours, but eventually the Legate brought his triumphant procession into the city. The procession was triumphant for all of five seconds before they, too, were overcome with revulsion at the sight that greeted them. The blue-eyed man did not come out to meet them. He had set up camp at the far end of the city, just outside the walls. He had already lit enormous fires to combat the smell. He knew the Legate would come to him.

He did not have long to wait. The Legate shoved aside the flap of his tent and entered ashen-faced.

"This is not the plague."

The Tribune took a long drink from his goblet of wine, his fourth this early in the day. He had been quite explicit on that fact and did not feel the need to reiterate it or engage in any after-the-fact recriminations. It was too late.

"What comes next will be worse," he said.

It was only a matter of hours before the men themselves began to feel the effects. There was coughing, then sputum, then black fingernails, skin began to flake and flesh began to fall off, then madness.

The blue-eyed man stayed in his tent, drinking. On occasion, a wild-eyed soldier would stumble in and he would decapitate him, the torso falling into the growing pile of bodies in the doorway and the head rolling randomly into one of the corners. The man would examine each body with mild morbid curiosity, noting each mutation and marveling at the abominations that god could create. He did gain a minor bit of satisfaction when the Legate stumbled in sporting a set of breasts even more pronounced than that which nature had blessed him with. The man cut him down without a second thought. He lifted his flask from the table, deeply saddened that it was now empty. He determined in his semi-drunken state that his need for wine far outweighed his need for survival, and he exited his tent, sword in hand.

Most of the men ignored him or were already dead. A few fought with one another in bizarre, contorted contests or simply writhed about on the ground. Those few who were bold enough or perhaps insane enough to challenge him were swiftly dispatched. He again marveled at how rapidly the gods had abandoned their cause, punishing them with the most painful and ignominious of deaths. He wondered why he was not yet affected and thought perhaps the gods had reserved some special fate for him.

The man staggered slightly, but it was a fortuitous stagger as it brought him eye level with a flagon of ale. He picked up the vessel, deeply disappointed to find it empty. He tossed it aside and it clattered loudly in the spreading silence. He stood, struggling to regain his balance and focus on the three figures in front of him.

The man sobered abruptly, his gaze focusing with sudden acuity on what was before him. But he was having difficulty believing his eyes.

There was a woman and two men standing before him amongst the bodies and the destruction. Two men and a woman dressed in strange garb that he did not have the words to describe. Two men and a woman that he had seen in the exact same circumstances a quarter of a century before. Two men and a woman who had not changed in appearance at all as he had grown from a child to a man.

"What is this?" the woman asked, examining the remarkable specimen before her. She was surprised that anyone was left standing in the carnage they had unleashed. Over the years they had changed tactics. With their few successes it was evident that this species was either tolerant or not, and there was nothing in-between. Because of that, they had accelerated their search by accelerating the death toll, knowing they would not inadvertently kill anything promising.

The man did not understand the strange language. It was unlike any language he had ever heard, with gaps and pauses where sounds were missing. He wondered if he was just unable to hear them in his current inebriated state.

Abruptly, the woman was before him although he had not seen her move, and he again attributed this to his drinking. Although he was extremely tall, she was slightly taller, and he realized she was the tallest woman he had ever seen. She was also quite beautiful, but somehow not quite right in a coldly reptilian way.

The woman examined him at length. He exhibited no physical defect, natural or induced. He was quite handsome and nearly the same age as the target, perhaps slightly younger. If he was indeed resistant and capable of being transformed, he would be perfect.

"Take him into custody," the woman ordered, "if this works we might be finished."

The man sat in the cage for days, then weeks, then months. He was fed and kept comfortable, even offered "companionship" in the form of terrified women who within hours succumbed to the disease that had taken his family as a child then his army as an adult. He kept his distance from them, as he did everyone who was placed in the cage with him.

Oddly, his best companion ended up being the one he initially most abhorred. One man, clearly infected, was thrown into his cage. The man had various tumors and growths about his body, a misshapen head, and a third ear on his forehead, slightly off-center that made eye-to-eye conversation with him extremely distracting. But the man was fully lucid, not driven to mental defect or insanity as all the others. The man was learned and well-traveled, and his conversation was a welcome respite from the Tribune's isolation. And after awhile, even the ear was no longer a distraction, or even noticeable at all. The blue-eyed man was actually saddened when the deformed one was taken from him, and as a result hardened himself, determined he would not soften so again.

The woman came to him daily. There seemed to be considerable conversation about him that grew more enthusiastic as he bore the various pin-pricks, examinations, and other maltreatments. The woman's interest in him grew pronounced and he was not surprised when she finally took him to her bed. He was very surprised, however, when she did not engage in any sexual activity in which he was familiar, but rather fastened onto his neck like an animal and began to take all the blood from his body. He was more surprised when she sliced her own neck and forced his lips to her vein. Very little blood passed into his system and what did burned like acid. Even so, it was a most extraordinary experience, right up until everything went black.

Ryan gazed up at the ceiling once more, still entwined with the father of her son. She wondered if Aeron was aware of any of this, even on a subliminal level. She herself had sensed her human mother's tragic memories simply because Elena's blood coursed through Ryan's veins, and even Victor's Sharing could not replace or ultimately repress those events. She wondered if Aeron, too, sensed his tragic origins and blamed Victor, or even her. It would explain his abiding hatred for her father and his attempts to destroy her, even if he himself was unaware of the motivation.

Ryan sighed, careful not to awaken her lover. Or, perhaps it was just the inherent killer in all of them that put them at each other's throats.

When Ryan awoke again, she was alone but she could hear the laughter of her son in the living room. She rose, combed her hair out her eyes, and went to see what he was doing.

Drake sat on Aeron's lap before the chess board. Jason sat across from them, a perplexed look on his face. He very hesitantly moved his knight, and Ryan smiled.

"I can tell that Ryan taught you play," Aeron said, "traditional tactics would assess that a ridiculous move."

Jason leaned back, pleased. He was still greatly intimidated by Aeron, but Aeron was Drake's father, and despite the considerable difference in their ages, Drake was his best friend.

Drake now pondered the board. He first moved his hand to his castle, an obvious and aggressive choice. He removed the hand, however, and instead moved a pawn in what appeared to be an almost random choice.

Aeron analyzed the board, as did Jason. "Sneaky," Jason said at last.

Aeron nodded. "I can tell you learned chess from your mother, as well," he said to the boy on his lap. "And I predict an endless round of 'draws' for the two of you over the years."

This seemed to please both boys.

Aeron became aware of Ryan's presence. He was still getting used to her ability to move so undetected, an ability he had seen only in Abigail to such a degree. Drake sprang from Aeron's lap and sprinted to her, hurtling himself into her legs. She lifted him, laughing, then hugged him tightly. She turned to Aeron.

"I think you should take Drake topside for a few days, get him out in the sun."

Aeron was surprised that Ryan would make such a suggestion. He had been allowed to spend as much time as he wanted with his son, but he had not been allowed to take him anywhere unsupervised. Jason shifted in his chair and Ryan interpreted his body language.

"You should go, too, Jason. You've been underground too long. And you should take your mother as well, she's been working too hard."

"What about you?" Aeron asked. "Would you care to join us?"

"My last outing didn't go so well," Ryan said, remembering the trip with Susan and Marilyn. Since the council meeting, Victor had apparently arranged some sort of informal rotation system with the Old

Ones and she felt like she had a constant babysitter.

"Kusunoki just left, and Marilyn isn't expected for another two weeks."

"I will make certain I return before that happens," Aeron said under his breath.

Ryan ignored the comment. "Victor is gone but a few days, then he will return. Besides, it's not as if I'm here alone. Edward watches me like a hawk and there's an entire staff on hand."

"I won't go far," Aeron promised, "and you'll call if you need anything."

"It will probably be Edward calling for help," Ryan said, sighing, "if I transform and begin tunneling my way through solid rock with my bare hands."

Despite her protestations, Susan had to admit that Ryan was right. She had desperately needed a break and although she was reluctant to leave Ryan, she was enjoying herself.

Drake and Jason were playing in the pool. They were staying at a marvelous estate out in the middle of nowhere, not far from the hidden entrance to the chambers. Susan did not know if it was someplace that Aeron had already owned or had merely purchased because he needed it for the weekend. She still had difficulties adapting to the material wealth these people possessed.

Susan examined her son. Although he had her coloring and fine facial features, he had his father's build. It seemed he grew taller every day and his shoulders were just starting to broaden. She was grateful that Jason was going to have his dad's athletic physique since he was continually surrounded by so much physical perfection. Even Drake, who was still a child, was clearly going to be built like Ryan, tall, lithe, and slender. Although still small, he already had muscular development comparable to a teenager.

Drake's father, however, was built nothing like a teenager and

155

Susan had difficulty not staring as Aeron strode out clad in only a pair of shorts. He looked as if he had been chiseled from marble, except the marble flexed and rippled beneath the surface of his skin as he moved. He took the lounge chair next to her, also watching the boys.

Susan wondered if it bothered Aeron that Drake so little resembled him, and feeling unusually bold, she asked.

"Drake has your eyes, and Victor's dark hair, but he greatly favors Ryan."

"No," Aeron corrected her, "he is nearly identical to her."

"Does that bother you?"

Aeron turned his blue eyes upon her. "Does it bother me that my son looks like the most stunning creature I've ever seen? In a word, no."

What was obvious to everyone else finally occurred to Susan. "You're in love with her."

Aeron's mouth twitched. "Just now figuring that out, are you?" Then after a significant pause. "So are you."

"What?" Susan asked, the indignation in her voice causing the boys to glance up. "I'm not."

Aeron smiled his shark's smile. "Marilyn is right, you really are a prude."

"I am not," Susan exclaimed, the second protestation sounding as weak as the first. "Ryan is my friend. I would never impose on that relationship."

Aeron's tone was filled with sarcasm. "So you're telling me that if Ryan chose to take your blood, you would not give it willingly?"

Susan did not really have a response. "As I thought," Aeron said.

"Well, it's not as if that will ever happen," Susan said.

Aeron sensed the disappointment she would not express. "The only reason why Ryan has not Shared with you is because you're too young and it would kill you," he said in his clipped, aristocratic manner. "Which is why if I were you, I would avoid her when she lacks memory because she will not restrain herself and you will most likely end up dead."

With perfect clarity, Susan understood why so many Young Ones went willingly to their deaths in Sharing. Aeron's matter-of-fact prediction of her fate was in no way a deterrent; instead it left her with a sense of warmth.

Aeron smiled. How typical. He was not willing to let Dr. Ryerson off so easily.

"And what will you do in a few years when those two wind up together?" he said, nodding to the boys in the pool. His tone implied many things.

"What?" Susan stammered. She tried to recover, "I mean, if that's what happens, then that will be okay, I certainly wouldn't object…"

"If that's what happens?" Aeron repeated mockingly, "that is Ryan Alexander's son, she who unintentionally seduces everyone around her. But Drake will be different. Ryan didn't grow up around the Others and had very limited contact with any of our Kind until she was almost a hundred years old. She was raised as a human. Drake, on the other hand, has been raised to be exactly what he is, with my influence, and Marilyn's influence, and Ala's influence, and god forbid, Abigail's influence, but most of all Ryan's influence."

"Drake," Aeron said with emphasis, "will seduce everyone. But unlike Ryan, he will do so with the full knowledge of what he is doing."

Susan watched the boys in the pool, aware of the closeness and connection between them. It was brotherly now, and protective. Jason was demonstrating all of the traditional signs of young male adolescence and his interest in girls was pronounced. His infatuation with Marilyn was more than evident, much to his embarrassment. But she wondered what effect Drake would have on him as the two grew to adulthood.

"Jason is not like me," Susan said slowly, "and although things at times have been confusing for him, he, like Drake, has been around the Others most of his life. He adapts to concepts that would have buried me. I will never forget when he asked Ryan to be his dad when he was Drake's age."

"Why his dad?" Aeron asked curiously.

"His reasoning was that he already had a mother."

The two fell into silence, then another question occurred to Susan, mostly because she was thinking about Jason's future.

"Who will Change Drake?"

"Ryan will," Aeron said without hesitation. "Her blood will make him stronger than anyone else's."

Susan thought about Ryan's current condition. "And if she can't, for whatever reason?"

"Then it will be Victor," Aeron said, again without hesitation. "In fact, I believe that's why he doesn't Share with her now, just to ensure that option with his grandson."

Susan was always amazed at how far in the future these people planned. Victor's actions today were influenced by something that might happen twenty years from now.

# CHAPTER 14

RYAN WAS BORED. True, her boredom was of her own doing. She was the one who had imprisoned herself in the lower levels then dismissed everyone. She had spent some time training in the simulator but it was not nearly as enjoyable as fighting with a live opponent. She almost wished her imaginary friend would return so that she could spar and banter with him, but apparently she had resolved whatever emotional issues had caused "Petrus" to manifest.

Ryan's pace down the rock hallway slowed. Someone was here, someone unexpected. She reached out, trying to assess the presence, but could not quite get a fix on it. Simultaneously, she felt a wave of dizziness come over her and she put out a hand to steady herself against the wall.

"Oh, wonderful," Ryan said aloud. She could feel the weakness overtake her. Her own weight suddenly became a crushing burden and her boredom disappeared into concern that she would not even be able to make it back to her quarters. She had left explicit orders that were she to pass into any phase, including this relatively benign one, none of the staff were to break the seals and come to her aid. She knew she was being monitored and it would be mortifying to be seen crawling down the hallway. She considered just sitting down right where she was to let the hours or days pass until she recovered.

"You don't look so well, my dear."

"And you," Ryan said, resigned, "as always, have the most impeccable timing."

Abigail moved from the shadows and took her elbow, a gesture that was gentle but insistent with a trace of possessiveness. Ryan had no choice but to lean upon her as the matriarch helped her down the hall.

"I could carry you, little one."

"No," Ryan said quickly, gritting her teeth at the exertion "that isn't necessary."

Abigail allowed her to struggle a little further, then swept her effortlessly off her feet. "Apparently it is," Abigail said with cool amusement, carrying her down the hall.

Ryan endured the humiliation of being carried like a child, primarily because she had no choice. Abigail was unbelievably strong, a match even under normal circumstances, and right now the circumstances were definitely not normal.

Abigail swept into her own chambers, closing the doors behind her.

"I see we are not going to my room," Ryan commented.

Abigail merely smiled, settling into one of her large overstuffed chairs. Ryan was now pressed fully against her in the confines of the chair, her legs draped over and supported by the plush arm-rests, her head held close to Abigail as one would hold a sickly child.

"Let me guess why you're here," Ryan said.

Abigail said nothing, but ran a fingernail just beneath her own collar-bone, opening a small wound on level with Ryan's mouth. Ryan stared at the drop of blood that oozed out, took a teardrop shape, then began to run downward, tracing the curved path of the body.

"Damn you," Ryan murmured, putting her mouth to the wound and stopping any downward flow.

Abigail gasped with pleasure but was fully in control. She allowed Ryan to drink for a few moments, then gently pushed her head back to the armrest. "You know what I want, my dear."

Ryan gazed up at her, mildly bitter but fully resigned. "Of course

160

I do."

Abigail's voice was gentle steel as she bent to slice into Ryan's neck. "Then you will show me everything."

The intense connection was like an electrical current throughout Ryan's body. Although she had Shared several times since her ordeal, this was the first time she had achieved full mental contact with anyone. Had she been the one to initiate the contact, she probably would have pulled away in shock, but Abigail held her tightly, taking her blood slowly, methodically, relentlessly. In Ryan's current condition, she was helpless.

The visions were haphazard, confused, a tumult of sight and sound that were a direct representation of the state of Ryan's mind. Abigail knew she was going to have to guide the girl fairly unmercifully to get the information she wanted.

"I want to see everything," she whispered, "starting from when Madelyn took you from us."

Ryan's body jerked, a physical manifestation of her unwillingness to comply, but Abigail pressed her hand to Ryan's torso, a gesture both soothing and controlling. Ryan's eyes unfocused, giving in to the influence that Abigail had always exerted over her.

And Abigail began to see what she wanted to see. Madelyn, as she had first appeared to Ryan, beautiful and horrifying, perfect and yet unnatural, powerful beyond reason and imagination. She saw Ryan taken away, bound and gagged, then sedated. She saw her awaken in the mountain fortress in a solid rock prison. She saw the guards, Madelyn's men, treat Ryan with disdain then pay dearly for their underestimation of her. She saw Madelyn stop Ryan's blows without effort, then take her blood, injecting her with a neurotoxin that paralyzed Ryan and caused her great pain.

At this memory, Ryan twisted about as if trying to free herself and Abigail held her tight. Abigail stroked the girl's stomach, the ridged abdominal muscles clearly defined beneath the thin cotton shirt, so tense was Ryan's body. Ryan relaxed a little, still struggling against the imaginary foe.

"I want to see more," Abigail whispered to her, softly and remorseless.

And the visions came. Ryan escaping from her captors, acquiring the swords that equalized their combat, then taking them down one-by-one. She saw Ryan gain hope at her success, hope that was dashed when Madelyn re-captured her with stunningly little effort. The creature Madelyn took Ryan to her chambers, and secured her cooperation by kidnapping Susan and Drake.

Then Abigail began to see what she had only glimpsed from Susan, subtleties that Ryan herself seemed unaware of. How Madelyn, while expressing disdain for Ryan, continued to take her blood again and again. How her orientation to the girl changed from one of contempt, to grudging respect, to outright desire and possession. How Madelyn had taken her into her inner chambers, then into the inner sanctum as well. And how their relationship changed completely when Ryan began to grow resistant to the neurotoxin and Madelyn seduced her rather than forced her.

Abigail sat back for a moment, digesting this particular angle. The fact that the girl had gone from a tortured, helpless prisoner to one who was in a semi-consensual relationship of near-equals was stunning. Ryan again twitched beneath her hand, and she firmed her grasp, returning to the task at hand.

Abigail next saw events she was familiar with. The arrival of Victor and the forces he had assembled to free Ryan. She watched Ryan's incredible speed in combat as she seemed to shift into a higher plane to defeat her enemies. And she saw Ryan's ultimate resignation to her fate as she sensed Madelyn's awakening.

Abigail leaned forward, holding the girl tightly. This is what she truly wished to see. The girl had confronted Madelyn and taken her blood, nearly destroying herself in the process but giving Madelyn intense pleasure. It was a tactic that almost would have worked had Ryan not revealed in Sharing what she herself was unaware of. Madelyn recognized how dangerous Ryan was, and more importantly, how dangerous she would become, and determined to destroy her.

Ryan moaned aloud and tried to twist away, but Abigail's iron embrace would not yield. This is where it got truly interesting. As Madelyn moved to kill Ryan, injecting her with a poison that Ryan's body could not adapt to, something came for Ryan. It was something she had sensed for years, something she had dreaded and feared, something she had entirely misunderstood.

"I want to see her," Abigail whispered, "show me."

And Abigail saw her, the creature who came through a rip in the space-time continuum, the slayer of millions, the undisputed ruler of an empire stretching across the cosmos, the unchallenged Queen of an extraterrestrial killing machine. She was beautiful in a chilling, alien, reptilian way, and her power was unimaginable, dwarfing everything around it.

This was Ryan's grandmother.

Abigail sat back, sated, holding the unconscious girl in her arms. There was more, but it was disjointed, the mass of history that Ravlen had passed on to Ryan about her species, then about the origins of their Kind on earth. This did not interest Abigail.

Rather she was transfixed by the great love and intense fascination that this near-omnipotent alien creature held for Ryan. Even more so was the girl's reaction to the alien Queen, one of unrestrained passion, obsession and longing, a desire so intense she was willing to sacrifice everything.

Abigail relaxed in the chair, stroking Ryan's hair. She was far less moved by the vivid and violent account than one would have expected. There was no fear evident, no worry or trepidation, no anger, no real emotional arousal at all. If anything, there was only an overwhelming air of pleasure and satisfaction.


The creature was bending over her, his snout-like nose inches from her face.

"Can I help you?" Ryan asked mildly.

163

"You sure sleep a lot," Petrus said.

Ryan sat upward, passing right through the twisted torso. "That isn't the first time I've heard that criticism." She waved her hands through him several times, trying to dissipate him as if he were a wisp of smoke.

"You trying to feel me up or what?"

"Yes," Ryan said, rubbing her temples, "that is exactly what I was trying to do."

She shifted so at least they were not occupying the same physical space, and he sat down next to her.

"I was actually beginning to miss you," Ryan said, "I thought perhaps I had solved all my emotional issues and you had disappeared."

Petrus slapped his knee and chortled. "Ah, we're just getting started, girly. Seems like you just got a lot more to chew on."

"And what would you be referring to?" Ryan asked. She put her fingers to the bruise on one side of her neck where she had Shared with Aeron, then the other side where Abigail had taken her fill. Aeron's bruise was nearly healed whereas Abigail's more recent damage was still tender. She turned her wrists, noting several additional bruises. As weak as she had been, Abigail had held her tight.

"You're kind of a trollop," Petrus said admiringly.

Ryan burst out laughing. "Yes, it's all fun and games with me."

Her eyes darkened as she thought about this statement, and Petrus grew cunning.

"So let's talk about your boyfriend."

"I would hardly consider Aeron my boyfriend," she replied.

"Well, he is the only person you've actually boned on this planet. I mean, there's been a lot of metaphorical sex, in fact, you've pretty much metaphorically screwed everything that's moved."

Ryan gazed at him. "Must you be so crude?"

Petrus shrugged. "Yeah, probably."

Ryan stood, restless. "You're just jealous."

"Damned right," Petrus muttered, "but stop changing the subject."

"So what about Aeron?" Ryan asked impatiently.

Petrus' expression grew crafty. "Are you going to tell him?"

"Tell him what?" Ryan said stubbornly.

Petrus' eyes fairly glittered in the dim light. "You can't play games with me, girly. I live in your head, remember? I know what's going on up there."

Ryan decided to test the creature, still not entirely sure he was what he claimed. "You're going to have to be more specific. What exactly would I tell him?"

The creature was not fooled. "Oh, I don't know. Tell him about his origins. Tell him how you're responsible for his suffering as a child, the death of his family. Tell him that his captivity and painful transition was on account of you. Tell him about the abominations that were created in your name, tell him how everything that happened to him and to all your Kind was just a step-by-step process to create you."

"It wasn't my fault!" Ryan said sharply, stopping the vitriolic tirade. The words echoed in the quiet chamber as the creature smiled a triumphant, bitter caricature of a smile. Ryan was becoming more convinced he truly was a figment of her imagination because their conversation so perfectly mirrored the chaos in her mind. She steadied herself.

"The end result of this 'horrible' fate I have inflicted upon him is unimaginable power and immortality, not to mention pleasure that few can even comprehend. And the first time I met Aeron, he was leaning over a table eating one of our Kind," Ryan said, "So despite the fact that Drake's birth has tempered him, he is a cold-blooded killer, vicious and unmerciful. I'm not certain this story would even matter to him."

"Oh," Petrus said, disappointed, "you're going to get all logical on me now."

Ryan felt a sense of relief, as if she had reached some sort of mental detente with herself. Her relief was short-lived.

"So let's talk about mommy."

Ryan turned, disdain in her voice. "If we were truly of one mind, you would know that my mother died giving birth to me."

"Or," Petrus replied, his tone even more disdainful, "I would know that you experienced all the wonderful things your father did to

Elena before she died. I would know you got to feel all of her pain and hopelessness in vivid detail because her blood flows through your veins."

Ryan's jaw clenched spasmodically and she had to control herself from charging him, knowing she would simply wind up crashing into the wall again.

"It's a wonder the number of crimes that have been committed in your name," he said slowly.

Ryan stopped. His words were brutal and true.

"That's why you're here," Ryan said, "isn't it?"

The creature cocked his head to one side warily.

"That's why I created you and why you look like this."

"Like what?" Petrus asked, his voice dripping with sarcasm.

"Like them," Ryan said, "like the Others who didn't make it."

"What do you mean 'the Others,'" the creature spat, his voice rising to a squeal of fury, "those fucking abominations weren't your Kind."

Ryan looked at him strangely. "Of course they were. What a stupid thing to say."

The creature was apoplectic. "You've killed thousands of your own Kind! Are you telling me now you're all soft on those monstrosities that didn't make it?"

Ryan tried to reconcile the contradiction and found that she could not. Their Kind had instinctively mimicked the species that created them, choosing the strong and the beautiful, culling the weak and defective. Allowing an extreme form of natural selection to take place in the Change itself, its physical and mental demands so intense it generally resulted in death. The cleansing was another instinctive culling, removal of the weakest among them.

"I'm just like her," she said at last, "aren't I?"

The creature was silent, but his judgment was complete.

Ryan thought back to the Purge she had conducted, how she had hunted down and slaughtered those deemed unworthy to survive. Even now she could not generate guilt or compassion for the dead.

"So I probably would have killed most of them, too," Ryan admitted.

"What do mean 'most' of them?"

"There were a few I probably would have let live."

"Oh, really now," Petrus said in disbelief, his tone acidic, "and just why would you be so merciful?"

"It has nothing to do with mercy," Ryan said, thinking back through her recent visions, "like the one in the cage with Aeron. There was nothing wrong with him."

"Nothing wrong with him!" Petrus sputtered, spittle flying from his lips, "he had a fucking ear in the middle of his forehead!"

"You really are inside my head," Ryan said with wonderment. She shook her head to clear it. "That ear was a little distracting, but it wasn't worth killing him over."

Petrus appeared to be choking on something. "Distracting? He was an atrocity, an abortion, a freak!"

Ryan herself was growing angry. "And he was smart, and brave, and loyal and strong. And I, who at times have been tasked as the gatekeeper of my Kind, have killed the venal, the petty, the cowardly, and the terminally stupid. But I would not have killed him."

It was difficult to tell if Petrus' mouth was agape because it did not close properly, but he stared hard at Ryan for a very long time. Finally his jaw snapped almost shut.

"So let's talk about mommy."

"Didn't we already have this conversation?" Ryan said tiredly, sprawling into a chair.

"I'm not talking about Elena," Petrus said, his crafty expression returning. His rheumy eyes flicked to the more prominent of the two bruises on her neck.

"Ah," Ryan said, "you're referring to Abigail."

"Yes," Petrus replied, "most people only have an oedipal conflict with one of their parents, but you seem to have it with both. In fact," he mused, "you seem to be having it with more than one generation."

"What does that mean?" Ryan asked, thinking he was referring to Drake.

"Well now you've got grandma in the picture as well."

167

Ryan tightened up. She wished he had been talking about Drake.

"Yeah," Petrus continued conversationally, "that's a big-ass cultural chasm before you; it might even swallow you whole."

"What are you getting at?"

"Well," Petrus said, "got be careful with those 'alien' relationships. It might be more than just metaphorical sex."

"You're a pig," Ryan said bluntly.

Petrus drew back, offended. "Is that a slur on my nose?'

Ryan glanced darkly at the proboscis. "No, although I wish I had been that clever."

# CHAPTER 15

ACCORDING TO EDWARD, RYAN HAD spent an uneventful period of about twelve hours where she had wandered about the lower levels exploring with great wonderment the things that had been familiar to her for hundreds of years. She presumed that this had been a period of amnesia, since she had no recollection of it. Edward also recorded an approximate two hour period in which she had taken on the violent persona. Edward, through remote control, was able to quickly isolate her to a single rock-walled room, and without stimulus or outlet for the savagery, she had simply sat in the center of the room and nearly burned a hole in the ground with the heat emanating from her body. After that, she had rolled over and gone to sleep.

Ryan sighed. Between the periods of amnesia, savagery, and weakness, plus the conversations with "Petrus," she felt as if she were completely losing her mind. She was actually looking forward to Marilyn's arrival so when the raven-haired one did not show up as arranged, Ryan was greatly disappointed. She assumed that something important had come up, but it was unlike Marilyn not to send word. After a few days without contact, even Victor was growing concerned.

"It seems that Marilyn has disappeared."

He returned the phone to Edward who returned it to his coat pocket.

"What do you mean she's disappeared?" Ryan asked.

Victor glanced to Edward, who took lead in the conversation. "I've spoken with several of Marilyn's staff and they indicated that four days ago Madame de Fontesque left for a walk about her estate in the south of France and has not been seen since."

"Well," Ryan said, searching for an explanation, "perhaps she found someone to toy with and has lost track of time."

"Under normal circumstances, I would suggest the same scenario except for the fact that there is no one," Edward, said, then repeated it with emphasis, "no one that Marilyn would choose to 'toy with' over you," Edward replied.

"I agree," Victor said, "and as wild and unpredictable as Marilyn is, she would never break an engagement without notice."

Ryan looked from one man to the other, her eyes settling on Victor. "There's something you're not telling me."

"At first the staff didn't realize Marilyn was missing. They assumed she had come here on her own," Victor said. "It was Edward's inquiries that prompted them to retrace her steps."

"And—?" Ryan said.

"They found signs of a violent struggle," Victor said quietly.

"That's ridiculous," Ryan said, unwilling to believe what he was saying. "Marilyn is as strong as any in this room and as much as she hides it, she is an excellent warrior."

"I agree," Victor said, "it doesn't make sense."

"Did they check all options?" Ryan demanded. "Did they trace her finances? Interview her latest paramours? Check any phones or computers she might be using?"

"I assure you they have done or are doing all that," Edward said, "and I'm duplicating their effort just in case."

Ryan's frustration was growing. "There are few people capable of harming Marilyn, and quite frankly, I would be suspect number one at this point in time. But I'm quite certain I'm on camera talking to myself in the basement when this occurred."

"Have you sensed anything?" Victor asked her.

Ryan shook her head. "No, but that doesn't surprise me. My abilities are greatly compromised right now."

"I haven't sensed anything, either," Victor said, "which would be very strange if she is in any type of danger."

Ryan felt her blood boil and for an instant was afraid she was going to transition into a savage phase. But she was merely angry and frustrated and feeling very helpless. She wanted to get up and destroy something but she was going to have to do the complete opposite.

"I will see if I can focus my meditation to reach her," Ryan said, "and you should contact Kusunoki and Ala to see if they can sense her as well."

Edward nodded and bowed, backing from the room to complete the task.

"I'm going to France," Victor announced. "I may be better able to get a sense of what has occurred there."

This only served to heighten Ryan's frustration. She should be going to France but instead she was locked in a dungeon ten stories below ground talking to an imaginary therapist, cycling between a pathetically weak creature who could barely stand and a raging lunatic who wanted to destroy everything.

Aeron and Susan returned with the boys and it took little effort to persuade Aeron to stay with Drake. Ryan felt distinctly uneasy about present events without any real insight why. She had sensed nothing and had no proof that Marilyn was in danger. "Signs of a violent struggle" meant nothing. She and Marilyn had once so trashed a villa that the structure had to be condemned, and there had been no violence nor any struggle involved in that incident.

Ryan tried to calm herself and meditate, but for the first time in centuries, she was unable to do so. Her mind was pure chaos and she could not slow it or focus it in any way. The attempted practice merely increased her frustration until she felt as if she was going to explode.

Only the presence of her son brought her any comfort or solace.

"I thought Marilyn was coming," the boy said, climbing into her lap.

"So did I," Ryan said, "but we don't know where she is."

"Is she hurt?" Drake asked, his blue eyes filled with concern.

Ryan knew she could not lie to him even if she wanted to. "I don't know. I don't think so. Marilyn is very strong and very smart. There are few people that could hurt her."

Drake paused, then his words sent a chill through Ryan.

"Madelyn could."

"Yes," Ryan agreed, "Madelyn could. But Madelyn is gone."

"The Queen killed her," the boy said softly.

Drake's words pained her. She had no idea how much he remembered from his personal experience and how much he absorbed from her, but regardless, he knew too much for one so young.

"Yes, the Queen killed her."

"She's going to take you away, isn't she?"

Ryan's head ached from the tears that wouldn't come. Although she could no longer cry, she could still feel the pain in her throat that accompanied unexpressed emotion.

"That's a long time, away, Drake. And we'll figure it out when it comes."

He settled back into her arms, as dissatisfied with her answer as she was.

Susan prepared the needle for the third try. She wanted to get an updated blood sample to see if anything had changed in Ryan's system, but as usual she was having great difficulty. She had scoured online resources searching for appropriate medical equipment and had finally begun designing her own. She had worked with a manufacturer to create a needle made of tungsten that tapered down to a point hardly larger than a few atoms that was attached to a syringe. Testing showed that it worked quite well on her own skin, and it worked well on Edward as well.

But of course it didn't work on Ryan.

"Maybe there is a force field about my body," Ryan muttered as the needle bent at a ninety degree angle.

"That would not surprise me," Susan said, trying to remain patient.

Ryan was through with patience. "This is foolish," she said. She lifted her wrist, slashed it with her own teeth, and thrust the bleeding arm toward Susan. "If you want blood, here."

Susan froze, staring at the rivulets of blood now running down the inside of Ryan's arm. She very carefully, very methodically took a pipette and touched it to the wound, drawing a small amount of the viscous liquid up into the glass tube. She just as carefully placed the sample in the tray on the table.

"I'm sorry," Ryan said, "that was rude of me."

Susan did not turn to look at her or the blood on her arm. She picked up some sterile wipes and handed them to Ryan, still averting her eyes.

"I know I'm not powerful enough for you to want to Share with me," Susan said quietly, "but you don't have to make it so hard."

Ryan snatched the wrist instead of the wipes and flipped Susan onto her back on the table. In an instant she was upon her, pinning her effortlessly with the full length of her body. She stared down, face-to-face with Susan, an indecipherable expression on her face. Susan quickly checked Ryan's eye color, but it was normal although her behavior most definitely was not.

Ryan examined the woman beneath her at length. She could have held her indefinitely with weight alone but she kept Susan completely immobile with a fraction of her enormous strength.

"You don't know anything," Ryan said at last. She pushed herself upward, then away from the table, then disappeared through the doorway.

Susan remained lying on the table, staring up at the ceiling for quite some time.

"Have you heard word from my father?" Ryan asked Edward.

Edward gave his master a surreptitious glance. She seemed quite out of sorts at the moment, even more so than what was becoming the norm for her.

"He called a little over an hour ago. He's learned nothing about Marilyn's disappearance and can't sense her anywhere. Kusunoki is going to join him shortly."

Ryan paced about the room. "And Abigail?"

"She remains in her summer home for the time being, but has sent forth a small army to assist in any way needed. She indicated she has sensed nothing but she can't mentally locate Marilyn either."

This boded ill, Ryan thought. If neither Victor nor Abigail could sense Marilyn, something was wrong. "And Aeron?" Ryan demanded, taking a full roll call.

"He remains with Drake and Jason as you requested."

Ryan stopped, suddenly realizing why she was taking the roll call as the worry flitting about the peripheries took form.

"And Ala?" she asked, looking Edward straight in the eye.

Edward cleared his throat. "She has not responded to our calls."

"What do you mean she has not responded?" Ryan said, "I know Ala isolates herself in the jungle, but she has always responded when we called."

"Well, we haven't eliminated the possibility of technical difficulties," Edward said delicately, "so we sent an envoy, one of our most trusted staff, to assess the situation in person."

"And?" Ryan said, her suspicions and concern growing.

"We have received no updates."

"You lost contact with him," Ryan interpreted.

"Yes, a little over twenty-four hours ago."

Ryan's anger was growing. "And when exactly were you going to tell me this?"

"Your father felt you might do something rash if you thought that Ala was missing," Edward said.

Ryan was fuming, her anger at a boiling point. "I'm going to Africa."

"Yes," Edward said under his breath, "something like that." He knew it was hopeless to dissuade her, but it was his duty to at least try.

"Are you sure that's wise at the moment?" he asked diplomatically.

"Of course it's not wise," Ryan snapped back, "it's probably horribly stupid, but it will fit in perfectly with all of my other actions lately."

She shook her head, clearing it. "Have my plane on the runway in the hour."

"It's," he paused, "it's already ready to go."

Ryan turned to the servant who knew her so well. "Thank you, Edward," she said gratefully, calming herself. She had one last order.

"Please take care of Dr. Ryerson in my absence."

# CHAPTER 16

RYAN EXPERTLY FLICKED THE SWITCHES on the console. She mentally ran through her checklist, got a signal from the linesman, then began her taxi on the runway. Within a minute, the jet lifted smoothly into the air.

"Are you sure this is wise?"

Ryan turned to the creature, not really surprised at his presence in the cockpit.

"No," she said, repeating her earlier conversation. "I'm sure it's as stupid as everything else I've done lately."

Petrus glanced out the window uneasily as the features of the ground disappeared into a postage stamp mosaic.

Ryan checked a few more gauges and then sent the plane into a dramatic bank before righting it onto its lengthy trajectory.

"So what are you going to do if you get all red-eyed on this flight?" Petrus asked.

"I'm not sure," Ryan replied, "From what I've heard, I doubt I can fly the plane in that condition. But," she replied, flicking another switch, "I know that I can survive a free fall impact from 15,000 feet, so hopefully we won't be any higher than that at the time."

She turned to him. "So if you really are my mental creation, you should be fine. If not..."

Petrus did not respond.

After two in-flight refuelings, the jet landed on the strip in Quesso. Ryan had chosen this particular airport primarily because of the corruption index of the locals; almost everything was available for a price. Although under normal circumstances the plane might have disappeared due to graft, simple contact with the stunning yet terrifying pilot rendered that idea implausible. No amount of money would be worth the wrath of this one.

The weather was characteristically humid and Ryan entered the jungle almost with a sense of relief. There were certain places such as Kusunoki's shrine where she felt immediate peace. Ala's homeland, even more than her own, was one of them.

Even so, Ryan could not shake the sensation that something was very wrong. She had a brief conversation with Victor prior to her departure, who, of course, was opposed to her journey. But he, too, sensed that events were spinning out of control. And she could tell from her abbreviated conversation with Kusunoki that he was greatly disturbed by Ala's lack of contact. They continued to search for Marilyn with no success.

Ryan moved through the jungle quickly, far more quickly than she could have by vehicle. When the undergrowth became too thick, she took to the tree-tops, flinging herself from tree to tree with abandon. The physical exertion seemed to provide some sort of release and she continued for hours on end until she neared Ala's home. When she got close, she paused in the top of a great umbrella tree to assess what was ahead of her. She could feel Ala's extended family and did not like what she felt. And she did not feel Ala at all.

There seemed to be a great deal of fear and uncertainty among the people ahead. And there was pronounced indecision and argument as to a course of action. Ryan paused without really knowing why. A normal response would be to arrive in the village, contact Kokumuo,

177

and investigate Ala's disappearance. But every instinct Ryan possessed told her this was a bad idea.

So she sat in the tree top as hours went by, extending her senses throughout the jungle to assess the unknown. She felt nothing and was disappointed. She began to fear she would transition into one of her phases, either forgetting who and what she was in the top of the tree, or grow weak and cling to the trunk, possibly falling hundreds of feet to the ground below. Or worse, she could transition into the savage who would then probably start eating everything it could find in the jungle.

Instead, she just sat as patiently as she could in the top of the tree.

Kokumuo moved stealthily through the foliage. He could sense something but it was ephemeral, something he could not grasp or identify. He had experienced the same sensation when his queen had disappeared. Something not quite right.

He stopped, his nostrils flaring and the muscles rippling across his chest beneath his ebony skin. He froze, extending his senses in all directions, desperately trying to diagnose the disturbance. He steeled himself, knowing that except Ala, there was no one more powerful than him on this continent.

Which is why he was quite surprised when he was snatched and hauled upward over thirty feet before he even realized what was happening. He was gripped tightly with a hand over his mouth. He stared into the eyes of Ryan Alexander as she balanced the two of them effortlessly on a slender branch.

"Shh," she said quietly, removing her hand from his mouth and releasing him.

"You came," he whispered in disbelief and gratitude.

"Of course I did," Ryan said, "I would do anything for Ala. Although," she confessed, "I'm not at my best right now."

Kokumuo nodded. "Yes, Kusunoki called. He said that if your eyes turn maroon..."

They looked at one another and finished the sentence together. "Run."

Ryan nodded. "Yes, that's good advice. I would run from myself if I could. Or so I've heard. Anyway, tell me what's happened."

Kokumuo shifted his position in the tree, resting on his haunches. "Ala went for a walk in the jungle as she always does, to commune with the spirits of nature and her ancestors."

He paused, thinking back to the incident. "Then she was just gone. There was no warning, no signs, no indication that she was even in trouble. Just one moment she was there, and the next minute she was gone."

"Did you trace back to her last location?"

Kokumuo's expression told her what she did not want to hear. "Yes, and there were signs of a struggle. Although we sensed nothing, it doesn't seem that she went quietly."

"That doesn't surprise me," Ryan said, thinking of the warrior queen. "But I have no idea what could take her, or, in fact, Marilyn as well."

Ryan again extended her senses and was again frustrated that she felt nothing. But somehow she knew instinctively what their path should be.

"You need to take all of your kin into the mountain," Ryan said, "and I'll stay here until I figure out what's going on."

Kokumuo started to object but she placed her hand on his chest, silencing him.

"You would be a good ally, but in Ala's absence, you need to protect your tribe. And if they're still vulnerable, then I'll be vulnerable because I'll have to act to protect them."

Kokumuo nodded his understanding. As much as he wished to stay by her side and fight whatever unknown adversary awaited them, he understood her logic.

Ryan stared out into the jungle. "If all that I love is protected," she said, "then I can act without restraint."

She turned back to him. "Now go, and I'll find your queen."

Ryan crouched on the lowest branch of the tree. She had been in exactly this position for almost thirty-six hours, an estimate of time based purely on the changing light filtering through the trees.

"You look like a gargoyle."

Ryan turned her gaze to the creature on the branch next to her. "You're one to talk."

"And what does that mean?" Petrus demanded with indignation.

"I don't know," Ryan said, glancing at his posture which perfectly mimicked hers, "you tell me."

"Oh," Petrus said. He plopped on to the branch, his legs dangling from the limb, his relaxed posture now in stark contrast to her alertness. "So how long are you going to stand here?"

"As long as it takes," Ryan responded, turning back to her assessment of the jungle. Her senses strained to pick up anything.

"Good thing you're immortal," Petrus said, picking a leaf from a branch, "we could be here for the next hundred years."

"No," Ryan said, "I'm quite sure I don't have that long."

"Ah," Petrus said, "that's right. Grandma's got you on a short leash."

Ryan was primed for a retort but it died on her lips. She turned to the west, extending her senses to their maximum. She focused, stunned at what she was feeling. This was not possible. Petrus jerked his head to the west as well and the movement caught Ryan's eye. A look of fear passed over his features and he glanced at his watch. Ryan's eyes narrowed at the peculiar movements.

"You sense that as well."

"I don't know what you're talking about," Petrus said, his fear evident. He glanced at his watch again.

Ryan turned her attention back to the west. She was not confident in her abilities right now, but she recognized that sensory signature. It was something very dangerous that should not be here.

Petrus seemed to be engaged in some sort of internal countdown, now staring at his watch non-stop.

"What are you doing?" Ryan asked in exasperation. She turned to the jungle around her. "And why is it so damned hot all of a sudden?"

Ryan bent over in pain, gripping the tree branch with a powerful grasp. Her torso twisted, almost as if she were attempting to writhe out of her skin. The seizure lasted perhaps thirty seconds before her locked muscles loosened into lithe, sinewy movement. She leaned her head back, cracking her neck loudly, then turned back to Petrus. She crouched on the limb like a beast. Her eyes were a dark maroon, the color of deeply oxygenated blood.

"Wow," Petrus said.

The creature examined him, the maroon eyes assessing, weighing, then determining that attack was not an option.

"You're smarter than you look in that form," Petrus commented. The creature smiled and turned away from him, looking off to the west.

"Do you know who I am?" Petrus asked curiously, and the creature turned back to him. After a long moment, she spoke.

"You are Petrusssss," she said, drawing out the last consonant in a snake-like hiss, as if conversation were unwieldy for her.

"Well, not 'Petrusssss'," he said mockingly, "just Petrus."

"Okay, pig-man," she said simply.

Petrus was indignant once more. "Oh, I see you're an asshole in this form as well."

The girl smiled and Petrus realized she was far more intelligent than she was letting on. She turned back to the west.

"Do you know what that is?" Petrus asked, nodding in the direction she was so intently staring.

"Yes," she said simply.

"Okay," Petrus said, still not certain of her IQ at this point. "Why don't you humor me?"

The girl turned back to him and he realized she was more than intelligent. "You know what that is," she said with dark amusement.

"Well, let's pretend I don't."

The maroon-eyed Ryan stared out into the jungle. "That's a blue man."

Petrus grew cold. She knew exactly what was out there. She turned her unblinking gaze back to him, still finding humor in the situation. "You're afraid of him, aren't you?"

It was a comment without accusation, but it engendered a defensive response. "Of course I'm afraid of him," Petrus said, "only an idiot would not be afraid of that."

"Hmm," was all the creature said, falling back into silence.

The silence wore on Petrus and he finally had to break it. "You're not afraid of him, are you?"

"No," the creature said, "I killed a lot of blue men. Hard to kill. But not impossible."

"You killed blue men?" Petrus said in disbelief.

"Yes," the creature replied. "I had a good sword," she admitted, then after a short silence. "Going to have to kill this one with my hands."

"Wait," Petrus said, "you're going to go after this one?"

"Of course," the creature said in amusement, "what else would I do?"

Petrus did not like this conversation. "Well, we could run, we could hide, we could do all sorts of things that are non-suicidal."

"Hmm," the creature said again, "that's no fun."

"You are more and more like your grandmother every day," Petrus said.

The creature merely smiled and with a great leap was off across the canopy of the jungle.

"Jesus Christ," Petrus muttered to himself.


Ryan, or whatever was left of Ryan in her current form, leaped from limb to limb with great savage joy. Even in her current manifestation, however, she was lucid enough to control her aura, prompted more by predatory instinct than strategy. She quickly closed on the sensory residue left by the "blue man," following tracks that were as visible to her as if they been neon signs.

She came upon a clearing, sensing that her prey was near, and she stopped, stilling herself and everything around her into absolute motionlessness. The man entered the clearing from the west and the creature, as fearless as it was, remained still.

He was tall and muscular, his features cruel and similar to the others like him. He was bipedal and could have passed for human if his skin had not had a bluish cast to it. Although the creature could remember little, she remembered this man, or rather those like him, possibly because she had only the most primitive feeling for them: hatred.

She lifted her head, sniffing the wind. This one was a scout and he was alone.

The man stopped in the center of the clearing, examining the jungle around him. The ignorant savages that populated this area were no threat to him. His party had acquired their quarry with little effort. Still he felt a sense of unease.

The girl crouched in the tree, but it was not indecision that stayed her hand. A multitude of images associated with the blue men rushed into the vortex of her mind, a series of geometric patterns and hieroglyphic lettering, a prison of solid rock, a woman who injected her with poison that ate through her system like acid. She could place none of the images or memories, had no context for the events or locations, and the fire in her body began burning through the mental montage, turning it into nothing more than white light.

The white light was pleasant, because then all she could remember was anger.

The man's unease grew marked, a feeling he was greatly unfamiliar with when facing such underwhelming opponents. He slowly turned in a circle, perusing the jungle around him, and when he had turned three quarters, he stopped abruptly, face-to-face with a girl.

He was stunned. It did not seem possible, but this was the primary target standing right in front of him. A cruel smile twisted his face. Could he be more fortunate? What stroke of luck had dropped this prize into his arms? Although only a low-level soldier, he could already see his own rise in station, the wealth and prestige that would follow from the capture of such a prisoner.

He examined her. Apparently reports of the danger she posed were exaggerated. She was not particularly large or powerful and seemed quite content to stand there in front of him, a slight smile on her lips and a somewhat maniacal look in her eye. He did note the strange color of her iris, something that had not been in his briefings. He would probably receive recognition for this discovery as well.

He nonchalantly removed a metal rope from his belt. It was a grayish-blue color, flexible, and incredibly strong with a tensile strength that vastly exceeded even Nanocarbon fibers. Under the right circumstances, it could act as a super-conductor, making it ideal for torture as well as restraint. He fingered the rope, analyzing his approach. He could probably pin her with his superior strength, then tie both her hands and feet. That seemed a good approach, especially since she was still merely standing in front of him with no apparent inclination to move.

He stepped toward her but that was far as he would get. She moved so fast she seemed to disappear, then yanked the rope from his hand with such force it amputated two of his fingers. He started to scream but could get nothing out as the rope was wrapped about his neck, cutting off the vocalization. With a vicious snap, the girl tightened the metal rope in a garrote maneuver so brutal it decapitated the man instantly. Blood spurted from the neck of the collapsing torso, spraying her arms and burning like acid. His head rolled off into the underbrush, a look of stunned surprise frozen on the bluish features.

The creature muffled a groan of pain. Even in her state of hyper-arousal, the pain of contact with the blood was extreme. She collapsed on the ground, trying to rub the liquid from her arms with the dirt and leaves on the jungle floor. The power it had taken to move so quickly had drained her completely. She felt darkness closing in on her, and with one last vicious kick at the torso to her left, she drifted into unconsciousness.

Ryan opened her eyes, staring up at the light filtering through the

184

tree-tops. She shifted slightly and then groaned. Her arms hurt like hell and she had no idea where she was. She looked down, trying to figure out what was causing her pain, and was shocked at the burns on her skin. Granted they were already healing, but the damage was extreme.

She sat up, gently rubbing the arms. Something caught her eye and in the fraction of a second that it took her to recognize what it was she had scuttled crab-like on all fours halfway across the clearing.

"Oh," Petrus said, rolling his eyes, "now you're afraid of it."

Ryan stared at the torso in disbelief. It lacked a head, but the muscular form, the blue-tinged skin, the strange clothing that had no origin on this planet, all were terrifyingly familiar. She glanced about, looking for the head, and spotted it beneath a tree, facing her with a startled expression.

"He shouldn't be here," Ryan said, shaking her head vehemently, "he should not be here."

"Well," Petrus said, eying the corpse, "he's not really 'here' any longer."

Ryan's ground her teeth, then she repeated her mantra. "There's no way he should be here, she put this planet off-limits."

Finally, she calmed herself enough to crawl back to the headless torso. "What happened to him?"

"Oh," Petrus said casually, "some nut job, about your height, your weight, maroon eyes, killed him with that rubber band over there."

"What?" Ryan said in disbelief. She had no memory of that at all. She had managed to kill some of Madelyn's men, in fact, had garroted one in a very similar fashion. But surprise had been the key in that attack.

"Did I sneak up on him?" Ryan asked.

"No," Petrus said thoughtfully, "you pretty much planted yourself in front of him and dared him to move."

"Oh Christ," Ryan muttered. She examined the torso once more, her thoughts racing furiously. Thank god she had come across the creature in her savage form. If she had encountered him in her amnesiac form, or worse, in a period of weakness, there was no doubt the out-

185

come would have been very different. As much as she wanted to continue searching for Ala, she was now afraid she knew what had happened to her.

"I have to get back to Victor and my son. I have to warn them."

# CHAPTER 17

RYAN WAS ONCE AGAIN TEN STORIES underground, but now the rock walls felt less like a prison and more like a comfortable fortress. Madelyn had found her before in the council chambers, but Ryan had been on the upper levels at that time. Still, she wouldn't stay here long.

"Are you sure it was one of Madelyn's men?" Victor asked.

"No," Ryan said, then wished to clarify. "It's definitely one of that species but I have no idea if he was associated with her." She searched her memory for a better explanation of what she intuitively understood. She also sought to interpret the nuances of a language that was utterly foreign to them both.

"This one," she said, wracking her memory, "and the ones that came with Madelyn are like low-level ground troops."

"And the ones that came the second time?" Victor asked.

Ryan was certain Victor knew of the second soldiers from Abigail, because Abigail had taken those Memories when she had taken her blood. Victor was speaking of the ones that had come with Ravlen.

"They were different, elite troops, more like a royal guard. But the one that I saw in the jungle belongs to a caste of infantry." Ryan again struggled to interpret the title. "There is no direct translation in our language, but the name is pejorative and carries a connotation of extreme expendability. The closest thing I can come up with is 'cannon fodder.'"

"Did you sense more than one?"

"No," Ryan said, "but that doesn't mean there aren't more. And I don't understand why they're here at all." She struggled to explain. "Having met the Empress, even so briefly, I can't imagine that anyone would disobey her. Her vengeance would be absolute, not only meting out death to those directly opposing her, but to anyone who was even tangentially related to those who would oppose her. She would not only kill you, but remove every trace of your existence from memory."

"That type of brutality can generate powerful hatred," Victor mused. "What better way to strike at her than to destroy what is most dear to her?"

"Then they are on a suicide mission," Ryan replied, "and you're a target, I'm a target, and Drake is a target."

Victor was quite certain that Ryan was the real target, but that did not mean they would not strike at him or his grandson to get to her.

"So the disappearance of Marilyn and Ala is not a coincidence."

"No," Ryan replied, "and now I fear for their safety and their lives."

A muffled noise attracted Ryan's attention. Both Edward and Susan had sat quietly throughout this conversation, but this pronouncement distressed Susan greatly. Edward placed his hand on her shoulder to comfort her. Ryan stiffened her resolve and turned back to her father.

"You and I must part ways."

It grieved him, but he knew she was right. "Do you wish to go east or west?"

Edward found this conversation curious as they both had clear destinations in mind, yet he could think of nowhere they might go.

"I will go east," Ryan said, "and you will go west with Drake."

Victor eyed her. The fact that she wanted him to take Drake told him that she, too, realized she was the real target. He nodded. "Do you wish to take Aeron?"

Ryan thought about it. Aeron's presence would comfort her, a heretical idea that even a few years ago would have been met with derision.

But now his company had appeal.

"No," she said at last, "I want him with Drake as well."

"So you're allowed to protect your child but I'm not allowed to protect mine?" Victor said quietly.

"Your child is very dangerous right now," Ryan said, "and my child needs more protection than yours."

This comment broke the flow of the conversation, and Edward took that opportunity to ask his question.

"Where are you planning to go?"

"Sometimes our paranoia is beneficial," Ryan said, waving her hand about the room. "There are two more facilities exactly like this one, their locations known only to the Grand Council and leader of the hierarchy. They have been kept and maintained as 'safe-houses' in the unlikely event they would ever be needed." She turned back to Victor.

"I'm guessing they are needed now."

"I will go with you, my lord," Edward said firmly.

"I will, too," Susan said.

Edward's pronouncement did not surprise Ryan, but Susan's did.

"No," Ryan said, "you and Jason will go with Victor. You'll be safer with him."

"If I had wanted safe, Ryan Alexander, I would have left you in the morgue all those years ago."

The vehement response startled all three, most of all Ryan. She was certain with her recent crass behavior that Susan would welcome to part ways with her.

Susan did not wait for a response but addressed Victor. "If you would be so kind as to watch my son, I think both Jason and Drake will be better off if they're together."

"Of course," Victor replied.

"And you," Susan said, turning back to Ryan, "are not even close to being well. And there's no way I would abandon a patient."

Ryan had no words to express her gratitude, and Susan's expression told her she did not need any.

"Abigail and Kusunoki have been fully apprised?" she asked Victor.

"Yes, and they will chart their own courses."

"Good," Ryan said, "then we should leave immediately.

# CHAPTER 18

MARILYN STARED AT THE ROCK WALL in front of her. This was all quite hideously boring. After the initial excitement of the furious battle, the subsequent kidnapping and transport, then the gauntlet of leering soldiers she passed on the long march to her prison cell, this was quite a let-down. She sighed and shifted on her slab of rock, aware she was being watched.

This fortress was very similar to the one they had stormed when rescuing Ryan, and these creatures were undoubtedly the same. The soldiers all had the same cruel features, the hard muscularity, the bluish skin that looked as if they were all slightly under-oxygenated. Marilyn toyed with that idea for a moment. Perhaps that was the problem. After all, they were from another solar system; perhaps they weren't getting enough oxygen to the brain.

The rock wall slid open, its mechanism unseen but so precise the massive door moved silently. A silver-haired man walked in and Marilyn sat up with interest. This one was distinctly different from the soldiers. Older, handsome, his features were less brutish and his expression less brutal, possessing a far more refined cruelty than the foot soldiers outside. He examined her with similar interest, and both looked at the other as if they had discovered some new variation of bug that intrigued them. Her bold scrutiny amused him and he thought perhaps when this was over he would take her as his slave.

"Oh really," Marilyn said skeptically.

The man was startled. Although this species was generally deemed insignificant, this particular form of mutation was known to possess telepathy, sometimes extraordinary in its extent. Having been responsible for much of the early, failed experimentation on this planet, he had been greatly surprised at the reported gifts they had begun to manifest. There had been various rumors and explanations for such developments, the most outrageous being that some member of the royal family, possibly even a distant relative of the Empress herself, had seeded this planet.

Marilyn examined the man. He felt very similar to her Kind, and extraordinarily powerful, but Ryan was right. Neither he nor anyone else here had the ability to read her thoughts. Odd how they lacked something she and the Others took for granted.

A commotion at the door attracted both their attention as Ala was flung through the opening, still fighting despite the restraints that hung from her. Her two captors were obviously frustrated over the fact that such a trivial prisoner had given them so much difficulty. Ala collapsed onto the shelf next to Marilyn, shrugging the remaining ropes from her body.

"Well, that looked like fun," Marilyn commented.

"Trust me," Ala said, glowering at the silver-haired man, "it was."

The man examined this wonderful specimen as well. He was still getting used to the fact that females were so prevalent on this planet. He motioned for one of the captors to remove the fallen restraints. No sense in providing them an opportunistic weapon. Ala was disappointed. She was already fantasizing about strangling someone with that silver rope.

The man exited and the massive door whispered closed behind him. Ala wasted no time but assessed the solid rock room. She, too, knew that they were being watched.

"This looks like the other fortress, the one where Madelyn kept Ryan," Ala said.

"Yes," Marilyn agreed, "and these are definitely the same type of creatures. Odd that I haven't seen any females."

"I don't remember any with Madelyn, either," Ala said.

"Under most circumstances," Marilyn said, "I would find that a most wonderful ratio. At the moment, I find it less than appealing."

Can they sense our thoughts?

Ala asked the question without speaking and without turning toward her. Marilyn responded in kind.

I don't believe so.

Ala glanced at her fingernails. We should use the gift sparingly, just in case.

Agreed, Marilyn responded.

The door opened, and almost in contradiction to their earlier conversation, a woman strolled in. She was tall with blonde hair that flowed down her back, elaborately intertwined with a decorative material similar to the rope, only finer. She wore armor-like clothing that although completely alien, gave the impression of military purpose, wealth and status. She had piercing eyes that were a dark blue, almost purple and she assessed her two captors with a penetrating gaze. She was quite physically stunning, but possessed the same unnatural and reptilian coldness of Madelyn, the same slight feral movements that betrayed her as something very different and non-human. And both Marilyn and Ala had the same impression at the same time.

This woman was far more powerful than Madelyn. And more deadly.

Try to control yourself, Ala warned without looking over. And Marilyn, who would flirt with anything and everything, responded the same way.

Not this one.

"You are correct that I cannot sense the content of your thoughts," the woman said smoothly in surprisingly unaccented English, "but I can sense when you are communicating in that manner." Her tone grew very cold. "And you will not do so."

The silver-haired man re-entered the room.

"The phalanx is in position," he said, "they are preparing for an assault on the compound."

193

"Very well," the woman said, "you may proceed."

The man drew a rectangular shape in the air. To Ala's and Marilyn's surprise, a vivid three dimensional picture appeared out of nothingness. It was contained entirely within the imaginary shape the man had drawn, and appeared to be some sort of audio/visual communication device.

The holographic picture was of a deserted area, flat, dusty terrain with a backdrop of jagged mountain peaks some distance away. It could have been any number of places on the continent, but Ala and Marilyn recognized it immediately: it was the ground above the chambers of the Grand Council. One of the blue-tinged, brutal-faced soldiers appeared on the screen.

"We have located the entrance and have sent in the first wave. They have met no opposition thus far, and we believe the target is sequestered in the very lowest levels."

"Good," the silver-haired man said, "make certain you go with sufficient numbers. Our reports indicate this particular individual is deceptively strong." He tried to make his tone serious, but his manner was gleeful.

The soldier could not disguise his sneer. "We'll take her down. Especially if we can get to the child first."

The picture shifted, and the transmission was now coming from the first wave within the chambers. Soldiers, bristling with weapons, were slinking through the hallways and into the great room the council had so recently occupied. Marilyn sighed. She had enjoyed many an hour in the council chambers. The lead group was getting close to the level of the private residences, slowly but surely descending.

The woman glanced at her two captors, noting that neither one appeared particularly disturbed by what they were seeing. She cleared her throat, a tinge of disgust in her tone.

"I would withdraw them if I were you."

The silver-haired man turned to her. "What? But we are closing in on her position. All our reports indicate she is cornered here."

The holographic picture flickered, went dark, then resumed, now above ground once more. The man turned back to his commander in the holograph.

"What is happening?" he demanded.

The commander appeared unperturbed. "We seem to have lost contact on the very lowest level. There may be some interference from certain elements in the rock. We'll re-establish communication in a—"

The commander stopped, an uncertain look passing over his features as he looked down at the ground. "There seems to be some sort of seismic activity here…"

Marilyn was quite impressed with the technology because even though the ground began violently shaking, the picture was crystal clear. Just behind the commander, a huge sink-hole appeared exactly above the previous location of the Grand Council Chambers. The sink-hole grew and grew as ten stories collapsed downward on themselves. The huge crater grew at such an accelerated rate it sucked in everything within sight, including the commander who was pulled into the hole then buried alive by an avalanche of rubble. For a moment, the holograph was nothing more than a dust storm, the particles swirling quite beautifully in the air in the imaginary rectangle.

The silver-haired man stared at the holograph as the dust settled, stunned. Nothing remained other than the gigantic crater, which made it look as if the Grand Council Chambers had been struck by a meteorite.

The blonde woman also stared at the holograph, but her demeanor was in stark contrast to the man's. She seemed completely unsurprised at the failure of the troops, and glanced to her prisoners.

Ala wanted to burst out laughing but did her best to maintain a neutral expression and avoid eye contact. Marilyn examined the crater, then turned to her captor.

"She likes to blow things up," she said simply.

"I see that," the woman replied, then turned on her heel, leaving the silver-haired man staring at the gigantic virtual hole.

Ryan watched the destruction from a distance, highly entertained by the disaster. It seemed the one weapon she could continually wield against these idiots was their own overconfidence, their own arrogance. They repeatedly underestimated her Kind, and she repeatedly made them pay for it.

She sobered abruptly, wary of falling into the same trap. She also knew that these creatures were willing to sacrifice legions simply to test an opponent's strategy, get a feel for how they would react, then move in brutally for a killing blow. They would throw wave after wave of low-level soldiers into a battle simply to find an exploitable weakness. She could not afford to underestimate them, or make any mistakes.

She motioned for Susan and Edward to join her. They had a long journey ahead, and she was never certain how long her current "normal" phase would last.


The three sat on the wooded hillside overlooking the small airport. It was dozens of miles from the gigantic hole Ryan had left in the ground, and they had covered the distance quickly on foot. She surveyed the tarmac and adjacent buildings. Although she could see nothing unusual, she was hesitant to move out into the open.

"Something's wrong," she muttered to herself. "Edward, do you sense anything?"

"No, my lord. But I trust your senses much more than mine."

"Susan?"

Susan was surprised that Ryan would ask her, given her youth and relative lack of abilities. "No," she replied, "I don't see anything, either."

"Maybe I'm just being overcautious…" Ryan said, then let her sentence die. A shadowy figure peered around one of the buildings, seemed to shimmer, then disappear. A chill went down her spine, the sensation spreading then settling like a chunk of ice in her stomach. Instinctively she pressed backward into the shadows of the trees surrounding them.

"That's something new," Ryan said, and the edge in her voice put both Edward and Susan on alert. "We can't go down there."

Edward's tone dropped to a whisper, mirroring Ryan's instinctive reaction. "If they found the council chambers, as well as this airport, it's likely they've mapped out all your properties. And probably your potential escape routes as well."

Her thoughts raced furiously. With the technology these creatures had at their disposal, there was a multitude of ways they could be tracking them.

"Destroy your phones," Ryan ordered.

Edward removed his cellular phone from his pocket and crushed it in his hand. Susan was looking about on the ground for a rock to smash her device. After observing Edward's actions, she hesitantly fingered the casing, then experimentally put pressure on the shell. The phone exploded into pieces, a result that brought a look of guilty pleasure to her face.

Ryan was expending a great deal of energy shielding their presence and was having difficulty concentrating. Edward was running possibilities through his head and did not like the conclusions he was reaching.

"I've failed you, my lord," he said at last.

"Well, I doubt that," Ryan said sardonically, "but what's brought about this dire pronouncement?"

"We…" Edward paused delicately, "we don't have any money."

Ryan gave him a sharp glance, finding this blackly funny. "Did you go on a shopping spree or something?"

"Let me rephrase that," Edward said, "we don't have any money that we can get to."

"They'll be tracing the accounts," Ryan said, understanding. She looked down toward the tarmac where the ephemeral creature had disappeared. "Even the hidden ones. That type of expertise is child's play to them."

"I have some money," Susan said quietly, but neither Edward nor Ryan appeared to hear her.

"I have cash stored at numerous locations," Edward continued,

197

"but I neglected to retrieve any from the council chambers, and I don't believe there is another reserve near here."

"And how much did I blow up back there?" Ryan asked absently.

"I believe it was several hundred million dollars."

"Hmm," Ryan said just as absently.

"I have some money," Susan said, slightly more forcefully but with the same lack of result.

"Under normal circumstances, I would suggest we just hide in the wilderness," Ryan said. "That tactic is almost fool-proof and we need very little."

Edward finished the thought. "But with your phase changes, that could be very dangerous."

"Yes," Ryan agreed, "you two would have a hard time corralling me if I shifted into a savage phase. And the amnesiac and weak phases leave me incredibly vulnerable. I think our original destination is still our safest bet." Ryan was still having difficulty concentrating. "We could steal a car."

"I'm afraid any type of ground transportation would be too slow. Again, there is the risk of an unexpected phase shift."

"Then we could steal a plane," Ryan said.

Edward continued to play devil's advocate. "Just yesterday there was a news bulletin regarding 'potential terrorist activity' involving the theft of aircraft." His brow furrowed. "Which I no longer believe to be a coincidence."

"We could steal a—,"

"I have some money!" Susan fairly shouted.

This exclamation caused Edward to start and Ryan to glance back down at the tarmac, certain that the shimmering creature would reappear. No such thing occurred, and both turned their attention to the red-headed woman.

"How much money?" Ryan asked.

"A couple hundred dollars," Susan said, embarrassed at her outburst, "it's not much, but it can get us away from here."

"And how is it going to do that?" Ryan asked.

"Well," Edward said, regarding Susan thoughtfully, "we could travel in a way that no one would ever expect."

"Flight 409 for Dallas departing out of gate 36 is ready for pre-boarding."

The announcement over the loudspeaker crackled at a stupendous volume, causing Ryan to wince at the noise.

"I was really hoping you were going to say hot air balloon, or something like that," she commented, trying not to sound as surly as she felt. The line they were standing in snaked through a series of cordoned aisles, barely moving. It was like being in a jam-packed maze.

"And can you explain to me again how this is a good idea?"

Edward tried to suppress his own misgivings. He was taking quite a gamble that commercial air travel was so out-of-the-question it would not be strictly monitored. He did not know how many of the creatures were present on the planet, but it did not seem they were so numerous they could be everywhere. Although he, Ryan, and Susan all had false identification cards, a practice utterly common for their Kind, he wondered if their pursuers possessed facial recognition technology that would identify them immediately as they passed the gauntlet of surveillance cameras.

"My hope is in speed," Edward responded. "The flight is four hours, and if we can get there without incident, we may remain undiscovered."

"Or," Ryan said, "I may phase shift at 40,000 feet and send the plane hurtling into the side of a mountain."

Edward was unfazed. "Then to prevent that, when your eyes turn maroon, I'll lock you in the bathroom with Dr. Ryerson and you can join the mile high club."

Susan was feeling slightly edgy and irritable herself. "I'm quite sure she's already a member."

Ryan looked from one to the other. "I don't have the slightest idea what the two of you are talking about." She settled into her own irritable silence.

They were approaching some sort of bottleneck in their maze. Susan leaned forward to whisper to Ryan and Edward.

"This is the security screening. You'll have to remove your shoes and any metallic objects from your pockets, then pass through that machine over there."

Edward looked at her in disbelief, and Ryan put voice to his expression.

"You've got to be kidding me."

Susan shook her head and Ryan continued. "I can't believe people travel this way."

As if to emphasize the ridiculousness of the process, the line stopped, giving Ryan the opportunity to read an adjacent sign. The travel alert declared that "snow globes" were forbidden for transport due to the danger they posed.

"Ah," Ryan murmured, "I have always felt that snow globes would bring about the fall of western civilization."

It was now their turn and Susan removed her shoes and a few items from her pockets, placing them in a tray on the x-ray belt. Edward followed suit, then Ryan dutifully did the same. Susan was motioned through the detector and passed without incident. Edward was next and also passed without incident.

"Wait."

A short, black lady approached, her uniform bearing the insignia of the security supervisor. "In here," she waved, motioning to the full body scanner.

Ryan glanced over at Susan, who nodded cautiously. It was likely this was a random assignment, brought about by Ryan's position in line rather than anything particular to her person. Still, Susan felt uneasy as Ryan obediently entered the machine and raised her arms above her head. Susan was not certain how detailed the scan would be and was a little concerned since Ryan's anatomy was so radically different from a human's.

Susan's concern grew as there was a long pause from the operator behind the machine. He slowly leaned around the drapery that concealed the image. He took a long look at Ryan, then turned back to the screen. The supervisor walked over to join him, also disappearing beneath the curtain. A brief moment later, they both leaned out around the curtain to again look at Ryan.

"Damn," the operator said, unable to help himself. The supervisor was trying to maintain some professionalism, but she, too, was having difficulty hiding her appreciation.

"Um, you can go, dear."

"Thank you," Ryan said politely, then gathered her things. Both watched as the perfect form loped gracefully down the ramp into the terminal.

"I can block their perception," Ryan said as she reached Susan and Edward, "but I can't block the machine's. And I must say," she said as she put her shoes back on, "that out of all of the indignities I've suffered in my life, which have included such memorable events as the near-rape by a member of an alien species, I don't think I've ever felt so violated."

They were able to board the plane without further spectacle. Ryan made certain she was nearly undetectable to everyone around her and had determined to try and meditate to pass the flight. She sat on the aisle, Susan to her left, and Edward at the window. All three were cramped, but Ryan especially so as her knees were pressed against the seat in front of her. The plane took off smoothly and quickly reached an altitude where the lights above them went off, indicating something had just occurred or was allowed to occur, although Ryan was not quite certain what either of those things might be.

A clatter to her right attracted her attention. A thin, pale young man was wrestling with a laptop computer that was suddenly jammed into his chest when the seat in front of him came hurtling backward. Ryan gazed at him with sympathy. He was already crushed on his right by the overweight woman spilling over the shared armrest into his seat. Now he was crushed from the front by the rude individual who fully reclined his seat back.

Ryan's attention was immediately drawn forward as the seat in front of her came hurtling rearward. It came to a stop inches from her face. A feeling of claustrophobia overtook her.

"Now this is just poor design," she muttered to herself. She leaned forward and tapped the shoulder of the person who was now practically sitting in her lap.

"Do you think you might move forward a bit?" she asked politely.

"Get bent," the man in front of her said, "it's my seat."

Edward started to get up out of his seat, the slight to his master enraging him, but Ryan waved him off. The pale young man next to her watched the situation unfold, wishing he had the courage to intervene. Susan was amazed at how calmly Ryan was responding to the rudeness, an estimation that quickly changed.

Ryan adjusted her position in her seat, resting her knees on the framing of the seat in front of her. Without effort and in an extremely casual maneuver, she shifted her weight and began pushing her knees forward. Not only did the seat back begin to move, but with a shriek and protest of metal, the entire framework began to move as it bent, shifting both the seat and occupant forward.

"What the—?"

The man in front of her turned around in his seat and froze. Ryan was no longer hiding from him. He stared into gray eyes flecked with violet, eyes that burned a hole right through him. All words died on his lips, then coagulated into a thick mass in his throat that nearly choked him. Wordlessly, he turned back around, pressed the button on his armrest, and brought his seat into its upright position. In his new location, he no longer had any room between him and the seat in front of him, but he no longer cared.

Ryan cast a dark glance at the man forward and to the right of her, the one who had crushed the pale young man. He had watched the exchange with wide eyes and now he, too, wordlessly brought his seat to its upright position and promptly returned his attention forward.

Ryan stretched in her new-found space, turning to the red-haired woman next to her.

"And what is this—?" she said, waving her hand about her, "What is this called again?"

"Economy class," Susan replied, suppressing a smile.

"Never again," Edward said sternly.

# CHAPTER 19

THE GAMBLE OF THE COMMERCIAL FLIGHT paid off. Although Edward had spent the entire time feeling trapped in the metal tube, certain they would be captured the minute they landed, the remainder of their trip had gone smoothly. Ryan had suffered no bouts of amnesia or loss of control, and once on the ground they had reached their destination quickly.

And now Edward analyzed the encrypted message before him. It would be their last contact before going underground, at which time they would enter the agreed period of non-communication. Both Ryan and Victor were wary of the technology of their opponents and agreed that silence would be a good temporary tactic, at least until they could figure out what to do.

"What does it say?" Ryan asked.

"Your father, Aeron, and the boys have reached their destination. They will not contact us again for two weeks."

A surge of relief filled Ryan. But it seemed there was something Edward was not saying.

"And what else?" she asked.

Edward re-read the message, just to make certain he was interpreting it correctly. He sighed.

"Abigail was contacted and apprised of events. However, attempts to contact Kusunoki were unsuccessful."

"They were unable to reach him?"

"No," Edward said.

The words were like a blow. "Let's get below ground," Ryan said, turning on her heel and stalking away.

"Tra'e'ela," the servant said, bowing.

The blonde woman eyed the servant. As was common, it was both a name and a title, one greatly respected and feared throughout their vast empire. And one seemingly at odds with the minimal requirements of this mission. Even odder was the fact that this was the second time she had been sent to this planet, a speck of dust that appeared to have little if any value. Granted, a few of these mutations exhibited interesting abilities, but the Empress was not known for her patience. Normally this place would have been razed long before the experiment achieved its few successes. With so many options and overwhelming force at her disposal, her Majesty generally just cut her losses and moved on.

"Yes?" she prompted.

"We followed the father and the son as you directed and have assumed positions outside their new sanctuary. They are sequestered in another underground bunker similar to the first. Per your instructions, the men you chose are providing surveillance but haven't made a move on the compound."

This was good news, but not entirely what she wished to hear.

"And the girl?"

Her servant cleared his throat uneasily. "As you anticipated, she fled just prior to the arrival of our troops. Although she was tailed by the Trackers for a short distance, they were unable to stay with her. "

"So she eluded them," Tra'e'ela said.

This was interesting. It was nearly impossible to escape from the Trackers because of their extraordinary sensory abilities. They could detect even minor temperature variations and the subtlest of scents.

They were generally able to adapt quickly to whatever biological defense mechanisms prey utilized. And if their personal abilities were inadequate to the task, they deployed a wide array of technology that could identify and capture just about anything.

"So you have no idea where she is now."

"No."

Tra'e'ela mused over this turn of events, again unsurprised.

"And her closest companions?"

"Another has been captured and is in transport. One is with the father and son. And we are moving in on the last."

"Very well," she said, "keep me informed."

Abigail sat in her drawing room, enjoying the cool breeze that lifted her filmy curtains, causing them to flutter ever-so-gently. She had dismissed most of her staff and the vast estate was quiet. The few servants that remained had been given explicit orders; now she was merely waiting. She lifted her head, tilted it to one side, then smiled ever so slightly.

Outside, the shock troops stealthily approached the mansion. They knew this mission was dangerous; this target was rumored to be very powerful. Their tension grew the closer they got and they moved furtively up the great stairway. Their stealth shields flickered, changing with the terrain as light bent around the surface. They paused, silently communicating via hand signals to surround the structure and all exits. There was a collective pause in preparation for the launch of the attack, then they began skulking across the huge front porch to the double doors.

And they were greatly surprised when one door opened and a very calm man greeted them.

"Can I help you?" the chief consort asked politely.

Normal procedure would have been to rush him, take him to the ground and deliver a killing strike before an alarm could be raised. But for whatever reason, they did no such thing. They stood upright from their crouched positions, suddenly feeling foolish. The stealth shields flickered, then apparently underwent some sort of technical glitch and went off entirely.

"Please come in," the consort said with ineffable courtesy.

The heavily armed band squeezed into the house, jostling one another uncertainly in the doorway. It could be a trap, but they seemed to have morphed from highly trained commandos into a rag-tag group of ill-trained novices.

Abigail looked up as they pressed into the drawing room. "Can I help you?" she said, replicating both her servant's words and his calm manner.

The soldiers were now completely at a loss. They had expected a fierce battle, anticipated numerous casualties, had even drawn up contingency plans were the mission to fail. What they had not expected was that their quarry would be casually waiting for them, nor that they would act so completely out of character in response. The commander stepped forward.

"You are to come with us," he said gruffly, for some reason still feeling foolish. He was beginning to hate these people.

"Very well," Abigail said sedately, "let me get my things."

And the men stood there while Abigail left the room. They seemed rooted to the spot, looking at one another uncertainly, knowing that at least one of them should have followed her but none seeming capable of the act. Abigail returned carrying a small bag.

"I'm ready to go," she said. She glanced to her consort. "Please care for things in my absence."

The servant nodded and the men escorted their prisoner from the room. As she swept gracefully down her staircase, she hardly appeared a prisoner as not a single soldier was willing to touch her, or even in fact get too close. She appeared almost a dignitary, her escort provided unwillingly and involuntarily by the bemused commandos.

Susan shined the penlight in Ryan's pupils, then replaced the instrument in her pocket.

"You seem to be doing well," she commented, "you've gone almost a week and half without a phase shift."

"That figures," Ryan said, "the one time I might welcome some forgetfulness to pass the hours."

"I still wish I could figure out the timing and pattern of the phases," Susan said.

"Do you think there is pattern?" Ryan asked. "It seems so random."

"I agree," Susan said, looking at the chart in which she had studiously recorded the time, length, and frequency of the shifts. "But it keeps gnawing at me that there's something I'm missing."

Movement caught Ryan's attention, something from the corner of her eye. She turned to find Petrus perched on a chair. She frowned at him, and Susan turned to see what she was looking at. It was clear she saw nothing, and turned back to Ryan with an assessing gaze.

"Have you been able to meditate at all?" Susan asked.

"No," Ryan said, "nor have I been sleeping. My entire life I've slept an obscene amount of time and now that I want to, I can't sleep at all."

"I would offer a sedative, but I have nothing that would affect you."

Petrus was making various faces at her over Susan's shoulders. His reappearance and misbehavior were unwelcome to Ryan.

"You're such an asshole," she muttered under her breath.

"Excuse me?" Susan said.

Ryan was embarrassed. "Not you," she said quickly, "I was just thinking about someone else."

This struck Susan as particularly strange. Ryan was not one to use profanity, let alone spout it out spontaneously. She turned back to the empty corner. Perhaps this was a sign of some additional mental defect. She would have liked to run another PET scan on Ryan, but they had not had time to move the medical equipment.

"Alright," Susan said slowly, "well, as usual I can't find anything wrong with you."

"You mean other than the fact that I clearly have Tourette's syndrome."

Susan patted her on the shoulder. "Maybe you should try to rest."

The door whispered closed behind Susan and Ryan leaned back sighing. She turned a baleful eye toward Petrus.

"And why the hell are you back?"

"Didn't you miss me?" he said gleefully, bouncing across the room like some gelatinous blob.

"No," Ryan said, "I didn't think we were making any progress in our therapy sessions."

Petrus settled down in front of her, his eyes glowing.

"And how do you feel right now?"

"How am I supposed to feel?" Ryan said sarcastically, "Marilyn, Ala, and Kusunoki have disappeared. My mortal enemies have re-appeared. I have no idea if my father and son are safe, and I'm sitting in a bunker talking to—," she stopped, shaking her head, "I have no idea what you are."

"Ugh," Petrus said, "you wound me."

"No, but I wish I could."

"So what do you think happened to your friends?" the creature asked slyly.

"I don't know," Ryan said, growing somber, "the best case scenario is that they have been captured."

"And the worst?"

"They're dead."

"And which do you think is correct?"

"I believe they've been captured, because I think I would sense if they had been killed."

"And just why do think they've been captured?"

Ryan was silent for a long moment. "Probably a strategy to get to me."

"And yet here you are, hiding in the basement."

The words sliced through her, cutting no less deeply even though she agreed with them. She rubbed her forehead with her fingers.

Tra'e'ela watched the prisoner through the thick wall. It appeared as rock within the cell but transparent on the other side. The prisoner sat calmly, doing something with a piece of fabric, a thin metal object, and some sort of thread. She sat doing this for hours in a mesmerizing, repetitive fashion, often causing her guards to fixate on her as if hypnotized.

This one intrigued Tra'e'ela but she was not certain why. She could not remember this prisoner's origins, although she was clearly as old as some of the first they had transformed. The captive did not seem significantly more powerful than the others they had captured. Perhaps it was the archetype of elder female that played a role, the matriarchal image so powerful in their culture that Tra'e'ela was projecting it on to this one.

This explanation did not completely satisfy her, and her disquiet continued. That disquiet actually increased when it seemed the prisoner paused in her needlework, slowly raised her gaze, and appeared to look right through the wall into Tra'e'ela's eyes, a slight smile on her lips. It was the briefest of contact and could have been pure coincidence, luck. The woman returned to her task, an expression of quiet contentment on her features.

Tra'e'ela stared at the woman long after she returned to her needlework.

# CHAPTER 20

JASON HELD DRAKE IN HIS LAP while the younger boy pressed against him, sleeping. He tried to tell himself that he was fine, but he missed his mother and he missed Ryan. He felt safe with Victor, and he knew that Drake's father would protect him as well, but something about Ryan's presence always comforted him, even as sick as she had been lately.

Drake shifted in his lap and flung an arm about his neck, smacking him in the cheek. Jason winced. Drake was incredibly strong, almost as strong as him even though he was so much younger. Jason felt very protective of the smaller boy. He had always wanted a brother but didn't think he was going to get one because he had no dad. But then Drake had come into his life and everything seemed complete. He had his mother, he had Ryan, and he had his little brother.

Jason sighed. But now it seemed all messed up again. Ryan was sick, Marilyn was gone, and Kusunoki was not around to give him the sword lessons he promised. Jason glanced around. The bunker had been cool enough for awhile, with all its hiding places and spaces to run about and play. But he and Drake grew bored as the days went by, trying to entertain themselves with chess, movies, and video games.

Drake stirred, then awoke. He sat up, stretching, a perturbed look on his face.

"What's wrong?" Jason asked.

"Someone's coming."

Jason grew very cold. Drake did not make pronouncements like this very often, but he was never wrong.

"We should hide."

Jason snatched Drake up and darted for the door. The two had discussed this exact scenario, although it was more fanciful than anything else at the time. But they had agreed there was a most excellent hiding place off the great room, a small space that was hardly even a closet, the entrance completely hidden if one didn't know it was there.

They scrambled down the hallway, now hearing signs of struggle off in the distance. It seemed very violent with crashing and explosions echoing down the rock passages. They reached the great room, sprinted across its width, then scrambled to find the hidden closet. Drake found the latch first, and the wall slid open, revealing the small space. They ducked inside.

The blue-eyed man was still struggling violently when he was dragged before Tra'e'ela. She normally would not lower herself to such mundane missions, but these were too high-value of targets for her to leave the results to chance or to her imbecilic cohorts.

She studied him as he was held captive in front of her. He was still a magnificent specimen, ice blue eyes, a haughty demeanor, his chiseled features set arrogantly in fierce resistance. She assessed him curiously, but there was no corresponding recognition in his eyes. That was just as well, no sense in complicating things

The second captive was dragged in, he, too, struggling fiercely. He actually appeared to get the upper hand on his captors, throwing one into the wall with such force a hairline crack appeared on the rock surface. He was quickly subdued by pure numbers, giving Tra'e'ela the opportunity to examine him as well.

He calmed himself, relinquishing his struggle, and turned to examine her in kind. He was extraordinarily handsome for these creatures, dark hair and dark eyes with just a nagging hint of familiarity to his features. Tra'e'ela determined that it was his mouth, perfect in shape and form, that reminded her of someone, she just could not place who. He was also very powerful, at least for this species, and although not particularly powerful for hers, there was something compelling about him. She had always wondered why he was the "ground zero" transformation on this planet and why so much effort had been placed on finding him suitable companionship, but perhaps now she understood. She could see his genetic potential, as even now he seemed able to stand against those who should be able to squash him. She knew of many females who would be willing to experiment with such genetic viability.

Victor could not read her thoughts, but absorbed the general gist of them. He had no idea how Ryan had survived direct contact with them.

"And where is your grandson, Victor Alexander?"

The perfect, unaccented English surprised him. He composed his features into inscrutability, hoping Ryan was correct in that they could not read his thoughts.

"He's gone," Victor said simply.

Tra'e'ela laughed, a short harsh sound. "Although I cannot read your thoughts, I am very good at identifying deception," she said, "not to mention the fact that I sense the little one not far from here."

"Take them above ground," she ordered, "and I will join you shortly."

Jason huddled in the dark with Drake pressed against his side. Drake jerked as if shocked, the inadvertent movement startling them both.

"They know I'm here," the little boy said.

Jason felt for him in the darkness. "Don't be silly," he said, "they won't find us if we stay hidden."

213

Drake desperately wanted to believe Jason's words, but he knew more than Jason knew.

"No," Drake said, "they're going to find me, I know it. But if I leave you here, they won't find you."

Jason squared his jaw and pulled the small boy to him. "I'm not leaving you," he said firmly.

Drake desperately wanted to push him away, but even more, he wanted to pull him close. He clung to his friend, his brother, his constant companion, knowing that he had just doomed them both.

Tra'e'ela stood before the hidden door as it slid sideways. The small one was tucked into the tiny space as she suspected, but she was surprised to find a human boy in there as well. She reached in and grabbed the dark-haired one by his collar, hauling him out by the scruff of his neck.

She dangled the creature before her, noting that he possessed the same striking blue eyes as his male biological parent, and the coloring of his maternal grandfather. He also possessed that same perfect mouth, the oddly familiar one that she could not quite place. He had the same charisma of his grandfather, a compelling magnetism that seemed incongruous with his relatively low-level power and abilities. He gazed at her with the fearlessness she generally associated with the unintelligent or ignorant, but he, despite his young age, seemed neither.

She glanced into the hole in the wall. Here was the counterbalance to that ridiculous fearlessness. This species wasted entirely too much effort protecting the vulnerable among them, creating an easily exploitable weakness. She motioned and one of her soldiers dragged the red-haired boy from the closet. She was impressed that, despite his clear inferiority, he, too, was belligerent.

The blonde-haired woman stared into his eyes and Drake calmed himself immediately. He clearly understood the implied threat to his friend, and when she set him on his feet, he stood at her side obediently.

She glanced down at him, amused, thinking that he would also provide prime genetic material when he was of age, and when she walked from the room, he followed in her footsteps.

Victor was sedated during his transport, deemed far too dangerous a prisoner to be left conscious. When he awoke, he was in a solid rock cell with Abigail.

They are watching, Abigail communicated to him wordlessly.

He glanced about him, trying to identify a camera or any type of surveillance system.

The walls themselves are transparent from one side, she said silently, seemingly occupied with her needlework.

Victor controlled his urge to look directly at the wall. He instead engaged himself in a prolonged examination of her current creation. This might have seemed odd to the guards were they themselves not so preoccupied with the same activity.

Is Ryan still free? Abigail asked.

Yes, Victor responded, but they have taken both Aeron and Drake. Ryan will not stay hidden when it becomes apparent they have captured her son.

How long? Abigail asked, poking the needle into the canvas.

A few days, Victor responded, no longer.

Tra'e'ela sat in her chambers, satisfied with her progress thus far. The primary target had eluded her, but she had set out multiple snares as well as the containment that was closing in on her. And just in case, there were a few wild cards she had left out there to deal with the unexpected.

The door opened and her servant brought the little one in as she requested. He gazed at her somberly, his blue eyes almost as dark as hers.

She motioned for her servant to depart, and he handed her the boy.

Drake sat upon her lap uncertainly.

"Do you know where your mother is?" she asked.

Drake shook his head.

Tra'e'ela assessed the truthfulness of the response, and deemed it valid.

"Will she come for you?"

Drake thought about this for a long moment. "Yes," he said at last.

"Good," the woman replied, "that will make my job easier."

"What is your job?" the little boy asked, his boldness startling her. What startled her even more was that his gaze lingered on her lips in an almost sensual manner, and that he seemed completely unaware of this act. He reminded her of the Ajeo, a beautiful and artistic race of people so sexually desirable they went immediately extinct upon discovery due to the brutal and humiliating slavery that was thrust upon them. But he seemed to possess none of the weakness or vulnerability of that species.

She did not wish to answer his question and therefore did not. Instead, she asked another question of her own, curious at his response.

"What would happen to me if I harmed you?"

The boy did not have to think about his reply. It was simple, direct, and unequivocal.

"Ryan would kill you."

This amused the blonde-haired woman and she sought to pursue the line of questioning further.

"And what would happen if I harmed Ryan?"

If possible, the boy's answer was even more direct and unequivocal.

"Then Ryan's grandmother would kill you."

The answer surprised Tra'e'ela. She had expected threats regarding the boy's grandfather or father. She had no idea who the girl's grandmother could be, and she had received no orders in regards to this person. Perhaps this was a fantasy creation of the youngster. Still, his absolute certainty was unnerving.

"And who is Ryan's grandmother?"

Drake smiled to himself. The creature who had taken him, the one who threatened Jason, the one who had captured his grandfather, his father, and now sought to capture his mother...

She did not know.

Drake remained silent and his silence, especially coming from one so young, stirred a bit of anger in her. She, in turn, allowed her gaze to linger on his lips, something that from Marilyn or Ala or Kusunoki would cause him no concern, but from this one created unease.

"I have to stay here until you're grown," she commented, "so perhaps you and I will revisit this moment when you are of age."

Drake was not certain how to interpret her words, but in a wisdom that far exceeded his youth, he maintained his silence.

# CHAPTER 21

"IS THERE ANY WORD FROM VICTOR?" Ryan asked somewhat unnecessarily.

Edward examined the wealth of transmissions. Most were garbage and electronic chaff, purposeful misdirection to disguise the one true message. The only problem was that the one true message was not there.

"Let me go through the series again to ensure I haven't missed anything."

Ryan's tension spiked dramatically. Edward missed nothing. There was no transmission. Still, she sat as patiently as possible while Edward reviewed his work.

"There is nothing," he said at last.

"Just so I understand," Ryan said, "the agreement was for us to make asynchronous contact, Victor first, after two weeks."

"Yes," Edward said, "that was the arrangement."

"They have taken my father."

There were so many things Edward wanted to say. That there were other possibilities, that it was not certain that Victor had been captured, that perhaps he had simply gone silent out of necessity. But he did not say any of these because he believed none of them.

"Which means they have my son," Ryan said.

Edward glanced at Susan who sat pale-faced and stricken against the wall. It meant that they had her son as well, if he was even still alive. Ryan seemed to suddenly become aware of this possibility.

"I'm sorry, Susan. I know that Jason is also at risk." Something suddenly occurred to her, and she shared the insight. "But he is more valuable to them alive than dead." She followed this train of thought. "As are Victor and Drake."

She thought through the potential outcomes, trying to utilize the alien cognition that had been thrust upon her from exposure to Madelyn's blood and even more so from Ravlen's. "If I'm the ultimate target, which is what I suspect, then they will all be used as leverage against me."

Edward had to say the hard thing. "Then you must resist the obvious course of action, which is to bolt from here in an attempt to rescue them."

"Ah, wonderful," Ryan said bitterly, "so I'm to continue cowering in the bowels of the earth while everyone else pays the price for my inaction."

Edward was brutal. "We don't know what these creatures want, although it seems obvious they want you. If you give them what they want, what will stop them at that point from destroying everything else?"

Ryan was silent. She hated Edward at that moment. Hated him for his judgment. Hated him for his perfect logic. Hated him because she knew that he was right.

# CHAPTER 22

"WELL," THE MAN WITH THE SCAR SAID, "we're going to have to do something. She seems quite content to wait us out."

"We have two of this planet's decades," Tra'e'ela reminded him, "I don't see a need to rush this."

The man was almost livid. Although he was forced to respect his superior officer, he greatly chafed under her slow, methodical approach. He did not see how someone so meek and cautious had risen to such heights in the military.

Tra'e'ela, although not possessing the telepathic abilities of her captives knew full well what he was thinking and briefly considered twisting his head from his shoulders. This was the second mission she had been forced to serve with him, and if possible, he was more annoying this time around. She looked forward to killing him at the end of it. In their tightly-ranked caste society, his insubordination was already sufficient cause for her to take his life, but at the moment she did not have a replacement for him.

Which was another odd thing about her mission, Tra'e'ela thought. She had been sent with minimal troops, most very low-level. Even the two higher-ranking males that had accompanied her both times had no idea of her real name or place within their society. They would have been shocked to learn that, not only were they unworthy to serve with her, she so outranked them that technically they were not even allowed to make eye contact. They would have been astonished to learn she was a member of the Stealth, an elite cadre of spies and assassins responsible for conducting the Queen's most deadly business, silently and unnoticed. Tra'e'ela might have been uncertain why she had been tasked with this planet, but as always, she would do her duty without question.

An alarm sounded off in the depths of the fortress, one that sounded as if it was coming from the prisoner ward.

"Let me guess what that is," Tra'e'ela said. She drew a small, quick triangle in the air, and a holographic image appeared as before. "I see that there has been a breach in security," she raised her eyes and gave the man a look that froze his internal organs, "and it's within your sector."

Ryan sat before the chessboard, fingering her pieces. Edward sat across from her, contemplating his options. His master was a most difficult opponent and he could count on the fingers of one hand the times he had defeated her. She seemed very distracted at the moment, but he would not underestimate her.

As Edward pondered his strategy, she got to her feet, suddenly restless. He glanced up at her, then over at Susan who also watched Ryan's actions. Ryan seemed a little agitated and both were looking for signs that she might transition to another phase. Susan was particularly watching the color of Ryan's eyes.

Ryan sat back down abruptly. She tapped her forefinger on her queen, almost as if trying to wake the piece from its slumber. She then moved her hand to the king, rubbing her forefinger lightly along its smooth surface. She stared at the piece, her expression very distant. Her focus returned to the piece and she picked it up, squeezing it tightly in her hand. She then opened her hand and sat looking at the beautifully carved wooden piece.

Edward and Susan observed her actions with great concern.

Aeron ducked into an alcove. He had no idea what kind of technology he was facing so he just assumed his captors could track his every move and knew where he was right now. That did not mean, however, that he was going to just stand out in the open and wait for them. The alarm echoed throughout the corridors so loudly it hurt his ears.

He had no real plan. He had simply seen an opportunity and taken advantage of it. The fact that he had cracked the skull of one of his jailers had simply been a fringe benefit. If he could kill one or two more, then however this venture ended, it would be worth it.

His son was somewhere in front of him, he knew that much, and that was the direction he was heading.

The two boys huddled together as Tra'e'ela entered the cell. Interestingly, the larger of the two stood protectively in front of his friend even though the smaller boy was far stronger. She looked to Drake.

"Come here," she ordered.

Drake chewed his lip. He could feel his father near, and he did not at all want to go with this woman. But he knew by the way she looked at Jason that his friend would suffer if he disobeyed. He slid off the slab and onto the floor.

"Drake, no," Jason said.

"It'll be alright," Drake said, taking the outstretched hand of the woman. She lifted him into her arms and strolled from the cell as Jason watched the massive door shut behind them.

"Ryan, is something wrong?"

The chess piece was still in her hand and she slowly set it down on the square it had previously occupied. She looked at the other pieces, their relative positions, their potential movements, as if trying to glean far more than the chess board could offer.

"I don't know," she said.

Aeron was having remarkable success eluding his pursuers, but when he rounded the corner he suddenly understood why. His pursuers weren't actually trying to capture him, they were just trying to herd him into position.

The silver-haired man was there, and the brutal looking one with the scar. They were accompanied by at least a dozen soldiers, all who looked as if they wanted to tear him limb-from-limb. The worst, however, was when the doorway slid open and the woman with the long blonde hair entered. This was terrible, not only because she was more powerful than everyone else in the room combined, but also because she was holding his son.

Aeron froze, his eyes on Drake, clearly understanding the implied threat. He would have gladly fought everyone in this room, but he was not going to move if his son was in danger. Two of the soldiers approached and took him roughly by the arms. Tra'e'ela smiled. This species was so predictable. She handed the boy off to the silver-haired man and turned to deactivate the alarm, an action which required her security clearance.

Drake saw his opportunity and squirmed from the man's grasp. He ran toward Aeron, who saw his son's actions. With an amazing burst of strength he flung one of his captors into the other, their skulls striking with a large crack. He started toward his son, only to be tackled by three more soldiers.

The boy was halfway across the platform when the scar-faced man's anger boiled over and he had enough from this inferior species. He took two steps and kicked the running child in the ribs, sending him sprawling to the ground. Aeron's reaction was immediate as he roared in rage and battered his attackers to the ground. He fought through four more attackers before he lunged at the man with the scar, only to be stopped short, seemingly almost in mid-air. He wore an expression of stunned surprise.

Ryan uttered a muffled cry and collapsed forward as if she had been stabbed. She clutched her midsection, holding an imaginary mortal wound.

"Ryan!" Susan and Edward said simultaneously, the latter leaping forward to catch his master. Susan held her arm, trying to support her. Ryan leaned back, her features twisted in pain and surprise as her companions returned her to her chair. Her eyes were unfocused but filled with despair and disbelief.

"Aeron," she whispered.

Aeron looked down at the appendage that had impaled him. It was some sort of claw that had appeared out of the torso of the scarfaced man. It was pumping a liquid into him, some poison that burned and spread throughout his system. Aeron felt his immune system attempt to fight, then slowly collapse under the injected onslaught.

With a clacking sound, the man brutally retracted the claw from Aeron's midsection and Aeron fell to the ground. With a derisive look, he turned away as Drake crawled over to his father's side. Tra'e'ela watched expressionless, greatly displeased at this turn of events.

Aeron stared into his young son's deep blue eyes. They had never been icy like his, always warm like his mother's. And now, they burned with a steady inferno that only Ryan in her fury possessed. The blue flame brought Aeron more pleasure than any glacier ever could. He stared intently into Drake's eyes, giving him a three-part message for Ryan, and Drake reached out to touch his mother.

"I have always loved you," Aeron began.

A world away, Ryan groaned in anguish. Tears filled her eyes at the unrelenting pain. She could hear the words in her head, hear Aeron's voice as if he was speaking directly to her. She could even see his face and the light dying in his ice blue eyes.

"I can't keep my part of the bargain, so you must protect our son."

Ryan doubled up in pain, her grief and torment immense. Edward and Susan were both intensely distressed, unable to sense or see what was affecting Ryan, knowing only that it was awful. Ryan was clearly locked in communication with someone.

"And the last?" she said, barely able to articulate the words through the anguish constricting her throat.

"Avenge my death," he said simply. Then the blue-eyed man touched his son's cheek and died.

"No!" Ryan's agonized cry reverberated across the compound. She stood upward with such strength and fury that she lifted both Susan and Edward from their feet as they sought to hold onto her. Her breath came in furious gasps, a throw-back to that most primitive part of her limbic system, the full flight-or-fight response. She brushed Edward and Susan from her like blades of grass and turned on her heel, but there was no place to go, nowhere she could escape the torment that was burning a hole in her.

"Ryan, what's happened?" Susan asked. She could sense nothing and Edward appeared confused as well.

Ryan stopped, the magnitude of her words sinking in.

"Aeron is dead."

"That—, that does not seem possible," Edward said.

"He is dead," Ryan repeated, "and my son watched him die."

"Why?" Susan asked, her own grief taking hold. "Why would they do that?"

Ryan turned in fury. "Because they want me!" she said, her fists clenched so tight blood ran from her palms, "and I'm hiding like a coward! I should be protecting our Kind; instead everyone I love is paying for my inaction!"

Edward knew that he could not dissuade Ryan from action; he could only hope to temper her fury into a controlled response.

"Then let's leave here," he said, "but not without a plan."

Ryan wanted to smash him, wanted to run from the bunker and keep running until she caught every one of those blue-skinned bastards on this planet. She wanted to tear them apart, limb-by-limb, then pick her teeth with their bones. She wanted to crush them one-by-one until they were each nothing more than a pile of blue dust.

Instead, she took a deep breath and with monumental effort, calmed herself. Edward assessed her and determined she was more terrifying now than she had been the few seconds prior. He watched as she strode to the chess board, picked up the king, then placed it in her pocket. She stalked from the room without another word as Susan and Edward quickly followed.

"Well that ought to draw her out," the man with the scar said with a cruel smile. He was quite pleased with himself.

Tra'e'ela did not comment at first. She watched as the small boy clung to his father. Then, with immense dignity, he placed his palm on the dead man's chest in silent salute, stood, and slowly returned to her side. She reached down and lifted him to her hip. She gazed at the beautiful little creature for a long moment, then turned a disdainful gaze on the scar-faced troll.

"Yes," she said mildly, "I'm sure it will."

She turned and left, carrying the boy on her hip. The soldiers lifted the dead man and carried him from the room. The scar-faced man simply stood there, staring after his commanding officer long after she had disappeared.

Tra'e'ela had agreed with him, yet never had an agreement filled him with such dread.

Victor sought desperately to interpret the images and emotions that rushed at him. Ryan and Drake were both in great pain, although it did not seem physical in nature, and Aeron seemed to undergo intense suffering which then stopped abruptly. He tried to sort through the emotions and sensations but they came at him too rapidly. He staggered from the mental and emotional barrage, but Abigail was able to sort through it instantly.

"Aeron is dead," she said, her eyes focused elsewhere.

"How can that be?" Victor asked, knowing her words to be true.

Abigail shook her head, silencing him, reminding him that they were being watched.

And Drake? Victor asked mentally. He seems in pain.

He watched his father die, Abigail said, but he has not been hurt physically.

Victor stood, pacing about their small cell, and Abigail watched the dark-haired man's helpless fury. She kept her own thoughts tightly concealed.

In reality, this turn of events surprised her. Thus far, she had been quite impressed with the strategy and patience of these people.

But this, she thought to herself, this was a mistake.


Kusunoki moaned from his position on the slab, also sensing Aeron's demise. Ala sought to comfort her fallen friend while Marilyn seethed. She, too, sensed Aeron's death and Drake's pain, both which infuriated her. She was not as connected to Ryan as Victor was and therefore could not feel her over the great distance that separated them. But she could only imagine what the girl must be feeling.

"How is he doing?" she asked, trying to distract herself.

Ala gazed down at the man who was like a lover to her. Kusunoki had put up the fiercest resistance of all and had been badly beaten. Worse, he appeared to be sick or perhaps poisoned because he was not healing as quickly as normal. He had made scant improvement since he had been thrown into the cell with them.

"He fights," Ala said, "just like he always does."

Marilyn nodded. She felt like fighting right now as well.

# CHAPTER 23

"SO IT'S SET," Edward said. "I will go to the surface, make arrangements for transportation, and you and Dr. Ryerson will join me in five hours."

"Good," Ryan said tightly. Her manner had been fiercely controlled since Aeron's death. "You must be careful, Edward. I don't know how they keep finding us."

"Can you find them?" Edward responded.

"Oh yes," Ryan said bitterly. Aeron's last physical location was burned into her memory, "I know exactly where they are."

"Good," her manservant responded. "Oh, and I showed Dr. Ryerson the confinement controls in case you should 'relapse,' in which case she will send me a short pulse message to let me know she requires assistance."

"Hopefully that won't be necessary," Ryan said, although the idea made her nervous. She had now gone weeks without a phase shift, which only made her worry that one was now due. "I think I'll be fine."

"Very well," Edward said, assessing his master. He was not at all certain of this course of action, but knew that Ryan was going with or without him. "I will see you soon."

Ryan sat in the den before an empty fireplace. She would have enjoyed a fire but was unwilling to provide any signal to the world above that something was occurring beneath the surface. So she sat before the cold hearth, counting the minutes until they could leave.

"So what exactly are you going to do?"

Ryan turned to Petrus, glaring at his unwelcome arrival. The sarcasm in his voice was even more unwelcome.

"Are you going to storm their fortress, you, your flunky, and your doctor friend?"

"No," Ryan said, "just me."

"Ah," Petrus said, "perhaps they will collapse from laughter and you will gain a momentary advantage."

Ryan glowered at him and he glanced at his watch nervously. Ryan was beginning to think it was an obsessive compulsive habit of his.

"Let me guess," Petrus continued, "you're going to try and trade yourself for the freedom of your companions."

"Maybe," Ryan replied.

"Yes, the selfless and stupid option."

"Shut up," Ryan said.

Just then, Susan came into the room, something clearly on her mind. She started to speak, then stopped abruptly, staring at the corner.

Ryan glanced up, followed her gaze, then returned her attention to the cold hearth. That was to be expected. Petrus' appearance could be quite shocking. She continued to ruminate on his words, something nagging at her that she couldn't quite get.

"Wait a minute," Ryan said, looking up again at Susan, then following her gaze to Petrus. "You can see him?"

Susan nodded wordlessly. She was quite stunned at the odd creature that was sitting in the corner, one that Ryan seemed perfectly aware of. The creature shifted uneasily as Ryan turned a lethal expression toward him.

"You son-of-a-bitch," she said, covering the distance between them in one leap. She pinned him to the wall, placing her forearm across his throat and dangling his feet several inches off the ground. She punctuated every word with a smack of his head on the wall behind him.

"I knew you were real, you bastard," Ryan said. "What kind of sick game have you been playing with me?"

"Nnbop thtkm," Petrus gasped, his words incomprehensible because of the arm across his throat.

"Who the hell are you?" Ryan demanded, smacking his head again.

"Nnkoj thiuhm!" Petrus gargled again.

"I think he's saying 'no time,'" Susan said, placing her hand on Ryan's shoulder. She was still astonished at the strange man.

Petrus clawed at Ryan's arm on his throat. "She's right," he gasped, "I'll explain everything, but right now there's no time."

Ryan loosened her grasp a little, but did not release him.

"What do you mean there's no time?"

"They're coming for you," Petrus said, his voice hoarse, "they're almost here."

Icy fear filled Susan. "He's right, Ryan. I was coming to tell you that Edward sent a distress signal, then disappeared."

"Damn it," Ryan said, releasing Petrus. The man fell to the ground, rubbing his throat. "We've got to get out of here," she said.

Petrus again glanced at his watch while Susan eyed him suspiciously. Ryan took two steps and a wave of dizziness overtook her.

"Not now," she muttered to herself. The world tilted violently and she would have collapsed had Susan not grasped her under the arm and supported her weight.

"Do you recognize me?" Susan asked anxiously, assessing Ryan's eye color.

"Yes," Ryan said, "I think this is just the weak phase. At a most inconvenient time," she added.

Susan again glanced suspiciously at Petrus, and at his watch. "You knew this was coming," she said.

Petrus took Ryan's other arm and the two began struggling to help Ryan out. "I don't know what you're talking about," Petrus said defensively.

But Susan's words resonated with Ryan and she suddenly understood Petrus' preoccupation with this timepiece. "You know the pattern of my phases."

"Maybe," Petrus muttered, maneuvering her through the door. If only she weren't so damn tall.

Ryan took a swing at him and missed, causing all three of them to stagger and nearly fall. "You bastard," she said. "All this time you knew when I was going to shift phases."

"Yes, yes," Petrus said unapologetically, "and you can continue to beat on me and we'll all be captured. Or," he said, pressing his hand to a seemingly random place on the wall, "you can shut up and we can get out of here."

A rectangular shape appeared on the wall which resolved itself into a doorway. The doorway opened into a secret passage, and within the passage were two more like Petrus. Both stared at the trio expectantly as Ryan stood stunned.

"How long has this been here?" Ryan asked, aware of the entire layout of the compound, but not this passageway.

Petrus' clownish manner disappeared and for once he was deadly serious. "We've been watching you, oh," he glanced around him, "long before this place was built."

Ryan stared at him, a sudden distrust now warring with her indignation and desire to escape. A clatter off in a distant hallway made the decision for her.

"Let's go," she said, and the two in the hallway moved into position to support her. Susan also glanced at the strange creature with distrust, but he made a mockingly gallant gesture for her to precede him, and she did so. He glanced down the hallway, then entered the secret passage, closing the hidden door behind him.

The servant entered Tra'e'ela's quarters, accompanied by the scar-faced man who had a look on his face that communicated far more than any words could.

"Well?" Tra'e'ela asked.

"It seems that the target has escaped once more."

Tra'e'ela turned her attention to the scar-faced man, who shifted nervously "And how did this happen?"

"It appears our contingency plan has interfered."

"Our contingency plan?" Tra'e'ela said with sarcastic emphasis on the first word. "You mean that your Plan B has decided she wishes to be Plan A."

"I'm sure she intends to return the target to us. She has been positioning her troops for some time to order an attack should one be necessary."

"Yes," Tra'e'ela said, her sarcasm even greater, "your strategy to gain compliance by killing off the majority of the mutated species."

"It is our way," the scar-faced man said belligerently, feeling at last that he was in the right. He was not, however, and this was immediately clear when the blonde-haired woman stood and towered over him, giving him the briefest glimpse of her true power. His over-simplified pronouncement infuriated her.

"It isss not," she said, seething, causing the "s" to be pronounced in a sibilant hiss. Her unaccented English disappeared into reptilian fury. "It is our way when it is beneficial, when it is efficient, or when it is productive. It is not our way, however, when it makes the task at hand more difficult or increases the odds of failure. We destroy as punishment, as revenge, to set precedent, to make a point, or even simply because we feel like it. But we do not destroy when it is counter-productive."

She turned her back on him. "You had better hope this works," she said, dismissing them both.

The stench was awful. Susan wrinkled her nose, looking about them. The narrow passageway had transitioned into a much larger, circular passageway.

"Are we in a sewer?" she asked.

Ryan stumbled, praying that she wouldn't go down in the filth. The two creatures that supported her under her arms, whom she had mentally dubbed "duckbill" and "whiskers," held her fast and she did not fall.

"Thank you," she muttered, and the two seemed surprised at her gratitude. They were also quite surprised at her continued effort as she was clearly exhausted.

"Did you know," Petrus said conversationally, leading the way, "that you can travel for hundreds of miles underground, through sewer lines, abandoned subways, utility tunnels, mines, etc., without ever going above ground? You can travel halfway across the US without ever seeing the sun. Hell, there are military installations that stretch for miles that no one knows about."

"We're not walking the entire way, are we?" Ryan asked, gritting her teeth. All she wanted to do was lay down.

"Nah," Petrus said. "We're coming up on an underground railroad, and I don't mean the slave kind, that will give us a bit of a boost. We'll be able to hop, skip, and jump our way to where we're going."

"And where are we going?" Susan asked. She didn't like this at all, and when Petrus turned his rheumy eyes toward her, eyes that seemed to glow yellow in the dark, she liked it even less.

"There's someone who wants to meet Ryan," he said. He turned forward, again leading the way.

No, Susan didn't like this at all.


It seemed like days had passed although Susan knew it could not be more than hours. They had traveled for some distance underground, then come out of a utility tunnel where more of Petrus' kind were standing by. They ushered them into several limousines and they set off for small local airport. Petrus sat across from Susan while Ryan leaned heavily against the side of the car.

"So why don't you tell me who you really are?" Ryan said. She was angry but her fatigue blunted her anger.

"Who do you think I am?" Petrus said, crossing his arms over his chest.

"No more games," Ryan said, "no more therapy, no more conversations. Just tell me who you are."

Petrus became aware that Susan was scrutinizing him.

"What are you looking at?" he demanded.

"Nothing," Susan said, embarrassed that she had been caught staring. Still, her scientific curiosity was overwhelming. "You are clearly our Kind, so were these mutations present prior to your Change or a result of it?"

"I'm not your fucking kind!" Petrus screamed, nearly frothing at the mouth. "Do I look anything like your kind?" He jerked his chin toward Ryan. "Do I look anything like this perfect specimen of humanity, or even anything like you, Red?"

"Stop being rude," Ryan said, "Dr. Ryerson's been treating me like a laboratory experiment from the day she met me, so you're in good company."

Susan wasn't sure which comment she should be insulted by, so chose neither. Petrus was not finished, however, and he leaned over into her face. To her credit, she did not flinch or react in any way, even when his spittle struck her shirt.

"Don't pretend you're not disgusted by the way I look. Don't pretend you would be 'okay' if you turned into something like me, or if your son transformed into an abomination with two heads or four arms or gills or wings." He shoved himself back into his seat. "Don't patronize me."

Silent before his onslaught, something in the way he moved caught Susan's eye.

"You're in pain," she said quietly.

Petrus slunk down into his seat. "No shit," he said, "we're all in pain."

"And who is we?" Ryan asked.

Petrus turned crafty once more, giving her a sideways glance. "You know who we are."

Ryan understood and she lowered her gaze. Susan did not, and turned to her friend.

"Ryan?" she asked uncertainly.

A long sigh escaped from Ryan, part exhaustion, and part unwilling acknowledgment to a truth she had known all along.

"Petrus is one of the Survivors," she said.

Petrus narrowed his gaze. They had been given many names over the centuries, most in the vein of "Abominations" or "Monstrosities," and they had given many names to themselves, such as "Unfortunate" or "Forgotten." But never had this name been uttered, odd since it was so undeniably perfect.

"I hate you," Petrus muttered.

"I know," Ryan replied.

Susan looked from one to the other. She wanted Ryan to continue with her explanation, but she was intrigued by the odd relationship that had formed between Petrus and her friend. It was difficult to assess, a bizarre mixture of familiarity, rivalry, humor, dislike, admiration...

And then it hit Susan. They acted just like siblings. She turned back to Petrus, but he was remaining stubbornly silent.

Ryan examined Petrus' deformed features, features that no longer even seemed out of the ordinary to her.

"When Victor was left on this planet, there was a 'search' for suitable companions for him."

"What kind of search?" Susan asked, noting the peculiar emphasis and the discomfort in which it was uttered.

"It was more of a large-scale biological experiment on humanity," Ryan said, "one that had fairly catastrophic results. Hundreds of thousands grew sick and died. There were mutations, deformities, suffering inflicted in an attempt to find the handful of humans who could successfully survive the hybridization with this other species. It's what we refer to as the Change, and it resulted in the first generation of our Kind, the Old Ones."

The story weighed heavily on Ryan as Petrus sat glaring at her. Susan had grown very pale at Ryan's account, appalled on so many levels it was hard to separate out what she was feeling. Ryan had recounted portions of this history before, but its brutality was still difficult to bear.

"Some who were not deemed 'successes' by this invasion force somehow managed to survive. And they have continued on in a parallel development with us."

This last statement was largely guesswork on Ryan's part, and it seemed there was something on the edge of her consciousness that almost came to light, something that she was almost able to remember. It slipped away, frustrating her because it seemed very important right now. Petrus took up the story line.

"So we went underground, in more ways than one, hiding in plain sight. Humans couldn't see us or touch us unless we wished them to, and neither could your kind. That is," he said with another sidelong look at Ryan, "until recently. Someone got another gift from grandma." He snorted. "I get a fucking pig nose, and what does she get? X-ray vision."

"And why are all of you in pain?" Susan asked.

"I don't know," Petrus said bitterly, "another one of our gifts, I guess. Our best scientists can't figure it out, and our best scientists were able to figure out nut-job's phase shifts when you couldn't."

"That was pretty clever," Ryan admitted.

"Thank you," Petrus said gruffly, and Susan was again struck by how odd their relationship was, beyond even the extremes of love and hate.

"So then who are we going to see?" Susan asked.

Petrus went abruptly silent, merely shaking his head. Ryan leaned back against the door, resting her head against the window.

"I don't know," she said, "but somehow I have a feeling that I should."

Ryan was asleep, her dreams haunted by a pair of green eyes that she simply could not place. Even in the dream the eyes were disembodied, floating unattached to any person, place, or event that she had ever known. The anxiety caused her to start from her sleep, and the green eyes quickly faded away, replaced by a more present danger.

"Where are we?" she asked.

Susan was overcome by Ryan's sudden apprehension and Petrus picked up on it as well.

"We're still a few miles from the airport. We had to take a detour through some city blocks."

"We're not going to make it," Ryan said.

No sooner had these words passed from her lips than the car they were in violently redirected, smashed sideways from the force of collision. The driver struggled to regain control of the vehicle but it spun out and crashed through a storefront. The car had barely come to rest when Ryan began struggling with the door, but it was trapped in a closed position by the damaged door frame. She cursed her present weakness, praying for a phase shift.

"Let me try," Susan said, and braced her feet against the door. Perhaps it was her newfound abilities or simply panic, but she gave a tremendous thrust and the door pushed outward in a squeal of protesting metal. Both Ryan and Petrus were impressed.

"Come on!" Susan said, pulling Ryan from the wreckage. The driver scrambled out the front passenger side. He was a thin willowy man whose deformities gave him a tree-like appearance. He grabbed Ryan's other arm a little roughly.

Petrus had also scrambled free and was looking fearfully out into the street. Ryan didn't need to follow his gaze; she knew what was there.

"I don't suppose you can beat 'blue men' in this state."

Ryan shook her head. "Not a chance."

The tree-like man and Susan dragged Ryan through the hole their vehicle had so recently created. Pandemonium was in full swing on the streets, and another vehicle from their caravan was now engulfed in flames. "Duckbill" and "Whiskers" were trapped inside, their terrified screams rising above the yelling and screaming on the block.

"Ryan, we have to go!" Susan cried, trying to pull Ryan away. Two very large muscular men with slightly bluish skin were exiting a black SUV, and Ryan did not even need to look to feel their frightening presence. But she could not let Petrus' companions burn to death, even if they were her captors.

"Susan, help me get this door off."

The two pushed from the inside and Susan pulled outward, and Ryan was quite certain she did nothing more than add her weight, but the door creaked open. The occupants tumbled out and Petrus grabbed Ryan's arm.

"We have to go!" he screamed as the men rounded the corner of the car. Two more were exiting from a car further up the street. "The subway is right over here!"

Susan and Petrus half dragged and half carried Ryan, who seemed to be growing weaker by the minute. They nearly lost control of her down the slick stairs to the subway tunnel, but regained their grip at the bottom. The mass confusion and crowded conditions were the only things keeping their pursuers at a distance, but even so, the brutal soldiers were cutting a swath through the mass of people by smashing pedestrians right and left out of their way. The doors of the train were sliding shut in front of them, but with a last great effort Susan and Petrus dragged Ryan onto the train and the tree-like man squeezed in behind them.

The train started from the station and the group turned to the horrified stares of the other occupants of the compartment. The stares lasted only a second, however, as the train made it less than fifty yards before jerking to a violent stop. Everyone in the compartment was thrown forward into a heap. Susan pulled Ryan from the pile, glancing fearfully over her shoulder.

Ryan assessed the situation grimly. They had made it just far enough down the tracks to be trapped within the confines of the narrow part of the tunnel. The yelling and screaming coming from the rear cars of the train told her that her pursuers were approaching. Even if they could get the doors open, there wasn't clearance enough on the sides of the train for them to squeeze through. She glanced up. There was the outline of an emergency hatch above her head.

Petrus followed her gaze. "We go out that way."

No sooner had these words left his mouth than the rear doors burst open. Ryan was tall enough to reach the latch on the escape door. Without thinking about how tired she was, she lifted Petrus up and shoved him through the opening. She turned to Susan and despite her protests, lifted her bodily upward into Petrus' hands. He pulled her free on to the top of the car.

Ryan glanced back and froze. One of the soldiers was pulling a weapon from his belt, a wicked looking three-bladed projectile. She turned to the tree-like man. "You need to get up there now."

The man's anger and indignation was palpable. "I'm as strong as you are, you go first."

Ryan glanced back, realizing they were out of time. "You don't understand—"

She didn't have time to finish the sentence because the soldier cocked his arm back and let the projectile fly. It spun out in a deadly arc and Ryan had no time for any action other than to shove the other man backward as the deadly weapon spun between them. Had she not shoved him, the weapon would have taken off his head. She groaned as it instead sliced through her midsection. The man stared down at the blood in shock.

"Those weapons will kill me!" she said angrily, gritting her teeth, "so I know they will kill you." She turned back to the soldier who was readying another projectile. It was clear to her that he was targeting her captor, not her, and the tree-like man's terror indicated he realized this as well.

Perhaps it was her anger that gave her strength, or perhaps it was the clarity that the pain thrust upon her. But Ryan saw with perfect vision as the soldier loosed the razor-blade missile at them. It spun toward them with frightening speed, a blur of deadly sharpness as it cut through the air. The smaller man stared in horror as the blade came right at his face, then flinched as it came to an abrupt stop right before his nose.

Ryan stared down at the blade in her hand, the weapon that she had just impossibly plucked from the sky. She looked down at her smaller companion and very slowly smiled. Despite her fatigue, despite her pain, despite her injury, she turned and with great joy flung the projectile back to its originator with such accuracy, speed and force, it decapitated the man in a spray of acid blood. It also caught the soldier behind him, landing with a solid "thunk" into the flesh of his shoulder and knocking him backward. Ryan surveyed her work with pleasure, then turned back to her captor who was looking at her with amazement.

"I'll lift you up, but you're going to have to pull me through. I'm too tired to jump."

The man nodded wordlessly and Ryan grimaced as she lifted him to her shoulder, paused, then pushed him all the way through. Petrus pulled on the other end. Then the two with the help of Susan pulled Ryan through the hatch. She went face down on the train for a moment, wanting nothing more than to sleep she was so exhausted.

"Come on," the tree-like man said, although far more gently than before, "we have to keep moving."

Susan helped Ryan to her feet and the four staggered down the top of the train. When they reached the front end, it was easier for Ryan to simply fall than to try and climb down. She stumbled upright, then began limping down the dark passageway toward a utility tunnel, supported by her three companions.

Petrus glanced back. It seemed that for the moment they were safe. If they could get back to the underground passages with which he was so familiar, they could easily outdistance anyone less familiar with the terrain. They should probably bypass the local airport now, but he was confident they were once again en route to their destination.

# CHAPTER 24

THE UNDERGROUND CHAMBER WAS IMMENSE, dwarfing even the expanses of the Grand Council Chambers, and Ryan had the impression that the facility itself went for miles in every direction. It was clear this place was for full-time habitation, not mere temporary residence. And the number of people present was far greater than any assembly ever called by the Council, including her coronation. There was a constant thrum of noise punctuated by an occasional, inarticulate shout.

Susan glanced around her as they made their way through the vast subterranean hall. The mass of mutations and deformities blurred together into one giant sea of strangeness, teeming limbs and gaping orifices, tumors, excess appendages, odd-angled joints, undersized and oversized body parts. And the mass of humanity pressed in on them in palpable anger, the beauty and perfection in their midst reviled and despised. Ryan limped along, still supported by Susan in her weakness, looking neither to the right or left but simply moving forward to the gigantic raised dais they were approaching. She sighed at the large number of stairs that greeted her. She had negotiated but a few when Petrus took her other arm.

"We don't have all fucking day," he muttered under his breath, and Ryan was grateful for the assistance.

After what seemed an interminable amount of time, they reached the top and were immediately stopped by two mammoth guards with protruding mandibles that gave them a canine appearance. The two appeared to be twins and reminded Ryan of the Egyptian god Anubis. The sharpened incisors they bared in warning added to the image.

The hum of the crowd died down and it became deathly silent in the gigantic hall. Petrus shifted nervously and a flatulent, squeaky noise emitted from somewhere on his person. Both guards turned a disapproving eye toward him and Ryan glanced down with a raised eyebrow.

"I really can't take you anywhere," she said, and Petrus cleared his throat.

The grinding sound of stone on stone silenced everyone. The raised centerpiece began to rotate and the elaborate alter slowly disappeared, replaced by an even more elaborate throne. The craftsmanship and detail of the piece was extraordinary, the twists and turns of the demonic relief both magnificent and frightening. It was a piece of art imbued with the dark essence of the artist's soul. But it was not the magnificent and horrible throne that attracted Ryan's attention, but rather the magnificent and horrible woman that sat upon it.

Ryan stared at her in wonder. She had two great horns curling from the sides of her head like a demon goddess. Her skin was a greenish-brown that changed color chameleon-like in the shifting light. The skin itself seemed leathery, or perhaps even reptilian in nature, with a pattern that seemed scale-like. She was not wearing clothing, the skin seeming to serve that purpose for her, and she had rather impressive proportions

"Wow," Ryan said under her breath. Petrus turned to her with a look, half disbelief and half indignation.

"Oh-my-god," he said, stressing each word. "You have got to be kidding me."

Ryan brushed him off. This woman seemed to be very angry at her. Furthermore, something was clawing at the back of her consciousness, some memory that was dying to get out. Ryan flinched as the connection was made. A series of images, conversations, thoughts, emotions, and memories rushed upon her, and now she stared at the woman with even more wonder.

"You are Lia," Ryan said.

The woman's nostrils flared and she turned with a look of fury upon Petrus who had strategically put some distance between himself and Ryan. Petrus shook his head wildly, raising his hands in denial. He had said nothing, as had been his instruction.

Lia turned her attention back to her prisoner. When she spoke, her voice was low, her tone malevolent.

"And how is it that you know me, Ryan Alexander?"

"I have your Memories," Ryan said slowly, "but I don't know how."

This comment seemed to stoke the woman's fury even more, causing her to sit upright, almost like the quick uncoiling of a snake. "How dare you presume to know anything about me," she said, her tone dripping venom. She seemed to catch herself, settling back in a sinewy movement that again reminded Ryan of a snake. "And what is it that you think you know?"

Ryan sorted through the images, trying to make sense of the history that had been thrust upon her.

"You were a mother," Ryan said, her eyes focused on a very distant point, "you lived in a small village. You were married and had three children, two girls and a boy."

"And—?" Lia said sarcastically. These were all banal facts a charlatan psychic could make up.

"And then the sky grew black."

Outwardly, Lia remained calm but her tension increased.

"It wasn't a storm," Ryan continued, "but an enormous flock of birds, scavengers. Then the soldiers returned, but they were sick."

Lia's tension was now outwardly visible.

"Your husband had been out hunting, and he, too returned sick. Your children were hiding under the table and you were relieved when Simon came home."

Lia flinched at the name.

"But Simon was too sick. He attacked you, and then he killed and ate your children in front of you."

"Enough!" Lia screamed. The word echoed about the vast chamber, stunning all within. She uncoiled again, rising to a fearsome height. But Ryan could not stop; she was caught up in the dream that had been hiding within her mind, struggling to get out.

"You wanted to die," she continued, "but you could not. And then they came and took you."

Lia's breath was coming in harsh gasps.

"They experimented on you, tortured you, caused you immense pain, changed you into what you are now. And then one man set you free."

"Why," Lia demanded, "why was I taken?"

"They were seeking companions for Victor," Ryan responded.

"And who is Victor?" Lia said, biting off every word but especially the last.

"Victor is my father."

A murmur swept through the crowd. Although the hated one was well known, many did not know this specific motivation for the hatred.

This admission seemed to temporarily calm Lia and she coiled back into a seated position on her throne.

"Do you know how many years I've watched you?" Lia hissed. It was clearly a rhetorical question and therefore Ryan did not respond.

"I watched your father for hundreds of years, hating him. Hating him for his perfection, for his beauty, for the gifts bestowed on all of your Kind. I watched as you slaughtered one another in your passion, mindlessly discarding that which any of my kind would sacrifice anything for."

"And then in the ultimate inequity, he had you."

Ryan understood. "You can't reproduce."

"No," Lia said, biting off the word. "We, like your Kind, cannot sexually reproduce. We can effect a transformation through our bite, but frankly, there are not many humans lining up to become one of us."

Ryan remained silent in the face of the indictment.

"We don't kill our young the way you do, but the suicide rate amongst our young is very high. Although some mutations are minor, others are catastrophic and the pain is omnipresent. Like you, we pass into a phase in which we essentially become immortal."

This seemed to cause Lia some private, hellish amusement, which she explained. "We have a sub-population known as the Suffering."

"And who are the Suffering?" Ryan asked.

"They are those who didn't have the courage to take their lives when it was possible and now live on, doomed to an eternity of pain and regret."

"And you blame me for this."

Lia leaned forward in a serpentine movement. "Of course I blame you. It's clear that all of this," she waved, indicating the mass of spectators, "was done to get to you."

As much as she wished to deny this, Ryan had seen into the mind of Ravlen and knew it to be true.

"So then what do you intend to do?" Ryan asked.

"I have you for twenty-four hours," Lia said. "I'm not allowed, and in fact don't believe that I can kill you, But I can make you wish for death. I intend to inflict as much suffering upon you as I can, to impress upon you the hell you have thrust upon us. And then when I'm done, I will send you and your little companion back to those who so desperately seek you. And I'm quite certain that they can kill you."

Ryan sighed in resignation. She turned to Petrus, who seemed unsurprised yet unhappy at this turn of events. He was not proud of his role in this escapade. The two Anubis guards took Ryan from Susan's arm, and she addressed the creature who had betrayed her.

"Please take care of Dr. Ryerson," Ryan said to him, not the slightest bit of condemnation in her voice.

He nodded, and as the two guards took her away, he finally admitted to himself that Ryan Alexander was not what he had expected at all.

# CHAPTER 25

PETRUS AND SUSAN SAT IN THE ANTEROOM. Neither had spoken a word in hours. Petrus continued his nervous habit of looking at his watch. Susan, for her part, felt both pity and disgust for the little man, and because neither was winning out, she simply ignored him.

Finally, Ryan was brought out from the Lia's chambers and although Petrus had anticipated the worst, it was worse than he anticipated. Susan gasped aloud at the condition of her friend.

Ryan's entire body was battered and bruised. She had whip marks, bite marks, blunt trauma injuries, several obvious broken bones, a knife that was still impaled just above her kidney, and a dislocated shoulder that was hanging. The two Anubis guards dragged her by her arms, then dropped her brutally in front of Susan. She rolled over groaning as the impact drove the knife further into her side.

"Do you think you could get that?" she said through gritted teeth.

Susan grasped the hilt of the knife and yanked it. Normally she never would have done such a thing. Standard medical procedure would have been to stabilize the impaled object in place until it could be removed in surgery. But Ryan's healing abilities were such that getting the offending object out was the first priority. The removal was met with a moan, then a gasp of relief from the victim.

Ryan sat up, moving gingerly. "And do you think you could get that back in place?" she said, nodding at her shoulder. Susan was less certain about this maneuver, so Ryan directed her. "Just hit it there, no, a little lower. And hit it hard."

Susan followed her instructions and fortunately her physical strength was such now that the maneuver was semi-successful. Ryan again sighed with relief. She was still, however, in incredible pain.

Petrus looked at the damage that had been done. He could not imagine what the last hours had been like for Ryan.

A look of chagrin passed over Susan's features and Ryan correctly interpreted the inevitable reaction to the sight of her blood.

"I hardly think now is the time," she said with black humor. She was still struggling with weakness, and the injuries only added to her effort. "I don't suppose you can tell me when this phase will end?" she said, addressing Petrus.

He shifted uncomfortably. "You still have a while."

"Long enough to deliver your cargo, hmm?" Ryan said. With monumental effort, she stood on her own.

"Then let's get going," she said, "no sense in delaying this any longer."

# CHAPTER 26

RYAN LAPSED IN AND OUT OF CONSCIOUSNESS for most of their journey. She had the impression of traveling via several modes of transportation: train, plane, then finally automobile. When they arrived at the base of a great mountain, she looked up, despondent.

"Don't tell me we're going by pack mule."

A large rectangular opening appeared in front of them and the doors slid open.

"I thought we would take the elevator," Petrus responded.

Several soldiers stepped out, as well as a silver-haired man who seemed quite different from the others. Ryan searched her memory, or rather the memories she had acquired from Madelyn and Ravlen. He was a higher caste, physically more powerful than the soldiers and far more intelligent. His uniform identified him as a biological combat engineer, an expert in biochemical and genetic warfare.

The silver-haired man examined her as well, hiding his surprise. Although she was badly beaten, she was absolutely stunning. By far the most powerful of these creatures, she was registering fluctuating strength levels that far exceeded what was expected from this species. He was going to enjoy studying and experimenting on this one.

Perhaps it was the offensive way the man was looking at her, but something triggered the memories of Aeron and Lia. Painful images flashed through her mind and she now recognized the man personally. She turned to Petrus.

"Did you know that this one was in charge of the experiment that altered Lia? That he is responsible for unleashing the agent that altered all of your people?"

Petrus turned a troubled gaze on the silver-haired man. He did not know that, and he wondered if Lia did.

The silver-haired man was now even more stunned. There was no way she could know that. They had left few alive and all had been mind-wiped. The look on this girl's face, however, told him that she knew far more than what she had just presented.

The soldiers stepped forward to take custody of Ryan, but she glared at them and Petrus and Susan did not relinquish their support of her. So instead, the soldiers surrounded the trio and they moved into the elevator.

The interior of the elevator was uncomfortably familiar to Ryan, the geometric shapes, the hieroglyphic writing. She could actually read some of the script, but stopped herself when the silver-haired man began watching her closely. She turned her attention inward.

The Others were here, Victor, Abigail, Ala, Marilyn, and Kusunoki. Her son was here as well. She briefly touched him, then turned to Susan.

"Your son is fine," she said. "Jason is frightened but unharmed, and he and Drake are together."

The silver-haired man was intrigued. He was wondering if he could gain permission from the commander to do exploratory surgery on her brain. Although he had many less invasive and more advanced methods at his disposal, vivisection was his favorite. While entertaining this pleasant thought, he looked back at the girl and froze. She was gazing at him with such a look of contempt, such a look of utter disdain that it took his breath away. He was not certain why because she was powerless at the moment, but something in that gaze was unnervingly familiar.

The doors opened and the silver-haired man's disquiet was so great that for a moment he did not move. He shook himself free of the spell and stepped out. Ryan, her supporters, and her cohort of soldiers followed him out onto the huge platform.

A gasp attracted her attention and she turned to Ala, who was on the platform to her left. Ryan had tried to prepare the Others about her appearance, but the earth mother was devastated by Ryan's injuries. Marilyn was also appalled. Ryan made eye contact with Kusunoki, and the two examined one another's various traumas, then both slowly smiled. They always were two of a kind.

Ryan turned her attention to Edward, then Victor, whose anger at the condition of his child was apparent. He was tightly in control, but just barely. Jason clung to Victor's side. Drake, in the arms of his grandfather, gazed at his mother somberly. He, more than anything, wanted to rush across the platform to her, but that action had killed his father.

Ryan mentally touched him, gently but firmly. That was not your fault, Ryan said to him, and it would pain Aeron to think you blame yourself. I will take care of this, she promised, I will fulfill your father's last wishes.

The last of the Old Ones stood apart from the Others. Although everyone was restrained by several soldiers, Abigail seemed to have a small army about her. This was odd because there was no agitation within her at all, she was serene. It was odder still because none of the soldiers stood too near her, rather monitored her from a distance as if some force field were surrounding her person. The elegant matriarch examined Ryan's cuts and bruises almost languorously and Ryan had to smile at the sensuality in that gaze. Ryan then turned her attention to the last person on the stage. She knew him as well. She recognized him from the early memories of Aeron and Lia, and more recently, from those of her son. He was the butcher from the original experiment, the brute enforcer of the party.

And he was the one who had killed Aeron.

The scar-faced man sneered at the girl who was brought onto the platform. She was hardly the threat that had been described. In fact at the moment she appeared little more than a weak, wounded animal.

She could barely stand upright and had to be supported by that pathetic little mutant and the anemic red-head.

Ryan's eyes burned into him. She wanted to direct all of her attention toward him but something else was approaching, something monumental and massively powerful. A woman with long blonde hair and dark blue eyes strode onto the platform. She moved with an alien grace and had a profound coldness at her center. She was undeniably beautiful, but it was the same unnatural beauty that Madelyn had possessed, and her presence shifted in and out of focus just like Madelyn's.

But here is where the comparisons stopped. This woman was clearly Madelyn's superior and Ryan struggled against the feelings of despair this created.

Tra'e'ela examined the girl, having quite the opposite impression as her dim-witted cohort. This infant impressed her far more than she had expected. Nowhere near as powerful as her, or even as her two officers, but far more than she had anticipated. But it was not this strength that caught her attention. No, there was also something else, something perhaps that only she was attuned to. The girl appeared to be hiding something, and doing so quite skillfully. It was a gift that, had she been born into their kind, would have marked her even at a young age as destined for the Stealth. And the fact that the girl had developed the skill with no training whatsoever was startling.

But meaningless at the moment.

"Ryan Alexander," the woman said. Ryan noted the same sibilance on the "x" that Madelyn had used in her pronunciation and it gave her a chill. She composed herself.

"And what is it you want from me?" Ryan asked.

"There is nothing that I want from you," the woman said, coldly amused. "There is nothing you can offer me, nothing you can give. You have nothing to bargain with."

It should have been a devastating pronouncement, but after a pause, it engendered the gentlest of responses.

"Did Aeron recognize you?" Ryan asked softly, subtle steel in the question.

This in turn generated a pause from Tra'e'ela. This girl was full of surprises.

"No," she said simply, "he did not."

This drew curious looks from everyone in the room, first at the blonde woman, then at Ryan.

"Good." Ryan said.

Tra'e'ela marveled at the girl. The response was relieved but carried a hint of veiled threat, as if there would have been consequences had she answered differently. She turned to the scar-faced man. "You may proceed."

The scar-faced man drew a large rectangle in the air, and while he was waiting for the image to form, he addressed Ryan.

"I understand you tried to sway Lia," he said sarcastically. "Did you really think a few hours spent with you would be enough to overcome a thousand years of bitterness?" He laughed, a harsh mocking sound. "You aren't that charming."

Ryan's shoulders slumped slightly and Petrus unconsciously mirrored the gesture. The holographic image formed in the air, a mutant minion appeared, then Lia herself. She was gloriously imperious and the Others looked upon her in fascination. Petrus had attracted quite a bit of attention upon his arrival, but Lia's presence and physical appearance attracted ten-fold.

"Yes?" she said with just enough disdain to irritate the scar-faced man.

"I trust your troops are in position?"

"Yes," Lia replied.

The scar-faced man turned to Ryan. "She has been waiting for this moment for centuries. She will unleash all her forces upon your kind. They are far more numerous than you and will hunt your people down one-by-one until all are slaughtered."

"And why would you do this if we are so insignificant to you?" Ryan asked.

The man sneered. "We left a lot of loose ends on this planet and I prefer things much 'cleaner.' I'm pleased at the chance to set things right." He returned to the holographic image. "You may give the order to proceed."

Lia engaged in some sort of discussion with someone off screen, then returned to the current conversation. "There seems to be some sort of parliamentary issue."

The scar-faced man bristled while the silver-haired man had a sudden sense of foreboding. "What kind of issue?" the brute demanded.

"Well it appears that this particular order can only be issued by the commander-in-chief of my military forces."

The man began grinding his teeth. "Then have him issue it," he said, spitting out the words.

"Well I can't," Lia said calmly, "because I just delivered her to you. You will have to deal with her personally. Goodbye."

The holograph vaporized and the scar-faced man stood staring at the empty air in fury.

Ryan had been studiously examining her fingernails during the transmission, and now looked to the scar faced man, her expression deadly. Her words were stunning and simple.

"I guess I really am that charming."

Tra'e'ela struggled to suppress a smile. The scar on the man's face was throbbing. Petrus looked at Ryan in disbelief and admiration.

"My god," he said under his breath but clearly audible, "you will fuck anything that moves." He knew he should stop himself but he just couldn't. "So, was it metaphorical sex? Or actual sex?" he asked with a sidelong glance.

"That's none of your business," Ryan said, not the least perturbed at the rude questioning or implication. She addressed scar face. "And just for the record, I won't be giving that order."

Tra'e'ela stepped forward. Although this was entertaining, she could not let it spin out of control. "This changes nothing," she said.

"Oh," Ryan said, "I'm afraid it does." She shifted, turning her head and cracking her neck loudly. "Petrus?"

Petrus glanced down at his watch. "You have about eight seconds, boss."

"Thank you," she said, "I thought it was getting a little warm in here."

Susan took a large step back.

The heat began to emanate off Ryan's body in waves that everyone could see. Ryan bent over, her entire body tensing, every muscle in stark relief, the veins on her arms coming to the surface in an attempt to dissipate the inferno rising in her. She slowly unfolded to her full height, neither weakness nor injury touching her any longer. She snapped out her right arm, setting the broken bone in place. She shifted her left shoulder in a violent movement, setting it back into position. Ligaments popped and cartilage crunched as joints re-aligned themselves, and her spine cracked as it adjusted into place. The cuts and bruises on her arms, neck, and face began to visibly heal. When Ryan opened her eyes, they were dark maroon.

Tra'e'ela looked at the girl in astonishment. Her power had just increased by orders of magnitude. Although she still was nowhere near Tra'e'ela's own abilities, she was now the equal of many of the soldiers in the room. In their curious, violent lexicon, the girl had gone from "insignificant-opponent-of-no-concern" to "slightly-dangerous-opponent-who-might-succeed-by-luck." It was not a particularly advanced category of adversary, but it made dealing with her far more complicated.

"Ryan?" Petrus said uncertainly, "do you know who I am?"

The girl turned with her slow, feral movement. She leaned down to sniff him, and Petrus was afraid for a moment that she was going to eat him.

"You are Petrus," she said, then clarified, "not Petrussss."

"Right," Petrus said, still a little nervous. The fact that she remembered their earlier conversation and found it humorous was promising. "Do you recognize the Others?"

Ryan turned her attention to the Others, one by one. She assessed Marilyn, then Ala, then Kusunoki. The examination burned through all of them, a violent, sensual, possessive appraisal that might as well have left a physical mark.

"Mon Dieu," Marilyn murmured.

255

Ryan then looked to Edward, then Victor, her eyes lingering on him, then to her son, her eyes lingering even longer. She looked at Jason, which then brought her attention around to Susan. It was almost as if she were rebuilding memories on the fly. Susan bore the burning assessment, quite certain a PET scan would reveal Ryan's brain to be on fire.

The maroon eyes then shifted to Abigail, pausing for an interminable length of time. Her scrutiny of the matriarch was intense, perhaps matched only by the matriarch's scrutiny of her. The creature smiled and turned back to Petrus.

"Yesss," she said, "I know them."

"Good," Petrus said, "and do you know them?" he asked, indicating the three standing in front of them.

Ryan turned to the silver-haired man who had moved to a position of safety behind several soldiers. He, too, felt the spike in the girl's power and although she was still no match for him, he was not taking any chances. The maroon-eyed creature gazed at him dismissively, and moved on.

Her eyes settled on the blonde woman, examining her from head to toe, and Tra'e'ela again marveled at the audacity of this little creature. The girl had transformed into a remarkable specimen, one with no inhibition and no fear, and one with quite a wicked sense of humor which was evident as her gaze lingered. Tra'e'ela actually felt herself respond to the girl's malevolent playfulness and quickly shielded herself. This caused only a twitch of a smile on that perfect mouth, and then the girl moved on.

Her gaze settled on the scar-faced man, and all playfulness disappeared. The malevolence, however, fully remained. The look in those burning eyes was so searing it was a wonder the man did not burst into flames.

"Yes," Ryan said, at last responding to Petrus' inquiry. "I know them."

The scar-faced man was incensed. As much as he wanted to, he could not turn his fury against the girl. To do so would mean the failure of their mission and the annihilation of his line. But he could certainly turn his rage against that traitorous little abomination.

"I knew your kind were not be trusted," he said, spitting the words out. He took a step forward and Petrus shrank back. Ryan stepped in front of him.

"Petrus and all his people are now under my protection." Her verbal abilities in the savage form seemed to be returning. "If you wish to deal with him, you deal with me."

The arrogance of the whelp was finally too much for the scar-faced man and he snapped. "Fine!" he said, stalking toward her.

It was beyond imagination that anyone would actually disobey the edict of her Majesty, and for that reason, Tra'e'ela was just slightly slow to react. Ryan went face-to-face with the scar-faced man and with horror Tra'e'ela recognized his intent. She saw the end of her career, the end of her life, and the end of anything and everything that had ever had even the remotest connection to her.

"No!" she cried out, but it was too late. The two combatants stood eye-to-eye, one now brutally impaled.

Several light years away, the Empress of half the known universe was overseeing the execution of her current conquered foe. It was a quadrupedal, silicon-based life form that had surrendered, but not soon enough for her satisfaction. She paused in her proceedings, turning her head slightly. She sensed the events as they occurred, transmitted across the thread that bound her to her grandchild, the filament that draped across the curvature of space time. She smiled at the enormous spike of energy, then returned to her decapitation.

The scar faced man stared into the maroon eyes, and Ryan stared back at him. Slowly, the light began to die in his eyes while all looked on in confusion, with one exception.

What no one could see was that as the man extended the deadly claw from his midsection, Ryan appeared to shift into a higher plane, moving so quickly that not even preternatural eyes could track her. From Ryan's perspective, however, the events felt leisurely and she had all the time in the world to step to the side as the claw slashed outward. And because the appendage missed its target, it overextended, leaving the cartilaginous connective tissue at the joint exposed. Ryan took advantage of the vulnerability and with incredible strength, snapped the claw at its base and shoved it back into the man's own torso, just as he was injecting his poison.

And now she stood eye-to-eye with him as he gurgled with the effects of his own venom and the amputated joint continued to reflexively inject poison into his torso. He slowly sunk to his knees, then keeled over to the ground with a thud. He twitched twice, then was dead.

Tra'e'ela stared on in amazement. She was not quite certain what had just happened, but she felt a tremendous spike in energy, something that she had felt only a few times in her life. It had lasted no more than a fraction of a second, but it had been immense. It could not possibly have come from this girl.

The soldiers were confused as well, so they began operating according to instinct and moved in to battle the girl. The entire thing was beginning to spin out of control, the potential for unconstrained violence almost assured. And then, if possible, the girl did something even more extraordinary.

"An'l'athas."

The effect of the command was immediate. Everyone froze, staring at the girl who had just uttered the phrase. And it wasn't so much the phrase, which simply meant "stop," but the manner in which it was uttered.

Not only was the command spoken fluently with perfect enunciation and diction, but in the seven distinct forms within their language, this particular one was reserved exclusively for the royal family. No one else was allowed to speak it, and most weren't even able to pronounce it. The soldiers shifted about, uncertain whether this was a legitimate order or the ultimate sacrilege. Ryan turned to the blonde haired woman, speaking distinctly and with authority.

"Aeron was Arl'antham to me," Ryan said. She nodded toward the dead man at her feet. "Therefore, by right, his life was mine to take in exchange."

Tra'e'ela was stunned, not only that the girl again spoke their language, but at the complexity of the legal argument she was presenting. She looked down at the dead man, weighed the proclamation, considered the evidence, assessed the applicability of the law, and made her decision.

"She is right," Tra'e'ela said. She turned to her men. "You will stand down." Then, as if it were no matter, she turned to the Others. "And set them free."

This latter action surprised Ryan, and as her father, son, and the Others were released, she stared at her captor in suspicion. She had the feeling that she had just passed some elaborate test. This feeling was confirmed when the blonde woman approached and stood before her, gazing down at her with cool amusement. For a long moment she was silent, simply examining the girl before her. She finally spoke.

"My loyalty to the Empress is absolute and I would never question her or her motives. But I confess that when I was sent on this mission I inwardly felt it ridiculous that I was to come to this planet to babysit an infant." She examined the maroon eyes, the high cheek bones, the flushed cheeks, and her eyes lingered on that perfect, familiar mouth. "I think now I begin to understand."

Ryan could not read this woman very well, but she could read this particular emotion.

"I thought there wasn't anything you wanted from me."

Tra'e'ela found the girl immensely entertaining. "We'll see," she said simply.

The response filled Ryan with disquiet and she turned away as her father approached with Drake in his arms. She made it only a step when Tra'e'ela's words stopped her.

"I'm not going anywhere, Ryan. I will be here until he is grown," she said, nodding at Drake, "and then you and I will return to the Empress."

Ryan turned back to her with the unblinking gaze of her Kind. "We'll see," she replied.

Tra'e'ela merely smiled, then turned and walked away.

Victor approached his child. He was cautious because he could still see the heat coming off her in waves, and could sense that she was just barely in control.

"Should I dare ask what 'Arl'antham' means?"

Ryan reached out to touch her son and caressed his cheek. She wanted to hold him, yet she did not trust herself right now, either. Although her memory seemed fully functioning and her mind stable, she was still struggling with impulse control, and all of her impulses were violent.

"There is no equivalent term in our language, but for them, it's a more intimate designation than family, more intimate than a lover or mate." The hue in Ryan's eyes briefly shifted, almost returning to normal, but then went back to the dark maroon. "A lyrical translation would be 'a life that hangs in the balance.'" She looked down at the dead man, then off at nothing. "But the most accurate translation is that Aeron was mine to kill, and mine alone."

She turned to Petrus. "How long do I have?"

Petrus looked at his watch. "About twenty-two more minutes, then you return to normal."

"I'm not entirely in control," Ryan admitted to Victor, "so I think I'm going to go cool off." She gave a quick glance to Petrus. "Why don't you come with me?"

"Of course," he said a little gruffly, unable to hide a flush of pleasure.

Victor bowed to the little creature. "Thank you, Petrus," he said formally, and Petrus turned bright pink.

Victor held Drake tightly and watched as the creature loped along at Ryan's side. Petrus' raspy conversation drifted back to them.

"So, now really, was it metaphorical or actual...?"

260

Petrus and Ryan walked from the platform into the hallway. Ryan wanted to leave the dreaded facility as quickly as possible, but knew in her current condition it would be wiser to wait for her phase to shift. She felt like smashing something.

A figure at the far end of the hallway gave her pause. Abigail stood waiting for her.

"Petrus, why don't you leave me alone for a moment?"

Petrus eyed the figure. "You should be careful with that one."

"I always am," Ryan said to him, and he left with one last look over his shoulder at the silhouetted figure down the hall.

Ryan approached the beautiful older woman. Abigail watched the animal-like stealth of the maroon-eyed creature with great pleasure. Ryan stopped before her, a volcano on the verge of eruption, innumerable emotions flowing through her.

"Hello little one," Abigail said.

Ryan did not respond, instead still analyzing her, studying her with great intensity.

"Do you know who I am?"

"Yes," Ryan said. She stopped, uncertain. "And no."

Abigail took this opportunity to move around Ryan, appraising her from every angle. When Abigail moved behind her, Ryan could not feel her and it took all of her willpower to remain still. The matriarch sensed the agitation in the girl and leaned forward to whisper in her ear.

"And do you wish to fight me?" she said, clearly entertained by the unrest she was causing within her quarry.

Ryan turned her head to look at Abigail who was still standing behind her.

"It is you who do not wish to fight me."

Abigail laughed softly. "And why is that?"

"Because you don't want the Others to know."

Abigail again circled Ryan, now stopping in front of the girl.

"Know what?" she said mockingly, "that you can defeat me?"

Ryan's maroon eyes fairly glowed. "No," she said simply, "that even now, I cannot."

261

Abigail gave a sharp inhalation of pleasure. The observation was startling and delightful. She leaned forward, placing her hand on Ryan's cheek.

"You are such a clever girl," Abigail said, "it is why your grandmother loves you so." She gave her a very gentle kiss on her other cheek, then again whispered in her ear.

"But unfortunately for you, you will not remember most of this conversation twenty minutes from now."

The elegant woman turned and swept gracefully from the corridor, and Ryan watched her until she disappeared. She then stood there, motionless, staring at nothing for nineteen more minutes.

# EPILOGUE I

THIS HAD NOT TURNED OUT the way she planned.

Lia looked at herself in the mirror, her thoughts not on her reflection but on the girl who had so recently vacated her royal chambers. For years she had dreamed of this day, the opportunity to inflict humiliation and pain on the object of her hatred, but almost immediately that fantasy had turned sideways.

The girl submitted without struggle to the blows that Lia delivered, but as the blood rose in welts on her skin, Lia had a most unusual response. She had experienced blood lust often in her years, but it was a violent and unpleasant urge, filled with anxiety and rage. When Lia gave into the impulse it was dissatisfying, not the least bit enjoyable and generally ended in a gory carnage.

But a different type of tension was rising in her at the moment, one that uncoiled in her midsection and was closer to desire than rage. Her blows from the whip slowed, the force lessened. The girl took that opportunity to stretch, a lithe, feline movement.

"You're enjoying this, aren't you?" Lia said in disbelief.

Ryan rolled over, her eyes twinkling with wicked humor. "I'm sorry. I can't help it. It seems to be some deep character flaw within me." She stretched again. "Granted, I can't say I would enjoy the chronic pain that you experience, but pleasure and pain have always been very close for me."

"I can't imagine what that must be like," Lia said with bitterness.

Ryan became serious, but there was still a gleam in her eye. "I could show you," she said. She took the fingernails of her left hand and traced them lightly over the vein in her neck, creating a deeper wound than any of Lia's blows. The blood began to flow down her already red-stained shirt.

It was too much for Lia. She set upon the girl, taking her to the floor, fastening on the wound that poured that dark gift. And the moment her lips touched the blood, she was connected to the girl in a way she had never been connected to anyone. She saw her own Memories through Ryan's eyes, her life as a human, her captivity, her release. And she saw Ryan's Memories, her childhood, her battles, her loves, her losses, the many pleasures and pains she had endured. She saw and felt Ryan's own horror at the species that had spawned her, and saw her ambivalence, despair and resignation at her fate.

But something else was happening as well. As the blood flowed through her veins, Lia could feel its fiery progress. It flowed through every artery, every vein, every capillary, diffusing out to organs and glands, burning and cleansing everything it touched. Atoms, molecules, genes began shifting, re-organizing, re-aligning. And as the adjustment took place, Lia's pain disappeared.

She finally broke away, her veins filled to bursting. She rolled over onto her back, staring up at the elaborate, demonic relief on the ceiling. Ryan rested for a moment, also staring up at the ceiling. She was still in her weak phase and she was now even more weakened by the loss of blood. She did manage to roll over on her side and propped herself up on her elbow, examining the demon goddess next to her.

"My pain is gone," Lia said.

"Good," Ryan said, and Lia noted that when the girl smiled such a gentle smile, she looked to be no more than a child.

"So where do we go from here?" Ryan asked.

And so Lia rolled over onto her side facing Ryan, also propping herself onto her elbow. She began outlining her plan, telling Ryan the exact timing of her next phase shift. Ryan thought it a very good plan with one exception. She looked down at her current battered condition.

"You're going to have to do far more than this to make it convincing," Ryan said, assessing the brutal injuries she had already sustained. "Kusunoki will recognize this as little more than foreplay."

"That's some character flaw you have," Lia commented, then spent a few hours following Ryan's suggestion.

Later, when it was time for Ryan to leave, Lia settled before her vanity. Her skin was already changing, growing smoother, less like leather and more supple like the silky skin of a snake. The scales reflected the light beautifully like tiny prisms. She stared at her reflection in the mirror.

"Will the rest of my appearance change?"

Ryan stood with some difficulty. Lia had done her job well.

"Honestly, I don't know," Ryan said. "And although your wishes on the matter are more important than mine, I hope your appearance doesn't change at all."

Lia turned from her reflection in surprise, and Ryan said her parting words.

"I think you're perfect the way you are."

And now Lia stared at her reflection in the mirror. Her skin had continued to change, growing even more smooth and supple, and now it was a joy to inhabit. It had become so like real skin, albeit still more snake-like than human, that she now wore clothing to hide the returning detail of her features. It was sensitive to touch and sensation, and Lia was experiencing things she had not felt in over a millennium. The contact of the clothing alone was blissful.

Her horns remained, and the coloration of her skin was still the greenish hue that shifted so beautifully in the light. And as Lia examined her features, she realized that she agreed with Ryan.

She hoped her appearance would not change, either.

# EPILOGUE II

TRA'E'ELA GAZED AT THE SECURITY holograph before her. Her personal servant, one of the few who actually knew who she really was, had wisely confiscated it and brought it to her attention. She did not think anyone else had seen it and it was her intent to destroy it as soon as she was finished with it.

And yet she could not help but watch it again. It was such an intriguing exchange, the powerful matriarch and the seething inferno that Ryan Alexander had become, the former clearly dominating the latter. It was an overhead shot from the hall entrance. The girl stood facing the camera, impatient but unmoving beneath the older woman's gentle taunting. The conversation itself was interesting, with Ryan clearly admitting she believed Abigail to be her superior, although nothing that Tra'e'ela sensed confirmed this fact.

"You are such a clever girl," came the words from the recording, "it is why your grandmother loves you so."

Tra'e'ela paused the recording. There was that reference again, to the girl's grandmother. After the boy, Drake, had mentioned this relative, Tra'e'ela had again searched through all known records to determine who this person might be. Yet nothing came to light. Victor Alexander had been successfully genetically transformed as an adult, but there was no information regarding his childhood or parentage.

This occupied Tra'e'ela's thoughts for a few moments, then she returned to the holograph. That was only one aspect of the incident that was intriguing, and not even the one that was of greatest interest. Of most interest was the way the recording ended. Tra'e'ela watched it for perhaps the tenth time, reversed it, then watched it again.

It could have been chance or pure coincidence, but the more she viewed it, the more undeniable it became. The elegant older woman leaned forward, kissed Ryan on the cheek, then whispered in her ear.

"But unfortunately for you, you will not remember most of this conversation twenty minutes from now."

Abigail then turned and walked toward the camera, moving with preternatural grace. And as she approached the entrance, she glanced up, looking directly into the recording device she could not possibly have seen or known was there, looking directly into the lens knowingly and with disturbing accuracy, looking directly, it seemed, at Tra'e'ela herself at this very moment, and right before she disappeared...

She smiled.